MORE THAN YOU KNOW

ALSO BY BETH GUTCHEON

FIVE FORTUNES

SAYING GRACE

DOMESTIC PLEASURES

STILL MISSING

THE NEW GIRLS

BETH GUTCHEON

a novel

MORE THAN YOU KNOW

WILLIAM MORROW • *An Imprint of* HarperCollins*Publishers*

HarperCollins books may be purchased for educational, business, or sales promotional use. For information please write: Special Markets Department, HarperCollins Publishers Inc., 10 East 53rd Street, New York, NY 10022.

Designed by Cheryl L. Cipriani / Brooklyn Bauhaus

ISBN 0-688-17403-5

For Wendy Weil

MORE THAN YOU KNOW

Somebody said, "True love is like ghosts, which everybody talks about and few have seen."

I've seen both, and I don't know how to tell you which is worse.

My children think I'm mad to come up here in winter, but this is the only place I could tell this story. They think the weather is too cold for me, and the light is so short this time of year. It's true this isn't a story I want to tell in darkness. It isn't a story I want to tell at all, but neither do I want to take it with me.

If you approach Dundee, Maine, from inland by daylight, you see that you're traveling through wide reaches of pasture strewn with boulders, some of them great gray hulks as big as a house. You can feel the action of some vast mass of glacier scraping and gouging across the land, scarring it and littering it with granite detritus. The thought of all that ice pressing against the land makes you understand the earth as warm, living, and indestructible. Changeable, certainly. It was certainly changed by the ice. But it's the ice that's gone, and grass blows around the boulders, and lichens, green and silver, grow on them somehow like warm vegetable skin over the rock. Even rock, cold compared to earth, is warm and living, compared to the ice.

For miles and miles, the nearer you draw to the sea, the more the road climbs; I always think it must have been hard on the horses. Finally you reach the shoulder of Butter Hill, and then you are tipped suddenly down the far slope into the town. My heart moves every time I see that tiny brave and lovely cluster of bare white houses against the blue of the bay.

The earliest settlers in Dundee didn't come from inland; they came from the sea. It was far easier to sail downwind, even along that drowned coastline of mountains, whose peaks form the islands and ledges where boats land or founder, than to make your way by land. In many parts of the coast the islands were settled well before the mainland. This was particularly true of Great Spruce Bay, where Beal Island lies, a long tear-shaped mass in the middle of the bay, and where Dundee sits at the head of the innermost harbor.

Not much is known about the first settlement on Beal Island, except that a seventeenth-century hermit named Beal either chose it or was cast away there, and trapped and fished alone near the south end until, one winter, he broke his leg and died. Later, several families took root on the island and a tiny community grew near March Cove. Around 1760 a man named Crocker moved his wife and children from Beal onto the main to build a sawmill where the stream flows into the bay. The settlement there flourished and was sometimes called Crocker's Cove, or sometimes Friends' Cove, or Roundyville, after the early families who lived there. In the 1790s, the town elected to call the place Sunbury, and proudly sent Jacob Roundy down to Boston to file papers of incorporation (as Maine was then a territory of Massachusetts). When he got back, Roundy explained that the whole long way south on muleback he'd had a hymn tune in his head. The tune was Dundee and he'd decided this was a sign from God. "God moves in a mysterious way, his wonders to perform: He plants his footsteps in the sea, and rides upon the storm" went the first verse. The sentiment was hard to quarrel with, though there were those who were spitting mad, especially Abner Crocker, who had to paint out the word SUNBURY on the sign he had made to mark the town line, and for years and years faint ghosts of the earlier letters showed through behind the word DUNDEE.

There are small but thriving island settlements on the coast of Maine, even now. On Swans, Isle au Haut, Frenchboro, Vinalhaven, the Cranberry Isles. But no one lives on Beal Island anymore. Where there were open meadows and pastures a hundred years ago, now are masses of black-green spruce and fir and Scotch pine, interrupted by alder scrub. Summer people go out there for picnics and such, and so do people from the town, and so did I sixty years ago, but I'll never go again.

Traces of the town have disappeared almost completely, though it's been gone so short a time. Yet the island has been marked and changed by human habitation, as Maine meadows inland were altered by ancient ice. Something remains of the lives that were lived there. When hearts swell and hearts break, the feelings that filled them find other homes than human bodies, as moss deprived of earth can live on rock.

* * *

When my children were little, they used to pester Kermit Horton, down at the post office, to tell about the night he was riding past Friends' Corner and the ghost of a dead girl got right up behind him on his horse and rode with him from the spot where she died till he reached the graveyard. I'd heard Kermit tell that story quite a few times. When someone asked him who the girl was, and how she died, he usually said that no one knew, though once he told a summer visitor she'd been eaten by hogs.

I didn't know Kermit when I was very little and made brief visits to my grandparents. But I remember him well from that summer Edith brought me and my brother back to Dundee. And I remember Bowdoin Leach. Bowdoin liked me; he always told me he had been fond of my mother. I was seventeen that year, and I needed the kindness. Bowdoin was bent with arthritis, but he was still running his blacksmith shop out in the shed behind his niece's house. There were some who didn't care to talk about Beal Island, where he had grown up. Bowdoin seemed to like to, if asked the right way. I remember him saying, the older he got, the more his thoughts ran on the years when he was a boy, as if life was a circle and as he got to the end of it he got closer and closer to where he began.

I got to know Bowdoin well because the people of the town liked to visit. Many still lived without electricity in those days, and those who were on the telephone shared a party line with half a dozen others; you couldn't hog the line. When they came to the village they wanted to have a good natter, see what all was going on. No one seemed surprised if I wanted to spend hours mooching around the post office or the library, or the blacksmith shop. They did a good bit of that themselves. No one needed to know how many reasons I had for wanting to be out of that house of Edith's.

The summer I was seventeen, Boston was pinched and stricken by the Depression, and there had been a polio epidemic the previous year. My father wanted us children out of the city. I don't know but what he wanted to see less of Edith too; I certainly could have done with less of her. Edith was the only mother I'd ever known, but she was my stepmother. My real mother died when I was a baby. Edith and I did pretty well together when I was little and cute, but things changed when Stephen came along. Now that I've raised my own children I have some sympathy for Edith, and I can imagine there's nothing like having your own little chick to make you want to kick out the great foreign cuckoo who lives in your nest. Whatever the reasons, for her and for me, that summer was the worst.

I'd been to Dundee for a week here or there when I was small. We never stayed long because Edith didn't like staying with my grandparents. My real mother's parents. At the grocery store, at the post office, when I came in total strangers would say to me, "Don't tell me who you are, young lady. You're the image of your mother." They'd have the mail all ready to hand over to me, or the groceries Edith had ordered. It's a rare thing, to feel you belong like that, and I think it brought out the worst in Edith, who was from away, and who anyway had felt like an outsider from the day she was born.

When Ralph and I had children of our own, and began to have a little money, we started coming back to Dundee in the summers. We camped out on an island Ralph's family owned back on Second Pond. We always had a fire, and after we'd scrubbed the dishes with sand and brushed our teeth in the lake, and Randall showed us all which star was Betelgeuse, they used to love to hear a ghost story. Ralph would stoke the fire and tell the story of the monkey's paw or Schalken the Painter. It's good sport to tell tales like that and raise the hackles on your neck for the fun of it. It doesn't matter if anyone really believes them or not. It isn't so much fun when the story you're telling is true.

Ralph was a good man and I loved him, but he wasn't the great love of my life and he knew it, though we never spoke of it. The first love, the one you never forget and never get over, was a boy from down on the Neck named Conary Crocker. That's the other reason I never told this story while Ralph was alive, that it was Conary's story as much as mine.

I'll visit Ralph's grave while I'm here. It will be a year ago he joined the Silent Majority, as Grandfather would have said, on January twelfth, his birthday. As if *his* life was a circle, and he closed it by dying on the day he was born. Ralph led a charmed life in that way, finishing what he started. He was a soul at peace, in life and in death. An old soul, and a restful one, with no wild strains to haunt him and no invisible burdens to carry. You can't mourn for a life like that. You can mourn for a life like Conary Crocker's.

For a long time the thought of that summer made me sick and sad. Then when I married Ralph and we lived a different life, away from Dundee, I was able to stop thinking about it. When you're young, you can leave a memory in your mind, like walking out of a room and closing a door behind you. Or like dropping a rock in a pond. When the surface clears, you look at the clouds and the treetops mirrored in it as if you didn't know what was on the bottom. I picture the pond, still and deep, in the old granite quarry up Dundee stream where we used to swim, though it was terribly cold. On summer mornings that pond catches the light so the surface turns a color we used to call skyblue pink.

I'd better bring in more wood. I can't start this story and then have to go out into the snow in my nightgown, on a night with no moon.

*   *   *

I'm reminded of how, one winter when my brother and I were little, we all came up here for Christmas. On Christmas Eve, right beside this fireplace, we read our letters to Santa Claus. Grandpa had a big fire going, very hot. He crumpled the letters and stuck them on the end of his pitchfork and held them in the fire. They blazed up, and were carried up the chimney with a whoosh. Then we ran outside to watch the sparks flying out from the chimney and off on the night wind to the North Pole, flickering orange against the cold white stars. It made you feel you could write a letter to anyone like that, living or dead, and mail it in the fire. Perhaps I believe it still.

You've seen how sometimes a young man falls in love not so much with a girl as with a whole family? I think that's the way it was when my father married my mother, Sara Grindle from Dundee, Maine. They met at college in Boston. He was alone in the world at the time, and my grandparents made him feel like a son. They never changed to him, even after their own daughter died and he remarried. They welcomed all of us, Edith and Stephen too. My grandparents had their faults, but as examples of how to live you could do a lot worse.

Edith hated that Christmas in Dundee. Stephen and I sat in the backseat and listened to her fight with our father the whole way home.

"I have family too, you know," she kept saying. That was true. She had a mother and two sisters, and they all seemed to hate each other. My father kept his mouth shut on the car ride, and after that we had Christmas at home in our apartment in Boston with Grandma Adele and Aunt Lou and Aunt Hester. Every year as she made her Christmas preparations Edith worked herself into a swivet over how her mother played favorites among her children, and every Christmas Day someone was in tears by lunchtime. Grown women slamming doors and weeping came to be part of the holiday tradition. You'd have thought that after a while they'd all give up trying to be together since it just made them miserable, but it didn't seem to occur to them.

The Christmas we spent at Dundee, Stephen and I bunked in together in that room behind the kitchen that had been my mother's when she was little. It's the warmest bedroom, when the stove's going. My children think I should sleep there now myself instead of going up and down stairs, but if I start making concessions like that, where will it end?

My neighbor, Phil, keeps a pretty good eye on me. When a house like this has been closed up for any length of time, the first thing you do when you come in is open all the windows. Even in midwinter. It's impossible to heat stale air, I don't know why. Air dies, I guess. Phil came in two days ago and aired it out, and then lit the woodstoves. When the house was warmed through, he turned the water back on and brought ice and food. In the fall, before the first snow, he banks the spruce all up around the outside too. It gives a nice feeling to have a blanket of evergreen tucked up around you.

You feel so close to the sky here. I think you feel everything more cleanly here, more keenly. There *are* times and places that alter your senses. I certainly saw things that summer I was seventeen that others couldn't see. And I was so raw, all that year, so exposed, like a peeled egg. A smile or a slight could pierce right through me and come out the other side, and the damage inside was enormous. I wouldn't be that age again for anything, but then, when you are so at risk, when you feel everything so intensely that the world seems almost to shimmer, you may be closer to God. Or for that matter to evil, especially the kind that looks for a heart to use. Everyone knows stories of people suddenly killed just at a moment of great fulfillment, great joy. Irony doesn't explain it. I'm not sure I believe in irony, I think it's just a conceit of ours to explain the way our notion of God's plan differs from the evidence.

I had a favorite rock on Jellison's Point, and on summer nights I used to sit for hours and watch the water go from silver blue to mauve to black, and listen to the loons. In the stillness of sunset, when the wind drops, a boat leaves a path like a scar across the water that remains long after its wake has flattened and the boat is out of sight. I always remembered that, in landlocked years, that scar across the water, a mere disarrangement of molecules, lovely and purposeless, but an illustration that everything matters, everything that happens changes something else.

I know what it is, that scar on the water: it's proof that inanimate things have memory. Dogs have memory, machines have memory, why not rocks and trees and water? What they don't have is judgment.

It's late. There will be fresh snow tonight, you can smell it in the wind. They say up here that if the bubbles on your coffee float together it will stay fair, but if they scatter it will storm. Grandfather could always tell when snow was coming. I couldn't as a child, but I can now. One of the things he left me.

One of the things I'll leave behind is that jar on the mantel of periwinkle shells I gathered with Conary. When you see periwinkles on the beach, wet and alive, they're blue-black like mussel shells, but dry they turn pale sandy colors from buff to gray. When you peel one from a tide rock, he pulls his foot into his shell as far as he can go. You can see it in there, like gleaming black rubber. Conary said they'd come out if you whistled, but that was one thing I couldn't do, though I tried and tried. I was so proud to be able at last to make a wispy little note with my lips that I scarcely minded when I came to find out the snails wouldn't have budged if I'd whistled "Celeste Aida."

Conary also taught me to dig for clams. We have huge tides here; we're so near the Bay of Fundy. The water depth changes by ten or twelve feet every six hours, and as much as sixteen in moon tides. Of course the distance between the low and high waterlines on a long flat beach is much greater than that. He showed me how to walk barefoot across the middle of the tide flat, carefully looking for squirt holes. When you find a cluster, you step gently near to see if your weight shifting onto their blind gritty world makes them spit. Where they spit, you dig. Conary's nails were always ragged from sifting through deep sand holes, telling live fat clams from stones or empty shells with his fingertips, like reading braille. I remember being up to my elbows in salty muck, my hands in darkness while all around us was tawny bleached sand and a high white sky, and the bay stretching toward the sea.

Once in a while in the sand you'd feel something long and muscular and think you had a giant clam neck, but it would be a sea worm. That's a long broad white disgusting thing which you would rather not have touched. I asked after my first if I could use a clam rake, or even a spoon, but Conary said if you dig with something you can't feel with, you always crush some shells and kill the clams, and he hated the thought of destroying the very thing he was looking for.

Well. I don't suppose you have to believe in ghosts to know that we are all haunted, all of us, by things we can see and feel and guess at, and many more things that we can't.

I remember that afternoon as if it happened last week. I remember the light. I remember being side by side on our knees on the sand, up to our elbows in muck, with the sun on our backs.

I love this room late at night. I love the firelight reflected in black windows. Grandma used to sit in this window seat looking down the meadow to the bay. Especially on rainy afternoons, we'd sit together to do jigsaw puzzles or play hearts.

What I don't love is going up those stairs alone at night.

Well. There's nothing for it. God hates a coward.

Claris Osgood's tenth birthday fell on a Sunday. She woke up with the light. Her sister Mary was sound asleep beside her in the big sleigh bed their uncle Asa had built them, with a mound of quilts pulled tight around her. In the early gray light, Claris could see the window crazed with hoarfrost; although the sun would warm the air by midday, early April in Dundee was still winter. Claris looked at the candle by Mary's side of the bed to see how long Mary had stayed awake last night; hours, it must have been. Mary was in love with Jonathan Friend, who was down at Harvard. She wrote to him every night, and they would be married in the spring. Mary and Claris looked very alike; "cut from the same cloth," their father said. (The boys were quite different in looks, all of them big and blond and heavy-boned.) Cuddled under a coverlet of cutting table scraps from the making of their aprons and dresses and the boys' shirts, Mary looked all arms and legs and long slender neck; she looked like a deer asleep under a pile of leaves. Claris knew that however alike they seemed, with the same fine brown hair and blue eyes, Mary had some happy, cheerful light in her that made everybody love her, and Claris . . . didn't. She knew it was true, but she didn't know why. It was the puzzle of her girlhood.

Claris got out of bed. The house was still silent; the little girls, Alice and Mabel, slept on trundle beds in her parents' room with baby Otis in the cradle, and the two big brothers plus middle Thomas were in the room next door. There would be two hours of church this morning. Good. Claris could sit for hours with her backbone straight as a ramrod; Reverend Friend often spoke about her remarkable composure. In a big noisy family people tended to label the children as if otherwise they would blend together into one burbling shouting mass; Claris was known as the serious one, determined, the one who would rather talk to animals. She was also known among her aunts as the one who had always had a pebble in her shoe, always the one who wasn't quite pleased by what was pleasing the others. No one wondered why children, even those cut from the same cloth, were so different from each other, or why they changed, or what things changed them. They were born with different wills and different ways, and all you could do was pray that the choices they made and the lives they met with brought out the best that was in them, and not the worst.

That tenth birthday was one Claris never forgot, and there wasn't another living person who ever knew that, or knew why. When she got out of bed that morning, she thought of three things. One was, it was the day that marked her first decade, and it was Sunday. The boys tended to fidget through church. Her parents, she suspected, relished it as the only two hours of the week when their children were silent, so they could think of things like how much butter to put down cellar and how much the yearlings would fetch. Mary of course thought only of Jonathan. But Claris actually thought of God. She believed that she and God understood each other. She prayed with real passion, and she waited for signs that she was marked for some special destiny.

The second thing on her mind was that there would be chickens for dinner instead of the boiled salt cod they had on normal Sundays. Her mother and Mary would catch two hens and kill and dress them before church, and when they came home the house would be filled with the fragrance of the roasting fowl, and of rolls and potatoes and lima beans. After grace, when the hens were carried to the table, brown and glistening on a white china platter, everyone would be glad about Claris's birthday. After dinner, the cousins would come in from next door and there would be music. (The cousins were actually double cousins, the two Osgood brothers, John and Asa, having married sisters.) The two families had once celebrated birthdays and holidays with family dinner together, but there were now so many of them they couldn't all sit down indoors at one time, even if some sat in the parlor. In summer they often ate together outdoors, but in colder weather they ate separately and gathered after the meal. They usually gathered in Mrs. John Osgood's house, since it was she who had the parlor organ.

The third thing was the rabbits. Claris's oldest brother, Simon, had caught a huge jackrabbit in a snare last fall; he had brought it home alive and left it in a sack in the barn, where Claris had found it. He had gone in to tell Mother that he'd caught dinner, and come out again to find dinner being rocked in his little sister's arms. He stood over her, arms akimbo, and watched as the big wild terrified animal gradually stopped trembling, and Claris stared at Simon with her small blue eyes.

"I suppose you give him a name already," he said.

"Esau," said Claris. Simon started to laugh.

"For my brother Esau is a hairy man?"

Claris nodded gravely.

"You beat all," Simon said. He went back into the house to explain to his mother there would be no meat for supper.

"Biscuits and grease again, Mother," said John Osgood. His daughters seemed always to amuse him. His wife looked sadly at the onions and apples she'd started cutting to cook with the rabbit.

"Get the molasses, Mother," said John, and his wife set about putting away the onions and getting out the flour and shortening with a resignation that also made her husband laugh. The set of her back and the way she plopped the onions back into their barrel was a wordless code old lovers understand. Mrs. Osgood was saying she'd rather eat biscuits in bacon fat six nights a week than have a set-to with her second daughter, even though Claris was only nine.

After supper, Simon went out to the barn and knocked together a cage for Esau, and that night after Claris went upstairs to bed, she could hear roars of laughter at Simon's expense from her father and brothers as Simon told again and once again of walking into the barn, the taste of stewed rabbit already on his tongue, to find Claris's blue eyes staring out at him and, right beneath her chin, the large terrified eyes of his former dinner.

Later that winter Simon caught a second rabbit. This one he never even tried to take to the kitchen; he just dumped it into the cage with Esau and went to tell Claris he'd brought her a Jacob. However, Jacob should more properly have been called Martha, for by the end of March, Claris knew for a certainty that Jacob was expecting bunnies. Simon discovered it too and thought it a huge joke, though he didn't tease Claris about it. Alone of his brothers and sisters, Claris did not take to that sort of thing.

He said, "I'll build you a separate cage for her."

"Why?" Claris resented his assuming he knew more about her rabbits than she did.

"Because it's what you do. Separate the mothers—you've been to Mrs. Leaf's." Mrs. Leaf was a widow in the village who raised rabbits for meat.

"No," said Claris, "they want to be together." Her rabbits were not like Mrs. Leaf's in any way. She took to slipping out to the barn every night after supper to sit in the steamy warm dark, listening to the oxen snort and chew, with Jacob in her lap, whispering into the warm fur. Claris had developed a growing conviction that the rabbit babies would be born on her birthday. She and Esau shared a running joke about how she was known in the woods, a heroine among rabbits, for having saved him from the stewpot. It was certain that this litter would be in her special care.

On the silver dim morning of her birthday, Claris dressed silently and slipped down the stairs. She knew exactly where to step so as not to make a creak or sound; it was hard, in that house, to be alone with your thoughts, or your God, or your rabbits. One creaking board, and she knew Mabel would be after her like a hungry shadow wanting hugs or stories or just to be allowed to follow her. ("Can I come with you, Claris-Claris? Claris-Claris-Went-to-Paris?" And, "How could he have babies, Claris? Is it a miracle? A boy having babies?") Jacob's belly had been so great with children last night that Claris didn't see how the moment could hold off much longer. Besides, Jacob had made her nest in the straw Claris brought her.

—⁓—

Claris paused inside the barn door to breathe the animal smells and let her eyes adjust to the dim light. The rafters were lined with barn swallows; they stirred and fluttered as a crack of morning light followed her in and then vanished as the door shut behind her. Tense with delight, Claris went to the rabbit cage and knelt beside it. Esau greeted her brightly. He pressed his nose against the wire, and she held her flat palm against it for him to nuzzle.

Jacob lay on her side. She looked sick. Her belly was stretched and deflated; it seemed somehow draped across the straw. Jacob's eye was glazed, and she made no notice of Claris. At first, Claris could see no sign of the babies. No tiny blind bunnies burrowed against Jacob's belly. Then as Esau stirred around, having lost her attention, Claris noticed the debris in the corner of the cage where he made his droppings. Tiny bits of fur were stuck to the straw with bright patches of blood. She saw a minuscule paw clinging there, and here and there a pink translucent needle of bone. The bunnies had been born, and Esau had eaten them.

I'll have to describe the house to you, because it was unusual. That's what Edith liked about it; she liked to have things different. When my father said he wanted us to go to Dundee for the summer, she couldn't think on what grounds to refuse, but she said she'd have to have a place of her own, two women can't share a kitchen. I don't know about that myself; I've seen women seemed to be having the time of their lives, chopping and stirring and laughing together, but I'll grant you two women couldn't share a kitchen if one of them was Edith. As it happened, my grandmother broke her hip that spring and had to be living downstairs all summer. It wasn't the year for her to have grandchildren underfoot, plus Edith, so that settled that.

I'm not sure how it was worked, whether Edith traveled up to Dundee to find a place to rent, or whether she did it through the mail. One evening, though, she announced she'd taken a place: an old schoolhouse, made into a cottage by two maiden ladies. Nice high ceilings, big windows, with big open rooms, "not all little and cut up and dark," Edith said, "like so many old houses." (Gracious of her, since she meant like this house, my grandparents' house.)

If you're heating with wood and lighting with kerosene, as this house was built for, you do want to keep your rooms cozy. And you do keep them stacked one on top of the other so the heat from the stove downstairs carries up and warms the bedrooms. Well, it wasn't what Edith wanted. And she was right about the schoolhouse; it was lovely. It was a white square thing, pretty good size, perched like a torso on a broad skirt of rock above the water. If it had had a school-house belfry for a head, it would have looked just like a person. Its face, door for mouth and bedroom windows for eyes, was on the north side, facing the road.

It was out past the post office, past the town park where the swings are. The downstairs was mostly one big room except for a kitchen in the back, with a nice back porch right over the water. There were three bedrooms upstairs, a little one in the front looking out toward the road to town that was mine, and a big square one at the top of the stairs for Stephen, and then one at the back overlooking the bay for Edith. And, of course, for my father, not that he managed to be there that summer more than a day.

I liked it better than this house, my grandparents' house, in one way; this house is too far from town to walk. When we were little and could play all day in the cove here, it didn't matter, but that summer alone with Edith it would have mattered a lot. This house, and those couple or three down closer to the shore, was built for the quarry workers in the 1880s. My grandfather came from Vermont to manage the quarry. He married Frances Friend, from one of the old Dundee families, and stayed. His stoneworks cut granite for the Brooklyn Bridge and the post office in Pittsburgh, Pennsylvania. Local people were proud of that, and often they'd travel to visit the buildings and monuments their stone made.

The one thing I thought when I first saw that house Edith had rented, it was an odd place for a schoolhouse. Down on that point, instead of right up in the village—I thought maybe they called it the Schoolhouse because one of the ladies who fixed it up had been a schoolteacher. Mrs. Pease at the library told me that.

The Ladies Social Library is that small brick building on the corner of Main Street and the Eastward road. In those days it was set about with huge elm trees. Gone now—Dutch elm disease took them all. The library has a big fireplace at the end, where you could curl up and read on a rainy day, and even when it was fine, it was a lovely place, with its welcoming musty leather smell, to get away from your stepmother.

"Don't tell me who you are, you're as pretty as your mother," said Esther Pease, when I came in that first afternoon. ''Are you paying a visit to your grandmother?"

"We're here for the summer. We're in the white house down on the point."

"Oh, did you take Miss Hamor's house? I always thought that was a lovely house." Esther Pease was a talker, as I was to find out. Her table behind the reference desk was stacked with hurt books, and spools of red binding tape, and bottles of glue, but I never saw her mending. She was always out in front helping some child understand the card catalog, or discussing the rental books with the women from the summer colony. The new best-sellers were for rent for two cents a day, which was a lot of money. Mrs. Pease liked to hear how each reader enjoyed her book; she'd tuck report cards in the front. "Mrs. Cluett says it's not his best, but she liked it quite well. B minus."

Many days that summer I helped with shelving returned books, or sat in back and mended with Mrs. Allen. Mrs. Allen and Mrs. Pease seemed glad of the help and content to have me around. They were cheerful and easy to be with because they so enjoyed each other's company. That first day I asked Mrs. Pease what she knew about the house.

"It's been empty a little time now," Mrs. Pease said. "Miss Fannie Hamor owned it. I took Latin from her; so did your mother."

I asked what Miss Hamor was like. "Tough as a pitch knot," said Mrs. Pease. "She lived there with Miss Kennedy, who drove the town taxi and sold jellies. She died, Miss Kennedy. And Miss Hamor, people were surprised at how undone she was. No one thought she'd been all that kind to Miss Kennedy in life. She stayed on in the house, but she wasn't herself. Nella B. Foss at the post office, she keeps track of those that live alone. If Miss Hamor didn't come for her mail two-three days in a row, she'd send someone over with a plate of berries or some pickles to call her to the door and make sure she hadn't died. That's how they came to find her after her fall. She fell right down her own stairs, and lay there all night. She'd had a shock. They took her to a nursing home, but she never came back to herself. She died soon after. Her nephew owns it now; he thought he had the house rented out last summer, but the people didn't stay. I don't know why. Have you seen our armor, over there? They say it belonged to Magellan."

The reading room was filled with scrimshaw and kimonos, ships' models and various oddments brought back by local sailors from their voyages around the world. It was surprising to think of the ships that were built right here at Dundee, brigs and barks and ships of a thousand tons and more. Right down there at the boatyard, where they build little peapods now and store a few yachts in the winter. There was a brickyard here too. The old brick houses you see anywhere from Dundee down the Neck and beyond, those bricks were fired right here in the village out of local clay.

But I'm supposed to be telling how it was when I first knew something was wrong with the house. He who hesitates is lost, my grandfather used to say.

You may have noticed I said just now that Miss Hamor had had a shock. I assumed at the time that Mrs. Pease meant a stroke. That's the usual name for it here. But later I was fairly sure something frightened her down the stairs. I'm sure something tried to. There was something in there that was furious, bitter, that other people were going on with their lives.

That first afternoon, as I returned home from the village, I saw that somebody had put a handful of beach roses in a glass and set it in the front window. The house was very quiet. Stephen was out in the side yard, where an old canvas hammock was strung between two pine trees. He was tucked into it reading about the Hardy Boys, and he had Whitey, his little terrier, in the hammock with them. As I stood with my armful of books, reluctant to go into the dark indoors, and thinking of going down to sit on the rocks by the water instead, I looked up and saw someone in my bedroom. She was standing at the window looking down at me, and I felt a wash of resentment. I didn't want Edith prowling around my things. I knew she had tried to read Stephen's Top-Secret Mirror Code Journal, and I knew she would read my diary if she could find it. I had put my clothes away neatly and carried all the suitcases to the cellar, as I'd been told. Edith had no need to be in my room, and no right either.

I went straight inside ready to charge up the stairs, but I didn't get any farther than the little mudroom, because I could see from there right through to the kitchen in the back. There was Edith at the sink, scrubbing out cook pans that hadn't been cleaned to her liking. I was confused and alarmed, and felt a pricking up the back of my neck.

I went back outside. I looked up at my window. There was no one there, but there *had* been. Who could it have been? The house was wide open, a stranger could have walked right in, but . . . had I imagined it? Was I so primed to be indignant at Edith that I made up things to be mad at her for? I forced myself to go in again, speak to Edith, and climb the stairs to my room. Everything was in order; the filmy curtains moved in the breeze. But the room felt cold, invaded. Altogether I decided to go down to the shore after all, and found a sun-warmed rock to lean against, and settled into a book that Mrs. Pease had recommended.

The rest of the afternoon was peaceful. When my bottom got tired of the hard rocks, I gathered my books and went up to my room to put them away. I helped Edith get the supper ready and washed the dishes afterward. It was a pleasant evening. When Stephen went up to take his bath, I said good night and went to read in my room.

There was my stack of the books on the bedside table. No one had been in the room; no one could have been. And yet, someone had picked up my book and done something to it. It was not placed the way I'd left it, and the bookmark was gone.

When Stephen came out of the bathroom in his pajamas, I followed him to his room and told him what had happened. I showed him the book.

"Are you *sure*?" He was solemn but seemed rather pleased. I had been frightened up to then, but his reaction calmed me down. He was practical and boylike; he wanted to set a trap so we would know for sure. Edith came in and shooed me out, back to my own room, and this time it seemed cozy and benign. I found my place in the tampered book and read on in peace.

The first time Claris Osgood remembered noticing Danial Haskell, it was the Fourth of July. The parade was forming on the lawn of the Congregational Meeting House, down the hill from the Osgoods'. Claris's youngest brother, Otis, was to drive the donkey cart carrying three little cousins, all dressed in stars and stripes. Shiny bunting of red, white, and blue was woven in and out of the wheel spokes. The cart was to be pulled by Elmer, the pet burro Uncle Asa brought home from California, but Elmer had chosen this moment to refuse to be driven. He was head down in the grass border of the minister's vegetable garden, and Otis, red in the face from hauling on the reins to no effect, was fighting tears. As Claris tugged on the burro's bridle and Colonel Dodge was calling to the marchers to Form Up, Please, Claris noticed the young man sitting by himself in shirtsleeves on the stone step of the meeting house, watching her. She didn't know who he was but thought with irritation that he might have offered them some help instead of sitting there idle; he could see that she needed it.

Later she saw him again, marching with the boys from the islands; he had his jacket on and stepped out proudly, shoulders back and eyes straight ahead, bearing the colors. He had a slight limp that suddenly touched her heart. Next came the marching band, in which her sisters Alice and Mabel played cymbals and drums, and then came Otis, earnestly flogging Elmer, while the little girls in the cart waved small flags at their parents and cousins and neighbors along the parade route.

The parade ended at the playground above the shipyard, across from the schoolhouse. There were tables set up on the grass, loaded with cold chicken and lemonade and all kinds of cakes and doughnuts. Elmer was taken out of the cart shafts and allowed to graze, to his delight. Otis and the little girls had run across to the school yard, where their school chums were playing under the elm trees, and the grown-ups had settled down on blankets to listen to speeches. Claris was standing alone when she found that the boy with the limp who hadn't helped her before the parade was now standing at her elbow holding two dishes of peach ice cream.

She looked at the dishes, and she looked at him. He had large dark eyes and a very high forehead. His hands were huge.

"I brought you this," he said and held one of the dishes out to her. She was so surprised, she took it.

"I'm Danial Haskell," he said, and took a bite of ice cream.

"I'm Claris Osgood," she said.

"I know who you are," said Danial. And then, to her bafflement, he walked away and sat down by himself on a rock overlooking the bay, and ate his ice cream.

Sometimes I was sure I heard bedroom doors open and close, or someone moving around the upstairs when we were all together below. Stephen believed me, but he never seemed to be near when it happened. I told Edith about it, but she thought I was just complaining.

Then one night when I was washing up after dinner I distinctly heard someone crying somewhere in the room behind me. My heart moved in sympathy, and I turned around, but there was no one there. It was not a child's weeping; at first I thought it was Edith herself in some kind of trouble and I wondered if I could help her. I left the kitchen but found that Stephen was upstairs and Edith was sitting in the living room reading *The Saturday Evening Post*. I went back into the kitchen, and in a minute the weeping started again. This time it slightly irritated me, as weeping that can be turned on and off tends to. I took a deep breath, turned around, and said as bravely as I could to the dark corners of the room, "Now *listen*. There's no need for this. And it won't do any good, so cheer up and get ahold of yourself." The weeping stopped.

I stood, hardly daring to breath. It was silent; I was silent. I thought, Well, that was easy, and turned back to the dishes. Suddenly I felt, or smelled, something cold and nasty right behind me, and then a glass I had washed and set carefully on the drainboard was swept violently back into the deep metal sink as if someone had hit it. I felt as if I'd been slapped, and cried out as it broke. Edith came running as I grabbed for the glass, thinking . . . what? That I could put it back together? I managed to cut myself across the web of my thumb, so there I was as she rushed in, bleeding into the sink with my heart hammering.

"Now what is going on in here? First you're talking to yourself and now you're smashing things! Oh!" she said, and took the broken stem of the glass from my hand. "*Oh!* Now look!" She was staring at it as if her whole heart had been wrapped up in that glass. It was a fragile one, an orphan we had found that matched no others in the cupboards, which Edith liked to use at dinner. The gash in my palm had begun to throb. I tried to stop the bleeding with a dish towel, but that made Edith madder.

"Don't do that! You're always destroying things that have value for other people!" She took the dish towel from me and threw it into the hamper. Then she went for her Red Cross box. When she came back she wrapped my hand so tightly that it took some effort not to wince.

I said, "Mother—there was something in here! I heard someone crying, and I spoke to it. Then it knocked that glass into the sink."

"What do you mean, something?"

"I mean—another person. Something. Not us." Our eyes locked for a moment, but I couldn't stand what I saw in hers, the dislike in the way she looked at me. I looked down; I guess that means I lost.

She said, "*Honestly,* Hannah!" She chewed her lip as she went back to strapping my hand. "I suppose you think if you do your chores badly, you won't have to do them anymore." Meanwhile, she wasn't doing such a tidy job with the adhesive tape herself. She seemed to expect an answer from me, but I couldn't give one. I was wondering if whatever had knocked the glass into the sink was enjoying this scene. How nice to know that now even creatures from beyond knew my stepmother was as much comfort to me as a bale of barbed wire.

As soon as I could I went up to be with Stephen. He was reading a Little Lulu comic and had his new "specs" on. The glasses had steel rims, like Father's. He looked very cute in them, like a tiny businessman. I sat on the end of his bed; his room had wallpaper with flowers on it, quite faded, but more welcoming than mine. It must have belonged to one of the schoolteachers. He had two narrow beds with iron bedsteads and an old pine table between the beds, which had been painted green, inexpertly. Stephen was very upset when I told him about the broken glass and my cut hand.

"You shouldn't have spoken, you made it mad at you!"

"I think it's mad anyway," I said. "Otherwise what's it doing creeping around our house? Does it think it still *lives* here?"

"Don't talk to it," he said. "Ignore it." I said I'd try and went reluctantly into my cold front bedroom. Stephen had put ghost traps in the form of bookmarks on special pages in all the books on my bedside table; I checked them every night. That night I also began checking the closet. What if it hid in there and waited for me to turn out the light? What would I do if I opened my eyes in the dark and found the closet door opening?

*   *   *

Some nights later, Edith was in her bedroom overlooking the sea. It had been a bone-chilling day of gray fog, and the night was thick and black. She had built up the fire in the cookstove in the kitchen so it would heat all night, and she had the radio going in her room. She used to listen to that late into the night and scribble, writing to my father, I guess. Stephen's light was out, and I was in my room in front, in bed more because my room was cold than because I was sleepy. Edith didn't let me use the stove in my room. She said I might do it wrong and burn the house down.

Distinctly I heard the front door just below me open and close. The old-fashioned thumb latch on that door made an unmistakable clacking sound, and it could not possibly open by itself. Or close. Fear pricked my scalp and down my neck, and my heart began to race. I waited for Edith to come out and investigate; what if there were a burglar in the house? The last thing I wanted to do was leave the safety of my bed, but I was more scared to do nothing. I made myself put my bare feet on the floor and went to the door.

Things were absolutely quiet downstairs. I could hear a dark cedar tree close to the front door move in the wind and scratch at my window, but this was a comforting sound. In the downstairs dark there still hung a faint aroma of cheese from the Welsh rabbit we'd had for dinner. I listened and listened, but nothing changed, nothing moved. Maybe there were rules: maybe as long as I stood and listened whoever was downstairs was frozen? But that was ridiculous. Far more likely I'd heard the sound wrong. It was some other door opening and clos-ing, the sound carried here on the wind across the water. I began to dislike standing at the door in my bare feet and nightgown. I got myself across the floor and back into bed, trying the old rule that it can't get you if you're under the covers.

At least my electric lamp burned steadily. The house had only recently been wired and had insufficient outlets; Stephen's room had only one, far from the bed, and Edith was afraid of extension cords so he had to use an oil lamp.

I stared at my book and succeeded in reading the same two lines over and over.

" 'Jeeves—there's something in there that grabs you by the leg!' "

" 'That would be Rollo, sir.' " A pause to listen, hard. To silence. Read.

" 'Jeeves—there's something in there that grabs you by the leg!' "

"That would be Rollo, sir.' "

What was that? I strained to hear . . . had there been something on the stairs? Read. Read.

" 'Jeeves—there's something in there . . .' "

. . . and there *was* something. I don't know what it was, but Whitey, who slept on the foot of Stephen's bed, began to growl. I could hear him through the wall. He was making the sound of low menace that comes right before he starts barking. The hair along my arms was standing straight up. Was the room suddenly colder? I was straining to hear something in the upstairs hall, waiting to hear a body with human weight and heft try to make its way toward me. But I heard nothing, except the sound of Stephen telling Whitey to hush.

Then, outside the door, I heard something that seemed like a weapon aimed at my heart. Someone right outside my door began weeping.

I was holding my book in front of me like a shield. I stared at the iron doorknob, waiting for it to turn. It never did. Instead, horribly, I suddenly knew that something had passed through the door and was in the room with me. I heard fabric rustle as it crossed the room. Then a soft creak of wood. Then the rocking chair by the stove began to move.

It made a creaking squeaking noise on the floor as it started, back and forth. It was facing me. Someone was in it, rocking and watching me.

I tried to call out, but I had lost the power to use my voice. I got off the bed, meaning to run for the door, but as I did, the chair moved violently and was left rocking. There was a dry scrabbling sound on the floor, like rats in dry leaves. At first I still couldn't see anyone, and then, I could. There was an old woman down on all fours, dragging herself across the floor. She turned and looked at me hatefully, with burning colorless eyes that seemed to have no pupils.

I must have screamed loud enough to be heard up in the village from the look on Stephen's face as he banged into my room. Edith was right behind him, and Whitey was barking and barking. I had jumped back onto the bed, and I must have been gibbering. Stephen jumped onto the bed with me, and I clutched him. Even Edith looked frightened. I was all pulled into a ball, hugging my brother; I remember being afraid to touch the walls or floor.

"Hannah, what is it? What happened?"

I said, "Something was in here." I could hardly make my throat work to speak.

"What was?"

I said, "Rustling. Like rats." I didn't know how to say what I had seen. "A woman, crawling across the floor."

"Crawling?" was all Edith said. Her face had begun to change from alarm to something else.

"Yes . . ." With her staring at me like that, it was hard to make clear what had happened. "Something got into my room. It was in the hall first, and Whitey growled."

Stephen was pale; he knew it was true, the dog had given warning, and he knew about the bookmark and the broken glass.

Edith was briefly stymied. "And then what happened?"

I told her. She looked at the rocking chair. Naturally, it was now utterly still.

"A woman was crawling?" she asked again.

"Crawling! Do you want me to show you?"

We stared at each other. *Why* couldn't she just believe me? *Why* couldn't she for once in her life put her arms around me and say, "It's all right. It'll be all right"?

"Do you want me to telephone someone to come search the house? Your grandfather?" She asked it as if we were playing a chess game and she had figured out her next move.

I certainly *did* want him, him or someone, but I didn't want her to be the one to call him. She'd make it sound as if I was crazy. I said, "No."

"Why not, if you're frightened?"

"He won't find anything."

Edith stared at me, and I stared back, wondering what she would say or do. Finally she said, "Oh for the love of Pete, Hannah. I know you don't like the house. I get the message. But I really have enough to deal with without you trying to thwart me every step of the way."

I was dumbfounded. What was this? A hateful thing that could move through closed doors had rocked in that chair right there and frightened me just about into the nuthatch, and suddenly we were talking about whether I like her house? I *did* like the house. It was the thing we were sharing it with I had problems with.

Edith was wearing a long quilted wrapper that made her look upholstered. Her graying hair was down, a somewhat alarming sight in itself. Her brown eyes looked tired, and the fingers of her right hand were stained blue; her fountain pen leaked. The thing was, Edith was not a woman who liked ambiguities. She didn't see what would be so bad about having your own mother die when you were too young even to remember her. If you didn't remember your own mother, and you had another mother, and enough food and a roof over your head, why couldn't you be happy with what you'd got? Why couldn't I be, that is. That was the Edith position on Hannah, and I didn't know the answer any more than anyone else did.

Edith said, "Stephen, honey, go to your room."

Stephen looked up.

"There's been enough excitement for one night. Go back to bed. It's late and you should be asleep." Stephen looked at me briefly as if to say, Sorry; he knew she was never as hard on me when he was in the room as when she had me cornered. Then he climbed down and went out without looking back at me. I was alone with the only mother I had, with my heart pounding as if it would knock itself apart.

"Hannah," Edith said. "You used to be such an attractive little girl."

I knew it was a preamble, not a compliment. Emphasis on the "used to be." She had liked me better when I was small and blond and cute, and people said to her, "What a lovely child." She never said, "Yes, we're proud of her," as if she knew the compliment was to me; instead she made the same reply she would have made if someone said that she herself was looking pretty. "No, no, but thank you."

Now she said, "I don't know what to make of you anymore. You look as if you don't own a comb. You should hear what people say about your grooming." (This was a favorite technique of hers. "Maybe you don't care what I say, but you should hear what people say behind your back." Try it sometime on someone you really dislike.)

There was more. "Your room is a pigpen. Your schoolwork is disgraceful. You could go to college if you'd *apply* yourself . . ."

"Except that you're the one who wants to go, not me." I said it to be rude, not because it was true. I liked school; I just couldn't stand the way she bragged when I brought home good grades. I felt erased, as if she were the one who had done it. She'd start dropping names like Bryn Mawr to the neighbors.

Edith answered fairly quietly, for the circumstances. She said, "I'll tell you, Hannah. You seem determined to hurt me, if you have to hurt yourself to do it. But I'm warning you. Do not try to make your father choose between me and you, because you won't like what happens."

I only stared at her. Finally she asked, "Do we understand each other?"

I said, "Is that a serious question?"

Here's how frightened I was; I was actually sorry when she went back to her room. Left alone, I didn't dare to turn out the light; instead I sat in bed and elaborately wrote in my diary everything that had happened. I think I was making notes to myself on how not to be a mother. I underlined the crack about my father. (What could I have made of it?) Even after all these years, I can't bring myself to soften much toward Edith, though I understand much better now what her troubles were. There was something hard and selfish in her, and though I could later feel for her, I couldn't respect her. It was as if she saw us, my father included, as hand puppets in a play in which she was the only real person.

I waited the long hours for daylight, when I would dare again to put my bare feet down on the floor.

Late in the fall of the year, when the nights were cold and the sun set at four o'clock, there was a day of bright open weather when Claris Osgood decided to take some eggs and a bag of her mother's doughnuts up the hill to old Miss Clossy and see if she could help her with any of her preparations for winter. Miss Clossy had been the village schoolmistress when Claris was small, but her eyesight was weak and she had been forced to retire. She lived in a tiny house, hardly more than a cabin, in an apple orchard, and survived on what she could grow and on what she was given. She had gradually fallen almost completely silent, and there began to be rumors about her. People kept her in their prayers, but many were so uncomfortable with the silence that surrounded her that it was all they could do to stop and sit with her. Claris felt a little that way herself, but she was in the midst of an argument with God about the goodness of her own character, and she thought she would improve the day by demonstrating that she was not a "dog in the manger," as a cousin had crossly called her in anger, but as spontaneously lovable and kind as her sister Mary.

The blueberry barrens had turned a deep crimson color as they always did in fall, and the trees stood black against the high November sky; it was a beautiful day of God's Creation. Claris enjoyed her walk, except for the wind that occasionally tore at her hat. She reached Miss Clossy's gate and went into the apple orchard. It was past picking time, but there were still some windfalls, mainly Winesaps and Transparents, which Claris particularly loved. She put down her bag and made a basket of her apron in order to gather the good ones for the old lady.

A small apple, quite perfect, fell from a tree above her, landing just within reach. She picked it up, rubbed it on her skirt, put it into her apron, then took it out again and took a bite. She picked up a cull; it was wormy on the underside. So was the next one. She hoped she wasn't eating the only good apple she was to find that day, when another one fell about a foot from her. It was perfect, and it was followed by another and another. Suddenly she straightened and looked at the tree. There was an apple ladder leaning against the trunk, and just where it tapered and disappeared among the upper branches, there was a pair of boots, with legs in them.

"Who's there?" she said, rather loudly. She was feeling foolish.

"Just us apples," said a voice.

"Well, it's very kind of you to persuade your little friends to jump into my arms."

There was a sawing noise, and then a gnarled branch fell to earth, looking like a withered arm amputated at the shoulder. The branch was followed by the owner of the voice backing down the ladder, so that Claris saw legs, then hips, then a yellow flannel shirt, and finally the dark head turning to her with deep brown eyes. It was Danial Haskell.

"Good afternoon, Mr. Apple," said Claris. Danial made a little bow.

He had a pruning saw in his hand, and now that she paid attention to what was on the ground among the windfalls, she could see that he must have been working in the orchard all morning. There were withered boughs everywhere.

Danial seemed a little taller than he had when they met in the summer; perhaps the difference was in his boots. He offered her the dark serious face, the deep eyes, as he had before.

"I didn't know you were an orchardist," she said for want of anything better.

"I keep apples and pears at home," said Danial. "I noticed last time I was onto the main that Miss Clossy's trees were about worn out, and I thought a little pruning might encourage them."

"That's very kind of you."

He shrugged.

"Is she kin to you?"

"No. But she's got no one to do for her, and I like apple trees. You don't remember me, do you?"

They were standing in the sunshine, he with his saw in his hand, and she with the apronful of apples he had thrown to her. Now she was taken aback.

"Certainly I remember you. You brought me ice cream at the town picnic."

"I mean from when we were small."

She was greatly surprised. He was right; she did not remember him, at least not yet.

"I came into the village one winter when my mother was doctoring. We stayed with the minister, and I went to the village school."

She still didn't remember.

"You were just a little thing. You sat up close to Miss Clossy's desk, in front of your sister Mary."

Something was coming back to her. A boy the age of her brother

Simon, but not nearly as far along in school. A boy who loved poetry...
who stood up in front of the class, so nervous he was shaking and her
heart had gone out to him. It was a lovely poem that she had remembered
and learned herself when she got bigger.

"You said the snow poem," she said to him. It was like trying to
describe a dream that changes and disappears the moment you touch
words to it. But she could see that she was right... he was the boy who
had said the snow poem.

"The snow had begun in the gloaming,
And busily all the night
Had been heaping field and highway..."

She said with him: "With a silence deep and white." There had
been a boy, as old as her brother Simon, who sat in back with the big
boys, but who kept to himself and seemed shy, and had long dark eyelashes and such dark eyes. He didn't go to their church, and she hadn't
known what his name was, but one day... this was so odd, it was like
the moment in Scripture when Mary Magdalene is looking into the empty
tomb, and yet when Jesus walks right up and speaks to her, she doesn't
recognize him. How could that be, that she could look right at him and
not recognize him? That story had never made real sense to her before.

"You gave me a marble," she said, and a slow smile came to his
face.

"I did. I won it from your brother Leander."

"And then you were gone, you didn't come to school anymore."

"My mother was better, and my father came in over the ice and
took us back home."

"I still have the marble," Claris said, trying to shake off a feeling of unreality. She did, she kept it in a tiny Indian sweet-grass box along with her locket and her collection of buttons. This was the boy, the mystery boy, the quiet one, who had only one set of clothes, and didn't know the games the others did, who noticed her alone at the edge of the circle of bigger children, and gave her his marble. All these years, when her family was roaring away with their songs and their games and their mock battles, and she didn't want to belong to a herd, she wanted one person who felt the same as she did, who would watch her with his dark eyes, as this boy had done, she had thought of him and kept the marble.

Suddenly shy of him, she said, "We better go in to Miss Clossy." Danial put his saw in the crook of a branch and picked up the bag of eggs and doughnuts she had left on the ground. She went ahead, holding up her apronful of apples, into the low dark house.

Miss Clossy had never been a beauty, and age was not improving her. She was big and bony, and her hair had gone very thin, but she didn't wear a cap as other women did, so you could see her scalp. In fact you couldn't avoid it. Her face was deeply pitted, and the scars were on her scalp too; maybe that was why so much hair had fallen out. Her cottage was very old-fashioned, without even a stove. Miss Clossy still cooked in the open hearth, as people had in the old days. She had only two windows, both small and high in the walls, so only a little light got in, and there was no view out. It had the feeling of a fortified place, a tiny cave, well defended. Miss Clossy herself, their old teacher, sat at a table. She seemed to be doing nothing, though a large spinning wheel, the kind you stand to use, stepping forward onto the treadle and back in a rhythm, stood by the fire beside a large basket of carded wool, which filled the little house with a lanolin smell. Claris guessed that the farmwives on the road gave her some of their work so she could exchange finished yarn for cheese and milk, or even a few pennies.

"Good day, Miss Clossy, it's Claris Osgood, come with some eggs from my mother, and doughnuts."

"We've brought in some of your apples for you too," said Danial. He walked over to the window and stood where the light would fall on his face, so Miss Clossy could see who he was. She peered at him, then ducked her head, as if to say, Good, it's you, I know you.

Claris sat down at the table in Miss Clossy's second chair (she had only two). She began to talk of the neighborhood news, a little loudly, as you talk to a deaf person, though as far as she knew there was nothing wrong with Miss Clossy's hearing. After a while she sputtered into silence, frustrated by the lack of response, though Miss Clossy listened with apparent interest, clucking a little, or ducking her head to indicate that she was following. Her responses came as from a distance, as if an invisible layer of some impenetrable stuff muffled her like quilt batting.

Danial leaned against the door, quiet and apparently content. Once he said into the silence, "I've cut some deadwood out of them apple trees, Miss Clossy. Ought to make pretty good kindling."

Miss Clossy ducked her head.

"Want us to stack it there beside your door where you can get at it?" Miss Clossy bobbed again. She kept her head to one side, as if she could see better out of one eye than the other. Claris was growing more and more uncomfortable.

After another silence Danial said, "We better get to it then, Miss Clossy. I have to catch the tide, but I'll see you the next time I'm in."

Miss Clossy, smiling now, bobbed her head at them. They saw themselves out, leaving her at her table. Danial went into the orchard and began collecting apple boughs, and Claris went with him, grateful to him for knowing just how to manage the visit.

Danial took a large heavy bough from Claris and sawed it into smaller lengths. Claris gathered them and followed him, taking up the cut pieces as he reduced the limbs to firewood.

"Do you see her often?"

"I try to whenever I come in. She was very good to me when I went to school. She made a shirt for me, seeing I had only one and the boys were teasing me."

Claris felt ashamed. She was sure the teasing boys had included her brothers and cousins. She looked at his calm, sober expression, which seemed to hold no rancor or self-pity. This was the boy who was teased, but stood up and recited that snow poem. Who was he? What was he?

He worked in silence for a bit and then said, "I don't think it matters if folks are odd. What matters is what makes them that way."

"There are so many tales told of Miss Clossy. But no one really knows, do they?"

"I do," said Danial.

"Can you tell me?"

"When she was a girl in Tomhegan, her mother took in a woodsman who asked for a bed for the night. The next morning the woodsman was dead of smallpox. One by one her whole family went down with it. When Miss Clossy came to herself again, the rest were all dead. She dragged the bodies into the woods one by one, then she walked away and walked till she came to rest here."

They worked in silence for a time. Finally Claris asked, "How do you know that?"

"She told me."

"Why?"

After a moment, he said, "I think she wanted to tell me people had teased her too. She wanted me to see that they wouldn't have, if they'd known what they were doing."

What a strange boy, Claris thought. She stood looking at him, and he returned her gaze, open and frank, and hopeful.

"Claris, Claris, Went to Paris..." he said softly.

"My jump rope rhyme," said Claris, and he nodded.

"Why did you give me the marble?" She surprised herself. She had not known she would ask that.

"Don't you know?" he said softly.

She shook her head, her eyes locked on his. But she did know.

When she could take her eyes from his face, she said, "You're a strange boy," and thought, not for the first time this afternoon, that he kept making things come out of her mouth that she hadn't meant to say.

"There's a streak of it in my family. As far back as can be remembered."

She nodded. She didn't doubt it.

"I had a great-great-uncle," he said, "he went completely strange, back at the time of statehood. In fact, when they drew the Maine border and he found out his farm wasn't in New Hampshire, he went right downhill and nobody could snap him out of it."

"Why?"

"He wouldn't say. They asked him was he afraid of more taxes, but he said no. They asked him if he didn't care for the new state government, but he said that wasn't it."

"What could it be?"

"They finally got it out of him. He said he dreaded them cold Maine winters."

She looked at his sober face for a moment, before she burst into laughter.

—⁂—

The hook was now set in each mouth, and each would become a barb through which the other would learn what life had to teach.

The morning after I saw the old woman in my room, I told Edith I wouldn't spend another night there.

"I'm moving in with Stephen."

"Don't be silly. You're too old for that."

"That may be, but I'm moving. Either that or I'll go back to Boston."

This threw her for a loop, briefly. "You can't go back to Boston."

"Why not?"

"Your father's working very hard. There's no one to look after you."

"I'm too old to need looking after."

She waited a moment too long to retort, so I went into my room and started cleaning out the dresser. She followed me to the door.

"This is just nonsense, Hannah. Stephen needs more sleep than you do, you'll keep him up—"

"No, she won't," said Stephen. That was brave of him. The last thing on earth Edith wanted was to find we'd formed a team, and she wasn't on it.

"Honey . . ." Her tone always softened when she spoke to him. "You don't know how late she stays up reading . . . the light will bother you, sweetie."

"I'll use a flashlight," I said, and went on to Stephen's room with my clothes in my arms.

When I was done, I went out and walked to the village, to the post office. I knew the mail wouldn't be ready, but I wanted to be outside, in the bright light of the summer morning. The air had a sweet crispness of balsam that seemed to wash me clean.

"Why, good morning, young lady," said Mrs. Foss when I came in. She had the most beautiful smile. She wore cotton dresses with mother-of-pearl buttons, and she sat on a stool behind the counter, holding court. It wasn't in that new building we have now, with the big parking lot in front so the summer people don't bash into each other on Main Street, backing into August traffic. The old post office was in that little building by the millstream where the man sells picture frames and fudge. When I was young it looked like the store it had always been (and is now again). It had a counter and shelves and a little woodstove in the middle of the room. Mrs. Foss had the mail contract in those days because she owned the building; her husband's people used to sell dry goods and notions there as well as run the P.O. Instead of fabric and buttons on the shelves, Mrs. Foss kept dime novels that summer people left with her to give away, and when the gardens started coming in, baskets of squash and beans and tomatoes that everyone had too much of.

"Good morning, Mrs. Foss," I said.

"How are you this morning, Hannah Gray? You know Mr. Horton?"

Kermit Horton was sitting by the window with his feet up on the cold stove. He had his dog Hoover with him. Hoover was a large yellow mutt, with tragic eyes. He had been mistreated before Kermit got him, and was very skittish.

"Mail's taking extra time," Mrs. Foss said cheerfully. "We got the Sears catalogs in it this morning. Good for a half hour right there."

"I don't mind," I said. I sat down beside Hoover, who shrank behind Kermit's leg. I had learned from Bowdoin Leach that Mrs. Foss and Mr. Horton kept company in some way that was left intentionally vague. Mrs. Foss called herself a widow, although it was well known that someone who looked exactly like the late Mr. Foss was living down in Portland with a young wife. Mrs. Foss was serene; she seemed to relish life greatly.

"How are you enjoying things down on the point?" she asked me. I said things were all right.

Mrs. Foss leisurely stuck envelopes here and there into people's mail slots. "You know of Miss Kennedy? She used to live in that house. She had a terrible time there." She said this mildly, and Kermit smiled and nodded.

"She did?"

"Yes, she used to come in all draggle-tailed some mornings, but Miss Hamor wouldn't let her talk about it."

I began to think that Mrs. Foss might be some kind of mind reader. "Why wouldn't she?"

"I don't know, dear. But Miss Hamor ruled the roost." Kermit agreed with that, evidently.

I said, "Miss Hamor taught at the Academy, I gather."

"Yes, she did."

"Is that why they call the house a schoolhouse?"

"Oh, no, dear," Mrs. Foss said. She seemed surprised that I had to ask. "That *was* a schoolhouse—it was the old schoolhouse out to the island. After it was closed, Miss Hamor had it brought across on the ice one winter."

"Really!"

"That's quite common around here. That schoolhouse was brought across, and some people in the summer colony, they brought over a barn and made it into their living room. I'm told that; I've never been in it."

This was news to me, and I was suddenly full of questions. Of course later I came to know a great deal about the island. Once the gasoline engine was invented, there wasn't the advantage there had been in living out at the edge of things, close to the fishing grounds and handy for the coasting trade. With an engine you could get out there almost as quick if there was wind or not; you just had to get up earlier in the morning. And the days of the great sailing vessels that called on the islands as they traveled from the Maritimes up to Boston, well, those days were mostly over anyway by the turn of the century.

"Course, there are islands where people stayed, gas engines or no," said Kermit. Mrs. Foss had paused in her dealing envelopes into slots to read some postcards. Everyone expected this, and, along with many others, in later life I'd often send a greeting to her on the edge of a postcard I was mailing to someone else in the village. "The truth is people started to remove from Beal back in the nineties, after the murder."

"The murder," I said. My skin pricked, and I stopped trying to get through to Hoover.

"Yes, there was a murder out on Beal in . . .'eighty-six, was it, Nella B.?"

"Eighteen eighty-six. I'm surprised you haven't heard of it. A girl called Sallie Haskell killed her father with an ax. There was a trial up in Unionville. . . . It was a terrible thing to happen in a little island village."

Killed her father! Was that what I had seen crawling across the bedroom floor? An old woman who had killed someone once? Was I so sure it was a woman? Was it a murdered man? The more I thought of it, the more I thought that I had heard something about it; it was the kind of tale that gets whispered among the sleeping bags at camp-outs. A girl murderer, a lonely island. But I certainly didn't know it was this bay, or that island.

"What happened to her? Sallie Haskell?"

"Why, they couldn't convict her. They tried her twice. The first time the jury was hung, and the second time they acquitted."

"Yes, reporters come up from all over New England for the trial," said Kermit. "My father went to the first one, every day. Course, the state was dry at the time, so reporters didn't have much to do with themselves except make things up. Not many wanted to come back up here for the second one."

"What happened to Sallie afterwards?"

"She came back here," they both said, as if this made perfect sense.

"But she didn't go back to the island," said Nella B. "She stayed in Dundee, where she had family, and lived in a little house by herself. She tried to teach school, but the children were so interested about who she was, she couldn't get much else through their heads. And every little while the press would dredge everything up. Anniversaries of the murder, that sort of thing. In her later years, she hardly went out."

"Wore nothing but black, and only went out after dark," said Kermit. "The children tended to follow her about, otherwise."

I was growing afraid to ask more about her. But I couldn't help wanting to know what she was like, had they known her?

"Yes, I knew her quite well," said Mrs. Foss. "She was quiet. She was always grateful for what you did for her. I'd take her her mail, when she got any, and visit a little. Max Abbott always sent a boy down with her groceries. She knitted a great deal. And she was wonderful during the influenza epidemic."

"Oh, I remember that," Kermit said. "Godfrey, wasn't that a time—half the town down with it; they turned the school here into an infirmary, and all that were able helped with those that weren't. No sooner one would get better than three more would go down with it, and we buried quite a few. When was that, Nella B.? Nineteen nineteen?"

"Nineteen nineteen. My daughter got it. She came through, though. Sallie Haskell was just as patient and kind, though she was awful frail herself by then. She was the only one nursing who didn't get it, and folks said she was the only one who really wanted to."

"She wanted to," I said.

"I think so, yes. Her life pretty much ended the day her father died."

"Though she went on breathing," said Kermit.

Nella B. began filing bills and catalogs into the mailboxes again. I sensed that I'd gotten to the limit of what she thought seemly to say on the subject.

I went out into the sunshine. Lovely as the day was, the shock and fear from the night before stayed with me like some foul-smelling vapor. I felt jumpy and anxious and wanted to go home to Boston. I missed my friends; I badly wanted to talk to someone who liked me. I guess it's in moments like that when you see if there's a meaning to things, because that was right when along into my life came Conary Crocker.

It was two years after the apple afternoon, and deep winter, when Danial asked Claris to marry him. The courtship had been sporadic because he lived on the island fishing and farming with his mother and brother and could not often come into town. Claris was twenty, and not only did her sister Mary have two children but her younger sister Alice had been married in the spring to one of the Crocker boys.

Danial had come to the main to take Claris to church at Christmastime, and she thought he might speak then, but he hadn't. He was often tongue-tied, but she believed she could read his silences better than a babble of talk from most people. She thought next that he would probably come across the ice for the horse races.

As soon as the bay was frozen solid, the village boys swept a course clean of snow and built great bonfires on the ice to mark the starting and finish lines. Men of the town and the farms gave their horses the day off, carriage and work horses both, and brought the likeliest of them down to try their speed. The whole town turned out to bet and cheer as the horses raced from one line on the ice to the other. Their hooves made a terrific booming sound, and they breathed steam like dragons as they galloped. This year Otis was wild with excitement; Leander had brought his mare, and Otis was going to ride with him in the pung. Their father and uncle Asa stood with the men at the fire, smoking and joking. Claris's mother and aunt kept track of the little ones who were shouting and falling down, holding skidding matches on the ice. The half-grown cousins were building snow forts. Meanwhile, far across the ice, Claris could see a sleigh coming down the bay toward the bonfires from the southern end of Beal.

When Danial drew his sleigh in among the watchers, Claris saw that he had his mother with him. Old Mrs. Haskell was bundled up under bearskin robes and wearing a man's fur hat. She peered out from beneath the brim with bright black eyes but did not attempt to leave the sleigh. Claris had met Mrs. Haskell only once and hoped this was a good sign, that she'd come into town, perhaps to be made acquainted with Claris's family. She waited for Danial to come find her and fetch her near. She began to feel almost impatient, as the Haskells, mother and son, hung back, apart from the gathering. Danial stood by the horse's head, and Mrs. Haskell stared before her in the direction of the races until the Baptist minister's wife, Mrs. Tull, climbed into the sleigh with her and asked her how she did. Danial called a small boy to come hold the horse and finally made his way to Claris.

"Miss Osgood," he said.

"Mr. Haskell." Claris bowed. It amused her when he got all formal. They looked at each other and became tongue-tied, two small figures on the edge of a gathering, in a vast white landscape of ice. They were both very conscious that half the town might be looking at them, since there is nowhere on a frozen bay to hide. Certainly the whole town knew they'd been courting quite long enough to be calling it on at last, or calling it off. Danial hoped they were not watching and Claris rather hoped they were. Finally Danial reached into a pocket and drew out a small wooden box with tiny handmade hinges. She looked it over thoroughly, guessing, correctly, that he had made it himself. She glanced up at him. The gray winter sun made a bright disk behind a screen of haze, and all the coves inshore were full of sea smoke. This was it. This was the moment, she was sure.

"Open it," he said.

After one more glance at him, both shy and excited, she opened the box. Inside, on a bed of soft silk, was a cat's-eye marble.

Claris was suddenly uncertain that this *was* the moment. Even poor gormless Byron Crocker had announced his intentions to Alice with a garbled speech, delivered on one knee, and an offered ring. She looked up at Danial, questioning.

"We got but one diamond in the family, and it's Mother's," he said. "But it will be yours in due time if you'll consent to become Mrs. Haskell." He said it stiffly, as if he were about to perish from embarrassment.

It *was* the moment. Well, thank heaven. Suddenly Claris would rather have had a marble in a handmade box than a ruby ring from the fanciest jeweler in Boston.

"Danial," she said, turning her face up to his. "My dear." Smiling, she closed the box and kissed it, then slipped it into the pocket of her coat. Then she gave him her hands and he took them, and they looked at each other, both grinning as if they would burst.

—⁂—

There were tears and anger at the Osgood house in the night and day that followed. Claris had known her family didn't like Danial as much as they had Jonathan Friend, or even cross-eyed Byron Crocker.

Danial was quiet. Her family liked people lively in company who told stories and sang. But through the courtship she had said she could read Danial's silences as she could the animals'. He was strong and a hard worker; Simon and Leander said so. He was fiercely protective of his aged mother. Danial understood Claris; she knew he felt the same way she did about things.

Claris had asked Danial to come to the house with her after the races, to ask her father for her hand, but he said he believed he ought to take his mother back home before it got dark. She said she understood. She spoke to her mother and father by herself after dinner, telling them Danial had asked her to marry him and she had accepted him. She expected kisses and congratulations as there had been for Mary and for Alice; she expected her father would send word out to the Haskells, asking Danial and his mother and brother to come to Sunday dinner so they could make wedding plans. Instead, there was a silence. A glance passed between husband and wife. Then her mother came and hugged her and left the room. Her father watched Claris, standing in the middle of the room; she looked like a sunny day turning to squall.

"What?" she said, staring hard at her father. "Do you know something ill of Danial?"

"No, I don't," said her father. "And what I've seen for myself, I respect."

"Then, *what*? You have something against him. Or is it that you have something against *me*?"

"Clarie."

She turned around, surprised by tears. She was too shocked and disappointed to let anyone see her cry. Why hadn't she expected this? Why didn't she ever learn? No matter what she did, nothing was ever the same for her as for the others.

"Clarie. Calm yourself. You're of age, and you're a fine, intelligent girl. If Danial Haskell is truly the man for you, you know we will support you in every way we can, and pray daily for your happiness, as we always have."

She whirled around. "You don't trust me! I know him—you don't! All you see is that he's different from . . . from . . ." She made a gesture of frustration. Even in her anger she couldn't bring herself to say to her father that Danial's difference from all that she had known was what she loved about him most.

Her mother came back in and closed the door behind her. In the kitchen Mabel and Otis were noisily washing the supper things, while Leander could be heard on the stairs threatening and cajoling the littlest Osgoods up toward bed, while they shrieked in mock fear. Mother sat down in the rocking chair near the stove and said, "Clarie, dear. Sit. We'll be as happy for you as you could want. Just let us talk it over quietly together."

Claris sat. Her cheeks were burning. She was furious.

Her father said, "This is a small village, Claris. We've known the Haskells—I knew Danial's grandparents well, and we both knew his father."

"I went to school with Elzina Haskell. Danial's aunt."

"It's not a happy family, Claris. There's a sour streak there. You're used to people who are happy and kind."

"*Oh!*" Claris almost shouted, but she damped her voice down at the last minute. She knew her temper made her family look at each other when they thought she didn't see. "Danial is not his family. Danial is Danial. I know him and you don't. I never heard anything so unfair. Or unkind, speaking of kindness."

Her father looked troubled and stared down at his hands. His wife leaned forward, though she looked as if she'd rather be anywhere than here.

"He seems like a decent man, Claris. We both think so." Claris turned a little in her chair, a twitch of irritation. They had been talking him over. They had been waiting for this, talking him over, because they didn't like his parents. "Does he mean to keep on on the island?"

"I don't know. What difference does it make?"

They both seemed about to speak at once. Claris's father shut his mouth.

"More than you know, Claris. Island life is lonely. And the Haskells are hard-shell Baptists—you don't know what that's like."

"Danial isn't."

"He may not be now, but he was raised that way. And people change with time. As the twig is bent, most often."

"I'd feel better about it if he meant to move into town," said her father. "We'd miss you if you moved way out there. And I'm afraid you'd miss us. Your cousins, all your friends."

You don't know me at all, Claris thought. You never have. You think I'm just like you, and that's the whole trouble. You think I should be like Mary. Her heart burned to protect Danial from people who would judge the boy by his father, by people who didn't understand that love can make everything right. She wasn't afraid of quiet, or loneliness. She'd never been so lonely in her life as she often felt in the midst of a crowd of people. All laughing and talking and not one of them seeing a single real thing about her. She believed Danial saw. Danial understood.

This is what happened the day that changed everything.

I had decided to go up to the library to see what I could learn about the murder on Beal Island. It would give me a project for the summer. What had made Sallie Haskell, a girl of almost my age, into a murderer? I was intensely curious about her story, but the plan had an additional advantage, which was that for some reason the subject irritated Edith. I asked her if she'd ever heard of Sallie Haskell, and she just flew at me, saying it was just like me to come to a beautiful spot and find the one morbid thing there was to dwell on.

"Morbid. Okay. Fine," is what my diary says for that morning.

I had hoped for newspaper reports of Sallie's trial, but Mrs. Pease said a squirrel came down the chimney one winter and made a pretty good mess of the old periodical files. They would have copies up in Unionville, but good luck trying to get Edith to drive me there and wait all day while I read through them. One amateur historian named Phin Jellison had written up his version of events sometime in the teens and published it himself. The library had plenty of copies of that. It was a pamphlet with a horrible photograph in it of this big bearded man in overalls lying on his back on a horsehair couch with his head split open. It was pretty hard to look at. I wanted to know what Danial Haskell had looked like when he still had a face, but I never have found a picture of him. I wonder if he never had his photograph taken in life.

There was a disgusting description of what he had eaten for his last meal, and much conflicting speculation on where the schoolteacher Mercy Chatto was at the time of the murder, and the wife, Claris, and the daughter, Sallie, and a boyfriend of Sallie's called Paul LeBlond. Mercy Chatto was a girl from the main, boarding with the Haskells while she kept school.

Mr. Jellison was an enthusiast, but not much of a writer, so I can't say I learned a great deal more. It seemed none of the three women who lived in the house would say a thing about how they had spent the morning except to assent to what they would have done, or usually did, of a Sunday. None of the women would have gone to worship. Mercy generally did her wash. Sallie went to the barn to tend her chickens and commune with the cow. Claris worked at her rug loom or sometimes stayed abed reading the Bible.

Mr. Jellison's money was on Paul LeBlond for the murderer. He was a queer kind of fellow, according to Phin, an artist and foreign, with a nasty temper.

When I exhausted the information in the library, I decided to hitchhike out the Eastward road to see my grandparents. I thought they must know something of Sallie Haskell. I was forbidden to hitchhike, so I'd have to tell them Edith had dropped me at the end of the road. I couldn't tell them anything about how it was with

Edith and me; Edith used to justify keeping us from my grandparents by claiming they didn't like her, and I didn't want to do anything to make her right. Besides, my grandparents wouldn't have liked it. Children were not encouraged to criticize their elders in those days.

We sat on the covered porch overlooking Grandpa's sheep meadow, which ran down to the edge of the bay and the great stone hulk of the granite wharf. You could see right over to the north end of Beal; it looked close enough to swim to. Mrs. Eaton, who helped grandmother keep house, brought out lemonade and gingersnaps.

"So what have you been up to, Miss Chick?" my grandfather asked.

"Nella B. told me about the murder on Beal Island."

Grandfather roared with laughter. "Oh, you've gotten around to that, have you?"

I felt myself blush. I suppose it *was* old hat to him. No doubt everyone in town had had a lifetime of having tourists come upon it all shiny and new and start asking the same questions.

"I knew about it before, sort of, I just didn't know it happened here," I said, on my dignity. "Did you know Sallie Haskell?"

"Oh, yes," they both said. Oh, yes, of course, we knew the murderess.

"What was she like?"

Granny could see how much I wanted to know, and was sympathetic. "Terribly sad. Kept to herself almost completely after the trials, though she kept up with her Osgood cousins, and there were a lot of them."

"Haskell cousins didn't truck with her though," said Grandfather.

"No. They wouldn't," said Granny. "We used to see her out walking on the Kingdom Road in the evenings. She was always pleasant, always greeted you."

"Not much for chatting." Grandfather would find this a good quality.

"No. She had a little dog for a while, didn't she, Ed?"

"Yes, some kind of terrier. Awful fond of it."

"And what happened . . . something sad . . ."

"I think it bit people and someone shot it . . ."

"No, that was Ella Staples's dog. I think Sallie's was killed by some animal. A raccoon. She was done up over it, and wouldn't have another. You know who Hannah should talk to, Ed? Cousin Amy Bell. Amy Friend Bell, she'd enjoy a visit," she said to me. "She always spoke of Cousin Sallie."

"*Cousin* Sallie? Was she our cousin?"

"Well, now . . ." Granny got a crease between her eyebrows when she pondered, and suddenly I could see in her old face the girl she'd been, with a beautiful smile and a sense of fun, a girl you'd want to be friends with.

"I used to be able to keep all this straight. Now . . . my father was Thomas Friend, and he had two brothers. The oldest one, Jonathan, married Aunt Mary, who was an Osgood—I *think* she was Sallie Haskell's aunt. So my Friend cousins on Jonathan's side were Sallie's first cousins, but we're just cousins by marriage. Cousin Amy will know. We'll go as soon as I'm back on my feet."

I'm still sorry that visit never happened.

"It's a good thing I came from away," said Grandfather, "or you'd have too many cousins in town to keep track of."

I could see my grandmother tired easily. She was mending, but she needed to take a rest in the afternoons. Grandfather offered to drive me home, but Jewel Eaton went home right after lunch, and I knew he didn't want to leave Granny alone in the house. I kissed them each good-bye and said I would enjoy the exercise.

I was walking west on the gravel shoulder of the tar road when

I heard a car bearing down on me from behind. I stepped off the shoulder to let it pass. But it didn't pass, and it wasn't a car. It was the strangest rattletrap truck—I learned later that it was a Model T, one of the very first ones, with the backseat taken out. It was kept on the road with ingenuity and spit, and it had one really distinguishing characteristic: there was no fuel pump, so in order to get gas to the engine when you went uphill, you had to go up backwards. On this afternoon it had a half dozen lobster pots in the back. The driver was a dark-haired boy with deep-set very pale eyes. He needed a shave. In fact, he needed a bath. He pulled the truck off the road and came to a stop so close to me that I thought at first there was something menacing in him. He sat at the wheel looking at me.

"You could stand there staring," he said, "or you could get in."

I hesitated.

"They both got their points, but one'll get you to town faster."

I had to smile at that. He leaned over to open the door for me, and I climbed in. He pulled the truck back onto the road.

"You the ones living in Fannie Hamor's house?"

"How did you know that?"

"Saw you walking the other day. You aren't any of the piano tuner's kids, 'cause I met all them, and those are the only other new people up that road. Anyway, Jewel Eaton's my grandmother."

At that I looked at him again. "Are you Conary?"

"Are you guessing?"

"Not really," I said. I had heard all about him, both from Mrs. Eaton and at the library. I gathered he was an all-around wild seed. I had the impression that Mrs. Pease and Mrs. Allen were crazy about him.

Conary, driving with his left hand, gave me his right to shake. He seemed pleased to think he had a reputation, and not surprised.

"I'm Hannah," I said.

He said, "Yeah, I worked that out. How you liking that house?"

I don't know why, but I felt there was something behind the question. I said, "It's a beautiful spot . . ."

The way he said, "Well . . . yeah," as if that was hardly the issue, I knew there had been something behind the question, so I asked him, "Did you know Miss Hamor?"

He said, "To speak to. Everybody did. She was pretty ancient. She taught my father Latin at the Academy."

"Really?"

"I don't believe he shone, at Latin." Something about this thought made Conary smile to himself.

I asked him why the house was empty for so long, just to see what he would say. We were drawing into town.

He said, "*I* heard it was haunted. Now . . . where can I set you down?" As he asked, he pulled in at the post office. I thanked him for the ride and got out, wishing the way had been twice as long.

T he Haskell place was on the southeastern shore of Beal Island, with a wide view of the outer passage to Frenchman's Bay. Claris knew this when Danial brought her home on their wedding day; what she hadn't exactly understood was that Danial's mother and brother, Leonard, were to go on living in the house with them. Danial had merely said that his mother would welcome her and all necessary things had been arranged, and Claris had assumed that things would now be for her as they had for her sisters. When Mary had married, Jonathan Friend's family built a house for them. When her sister Alice married, Byron Crocker took her all the way to Boston on a honeymoon.

Claris's honeymoon consisted of having an ancient coverlet quilted in a wedding knot pattern produced from a chest in Mrs. Haskell's bedroom and spread on the bed where Danial had slept since boyhood. Additional arrangements were that Leonard moved downstairs to sleep in the buttery, and that for her night soil Claris was given a rather grand china commode with a lid, from England.

In her first island winter Claris lost a child, a stillborn daughter. This was a terrible blow; her mother and sisters all gave birth to healthy babies at the drop of a hat; why should she alone suffer such loss, such failure? The brief dark days of that winter for Claris were endless. Ten months later she lost a second baby, also a girl. Her mother-in-law said very little about this (or about anything) but peered at Claris with apparent dislike from under her bonnet.

It was during this lonely passage in her life that Claris first began to doubt that behind Danial's silence lay a mind that divined her thoughts and a heart that beat in sympathy with hers. She was living in a thick atmosphere of paralyzing bleakness, waiting for Danial to show that he knew how it was with her, how it felt to have longed to be a mother but instead produced only death. When he merely came and went as usual and expected her to do the same, it finally began to occur to her that behind Danial's stolid silence might be . . . nothing she understood.

When her mother-in-law died the third winter, Danial brought the Baptist minister out from the main, along with the few old friends who remained, to pray for the soul of the inaccurately named Solace Haskell. While Reverend Tull was with them, he said prayers for the dead at the tiny graves of Claris's daughters, both named Sallie. The ground was frozen too hard to dig a hole for Solace, so Claris sewed her into a sailcloth shroud weighted with rocks, and Danial and his brother took her far out onto the ice, cut a hole, and buried her at sea.

Solace had been almost completely silent during her last year, and nearly bald, and so nearly dead it was hard to tell she was breathing. But her ways ruled the house both before and after death. In her house they did no work on Sundays, could read no books except the Bible and play no games of any kind. Solace opposed music, cards, and any form of alcoholic drink. Danial seemed distraught at his mother's death in a way that frightened Claris; it was nothing like his reaction to the deaths of her babies. Next, Leonard Haskell left to marry Ellen Gott, who lived around the tip of the island, and Claris finally found herself alone with her husband.

The family had chickens, sheep, a pig, a cow, and two horses at the time of Leonard's marriage. Leonard took one of the horses and half the sheep, and Danial bought out his share in the pig and the cow. The chickens they reckoned were Claris's, since she had taken on care of them when Solace stopped leaving the house. Danial butchered his sheep, froze the meat, and in the spring sailed into the main with most of it to trade at Abbott's store. When he came back he brought barrels of flour and molasses, some bright new cotton dress goods, and the most extravagant present: a whole stem of green bananas brought round the Horn from the Sandwich Islands. It seemed, at last, like the real beginning of their life together. Claris hung the fruit in the dark cellar to ripen, and it was the first and last time in her life that she had all the bananas she wanted.

When Claris went into labor for the third time in the spring of 1862, Danial sat alone in the kitchen while the midwife attended her upstairs. Twice in this marriage already there had been pain and blood and then silence. This time, after only two hours, Danial heard a surprisingly loud wail, and he took the stairs two at a time. He burst into the room to find Mrs. Duffy holding a long purplish baby boy by the heels. The baby was roaring, and with each lungful of air he took, his color became more human, white and pink. Meanwhile a coiling cord of an astonishing gray-purple color stretched from the baby's middle to between his mother's legs. Claris crouched on the edge of a chair, gripping the arms and weeping with relief, and Mrs. Duffy said, "Please, Danial. We're not quite ready for you here."

For the first days and nights of the baby's life, Claris wouldn't sleep; she wouldn't even lie down. She sat in the chair beaming and held him, sang to him, nursed him, while Danial looked on, proud and smiling.

Amos Haskell grew into a healthy and bright-eyed baby, the image of Claris's brother Leander. When he was sure the baby was going to live, Danial sailed into Dundee and came back out with Claris's mother, who stayed several weeks with them, sewing diapers, cleaning and baking, gossiping with Claris, and paying a round of calls on the island folk, getting to know her daughter's neighbors. Claris had never done this on her own, and some of the neighbors were quite surprised to see the Haskell wagon pull into their dooryards. They were happy to see Captain Osgood's wife, though, whom they knew at least by reputation, and glad to get to see that Claris was not so standoffish as she appeared.

Claris and Mrs. Osgood talked for hours over all the news of home Claris had missed. Both Simon and Leander had marched off south with the Thirteenth Maine, but both were safe so far. Her sister Alice had a baby girl, and Mabel was teaching school. Otis was now thirteen and as tall as his father, and could play the fiddle even better than Leander. Claris liked having her mother all to herself, although even now, from time to time, there were strains.

Claris had regained her health quickly once she felt sure the baby would survive. Baby Amos seemed to take on an aura of gleaming perfection for her. He was the coin with which she would be repaid for all the griefs, slights, and disappointments she had met in life thus far, and Danial and Mrs. Osgood watched with some surprise the intensity of the love she shone on the baby.

One night over a supper of fresh fish and wild greens Mrs. Osgood had gathered and cooked, Claris leaped from the table at the sound of a tiny mewling noise from the baby.

"Clarie, he's just dreaming," said her mother. "Don't wake him up. Finish your supper."

"I think I know my own baby best," Claris said. She picked the sleepy child up from his cradle and brought him to the table to nurse. Mrs. Osgood (who had always retired to a separate room to nurse her babies) looked across at Danial, and the two shared a moment of under-standing. Danial said, "Mother O, did I forget to tell you that that baby is the first and only baby ever born in the world?"

"I thought he might be the infant Prince of Wales," said Mrs. Osgood, smiling at Danial. Claris got up from the table and ran upstairs with the baby in her arms.

Danial and Mrs. Osgood looked after her, and then again at each other. Danial shrugged and went back to eating his supper. After a mo-ment Mrs. Osgood said, "Excuse me," and followed her daughter upstairs.

Claris sat, weeping, in the birthing chair, with the baby sucking happily at her breast. Mrs. Osgood came in and closed the door behind her. She looked around at the pine dresser, the bare floor, the bed with its thin mattress and wedding knot quilt. The bed linen looked none too clean.

"Clarie, don't cry, there's no need for that. No one meant to hurt your feelings."

Claris's brimming eyes met her mother's. "You don't know," she said. "You never *do* know how I feel. You never lost a baby as I have or you wouldn't mock me."

Her mother sat silent with downcast eyes for quite a while and then said, "Actually, I have, Claris. I lost a little girl between Mary and you. She was strangled during birth by the cord." Mrs. Osgood's gaze held her daughter's.

Finally Claris said in a flat voice, "I never knew that." (Mrs. Osgood couldn't help thinking that Mary or Alice, even in pique, would have melted at once, come to her and said, "Oh, Mother, I'm sorry.")

"No need to talk about it. You were born the next year, beautiful and healthy, and we were so glad to have you." The two women sat in silence for a while, watching Amos nurse.

The next morning Mrs. Osgood said to Danial that, with regret, she thought she ought to be getting home. Claris stood on the porch with the baby in her arms and waved as Danial sailed her mother away, feeling both sorry and angry.

—⁂—

That first year of Amos's life was mostly a happy one for Claris and Danial. Danial fished all summer, and the catch was good. Twice a week he'd sail into the main and peddle his fish, five pounds of haddock (no hake) for fifteen cents and clams for ten cents a quart. What he couldn't sell direct he traded to Abbott's. Sometimes he'd take Claris and the baby along with him into town, and Claris would spend the day with her mother or one of her married sisters. The rest of his catch Danial dried and salted and sold in barrels to the boats that called in at the wharf on the south end of Beal.

The winter Amos was three, Danial began work on a plan he'd had in mind since he was a boy; he wanted to try a sawmill at the mouth of their stream. He had suggested it years before to his father and been laughed at for trying to get fancy. There was a gristmill on the Neck and a sawmill at Dundee, and that was enough, according to Abner Haskell. Haskells didn't take wages, and they didn't go into trade, according to him. Danial went to study both of the mills on the main, and in the spring he ordered what parts he couldn't manufacture, and with Leonard and two of the Gotts he started building. All summer he worked on the mill instead of fishing. By fall he was in operation. They were nearly out of cash and goods to barter, and he told Claris they'd have to live close to the bone that winter, but by next summer all their hard work would pay off.

Unfortunately, he and Leonard quarreled over whether Leonard had worked for wages (still owing) or for ownership, and they stopped speaking with Leonard holding a large IOU from Danial. Business at the mill was less than Danial had hoped for, and he grew tense and silent. Their diet that winter consisted of dried apples, eggs, biscuits with salt pork gravy, and salted fish boiled in milk. In the spring Danial hired Percy Grindle to help at the mill, but they too quarreled. Soon after that, in a moment of pique or inattention, Danial sawed off two of the fingers of his left hand. Claris doctored the maimed hand in silence, pulling the bandage strips painfully tight. She had felt the mill was a bad idea from the start, and unfortunately had said so.

Danial walked away from the mill and never went back to it; he wouldn't even sell it. He went back to fishing and saltwater farming, and let the mill fall slowly down, year by year. Claris said little about this either, but her manner showed she was disgusted. Now and then she mentioned the courage and persistence the men of her family were known to show in good times and bad. She did not mention that in her family she herself was as famously hard to deflect once she had set her course as he could ever be, but Danial understood her well enough by now not to have to be told that.

In the spring of 1867, little Amos had outgrown all the clothes Claris could make him by cutting down outworn clothes of her own and Danial's, and she and Danial were threadbare themselves. Furthermore Amos was barefoot, and the rocks and sharp clamshells on the shore hurt his feet.

Claris took Amos down to the dock to meet Danial one blue and gold April evening soon after her birthday. The snow was gone from the meadows, and the air was warm and full of the fir-scented smell of spring. She stood watching Danial maneuver his little gaff-rigged sloop in against the falling tide.

"Fresh fish for supper, Mother," Danial said, when his boat was safely on the outhaul. He sat down on the dock beside a bucket of fish and began to clean them, throwing the guts into the water.

"Keep the heads; I'll make chowder," said Claris. Danial grunted.

"I'd like to go into town to the store tomorrow," she said, after watching him for a bit.

Danial didn't react; he just kept cleaning the fish.

"I need some buttonhole silk, and I want to order shoes for Amos."

"You want to sit and gossip with your sisters, you mean."

"Well, I haven't been to town in months, Danial."

"Mother didn't used to go to town from one year to the next."

"I'm not your mother," said Claris.

Danial raised an eyebrow and looked at her, as if to say, I'm well aware of that.

Amos was off on the beach, studiously gathering shells, selecting and rejecting rapidly according to some system of his own. She watched him, and then said to Danial, "The baby's helping you."

"Good. I can use it."

"My brother should be home from Bermuda," Claris said. Both her brothers had come home from the war, though seven boys from the village had died. So many boys had been lost from Deer Isle, to the south, that for thirty years it would be known as the Island of Widows. "I'd like to see him. And I have eggs to trade, and buttons." Claris had been carving buttons out of sheep bones all winter, to earn some cash money.

"Thought you traded them up at Duffys'."

"Not the buttons. There are things the island store doesn't have."

"Make me a list and I'll get them for you."

Claris went silently to Amos and let him fill her pocket with his shells and pebbles. She didn't want to speak, she was so angry and disappointed. She didn't want to give Danial the pleasure of seeing how much it mattered to her.

—⁓—

The next morning she watched from the shore as Danial sailed away up the bay with her bucket of eggs and the buttons she'd made sewn up in a bag. If he couldn't match the buttonhole silk exactly, she knew he'd get the wrong thing. And she wanted to weep, thinking of how Leander would have smiled at catching sight of her and Amos coming up the walk, and of Amos on Otis's shoulders, and of dinner at home. She wanted to know what her mother was reading, what new music her cousins had for the parlor organ, what games the children were playing in the town. She wanted to know if Cousin Mark's broken arm had mended and whether Alice was as sick with this baby coming as she'd been with the last. She wanted her brothers and cousins to have a blanket toss, to hear Amos's shrieks of joy as he flew into the air and fell back to the safety they stretched underneath him.

She doubted if Danial would even call at home, let alone ask any of the questions she herself wanted to ask. He seemed to think people thought ill of him for not going to the war, though he'd had an ancient mother and young wife to support, and babies coming. He'd march up to Abbott's and do his business as if the ground were burning his feet, then quick-march back to his boat. She knew how much he resented dawdling around town waiting for her to finish her visit when he brought her along. For her part, she resented his letting his temper show, for she fancied her father and mother, and aunts and uncles too, taking note of it. She pictured them talking her over after she left with her husband, saying, "We told her. We told her how it would be, but . . . you know Claris."

—m—

Claris saw Danial's sail coming down the bay at midafternoon and went down to the dock to meet him. She could see by the way he handled the lines of the outhaul that he was furious. He marched up the path toward her and went past into the house with her hurrying after him. His limp was worse when he was mad.

As she came into the kitchen, he threw a small pair of worn leather boots onto the table.

"Your sister Mary sends these to Amos," he said, the words exploding out of his mouth as if he were spitting bullets. The atmosphere was as charged as the minutes before a lightning storm, and Claris was both puzzled and annoyed.

"What's the matter now, Danial?"

"Your brother paid my bill at Abbott's."

"What bill?"

"My bill! I've been paying it off in my own time, and Abbott knew I was good for it, but your brother got wind that I owed money and he went in and paid it off."

"Simon?"

"Of course, Simon! What other high muck-a-muck would do such a thing?"

"Oh, Danial—that's just what a brother does!" She was exasperated.

"Not mine."

"Maybe it would be a better world if he did!"

"A better world if we were all Osgoods? I can pay my debts!"

"I didn't know we had one!"

"Why should you have? So you could tell your brothers?"

"Was Abbott charging you interest?"

"Why shouldn't he?"

"Is Simon?"

"I don't know what Simon is doing—trying to shame me!"

"I don't see that you need much help doing that!"

Amos looked from his father's face to his mother's and started to cry.

Claris was relentless when she was angry, and she was looking at Danial with fury, as if she couldn't remember ever having loved him in her life.

His face congested and red, Danial half-raised his arms, as if he were a bird about to take flight, then dropped them. He reached into his pocket and pulled out a reel of scarlet buttonhole twist. He threw it at her, and wheeled out the door, slamming it behind him. The spool hit her hard on the breast, but she never moved.

After Conary left me at the post office, I went up to the blacksmith shop. I'd never seen a blacksmith work before I came to Dundee. Horses were not used at all in Boston anymore, but they were still quite common here in the farming communities. Not so much for riding but for hauling heavy loads out of the backcountry and for pulling farm machines and bringing goods to town. The first day I discovered Bowdoin Leach, he was shoeing a team of Belgians while he and the farmer told stories. I could have sat there all day watching him heat the black metal until it passed orange and turned an angry white, and then he began to shape it with tongs and hammer as if he were bending an icicle. Best was the tremendous sizzle and hiss of steam when he plunged the hot iron into water to set and temper it.

This day, he was making a sign to mark the driveway of a house in the summer colony. The Elms, it was going to say. I wonder if that sign is still there in front of the house; I'm sure the elms are not. Anyway, I said, "Hello, Mr. Leach," and he said, "Afternoon, Miss Gray." He called me Miss Gray all that summer until somebody told me to call him Bowdoin. You pronounce it *Boe-din,* like the college, which someone in his family founded. Edith would have given birth to goldfish if she knew I was being familiar with my elders, even a blacksmith, but by then I had stopped listening to her just about altogether.

I settled myself on one of the big sawed-off stumps that stood around his shop. You could use them for chairs, or Bowdoin might use any one of them to hammer on. They were all covered with burnt-in scars. "You used to live out on the island, didn't you? Mrs. Allen said you did."

"She's right. I did."

"Did you know the Haskells?"

He stopped and looked at me. "You haven't been listening to that crate of flapdoodle of Abby Gordon's, have you?"

I hadn't, but immediately I wanted to know what crate of flapdoodle that might be. I knew Miss Gordon ran the little notions store on Union Street, but I hadn't known up to then she knew anything about Beal Island.

"No, I haven't."

"I'm glad to hear it." He held up the curlicue of iron he'd been heating and moved very carefully to his anvil. You could see in his movements how painful must be whatever force of nature held his back hunched over as relentlessly as he bent the iron.

"Abby Gordon never knew the Haskells. I knew them, and my father knew them well. He sometimes fished with Danial, and he often did odd jobs for Mrs. Haskell when Danial wasn't by. I took music from Mrs. Haskell up at the schoolhouse."

I was surprised. To look at him, you wouldn't have thought of

Bowdoin Leach "taking" music, any more than you'd picture him cro-
cheting doilies. (Which he could also do, I later learned.)

"What instrument do you play?"

"Mouth harp, anymore. Back then Mrs. Haskell wanted to teach
me the parlor organ, which she had one, down at her house. But she
could only do that when old Danial was off-island. He wouldn't have
music in the house. She taught me fiddle, instead."

"She played both?"

"She played anything. She was an Osgood."

"Why didn't Danial like music?"

"I don't know that he didn't. He just wouldn't have it in the
house. Pure meanness, like as not. I don't know anyone who knew
him who didn't think he needed killing."

You can tell when someone has said more than he meant to.
Bowdoin turned abruptly and carried his ironwork back to the fire hole.
When it was glowing, he flopped it onto a stump far from me and
began to hammer. I waited to see if he would come back to me, but
he seemed wholly absorbed in shaping his iron elm, so I went on
home.

There was rain for the next three or four days that kept us
trapped indoors. I stayed out of Edith's way as much as I could, which
was hard enough in a small house. I played Chinese checkers with
Stephen, and Edith showed us how to make pull taffy. I put on my
slicker and took Whitey up to the village to get the mail, and there
was quite a crowd in the post office, killing time and gassing. Kermit
Horton said the mackerel were running; the day before Buster Gordon
went out trolling in the rain and he got so many he was giving them
away. There was a bucket of them on the back porch, iridescent and
slick. I wondered aloud if Edith would like some.

"They're wicked good, fried in cornmeal," Mrs. Foss said to me. She winked as she said it.

Kermit said, "Wicked good fertilizer."

I decided not to take any. What I really wanted to do was go out fishing in the rain myself, but I didn't know anyone with a boat.

That night, Stephen went to sleep with forbidden bubble gum in his mouth, and the next morning it was all in his hair. Edith was sure I had given him the gum, though I hadn't. She announced I was on bounds for a week, and then she said there was no way to get gum out of hair but to cut it out, and that's what she did. She took a pair of kitchen scissors and cut off a handful of Stephen's beautiful black hair. Maybe she had to—I've never tried to get gum out of hair—but the way she did it made me mad. Edith said it would teach him a lesson. Later I tried to fix it by cutting the rest of his hair shorter, but he didn't look much better and it was going to take months to grow out. He looked just tragic sitting there on my bed with his Roosevelt Bear under his arm and his mouth all turned down. He said he was going to wear a paper bag on his head.

I asked him if he would feel better if I had short hair too. At first he just looked gloomy, but then I said maybe we could get the whole town to cut their hair, even Mrs. Foss, and even Mr. Horton, and even the coon cat that slept on the windowsill at Abbott's. The town would be famous; we'd all be in the newsreels. He finally started to laugh. Well, then I had to make good on it. We went into the hall bathroom between his bedroom and mine. He stood on a stool beside me so I could look at his shorn forelock while I cut my own, so we would match. There was a moth in the room, and it kept bumping against the lightbulb over the mirror.

I combed a hank of my hair forward over my face. My hair wasn't like Stephen's; his was silky fine, but mine was dense and straight, then as now. I felt for my eyebrows with my finger and made a cut with the scissors flat across my forehead, and then I could see from one eye. I met Stephen's eyes in the mirror; he was aghast with delight that I had really done it. I positioned the scissors carefully, taking care not to poke myself in the eye. I felt Stephen was holding his breath watching what I was doing. Slice—the blade cut through my hair, and suddenly there I was, transformed. Stephen was looking with amazement at my new face in the mirror and seeing nothing else. But my heart nearly stopped. Now in the mirror I could see a tall black-shrouded figure just outside the door, in the hall, silently watching us. It had arrived soundlessly and was hovering, intent, as if it didn't know it could be seen, its face shaded except for terrible piercing eyes, a gaze like ice picks. I screamed and dropped the scissors into the sink, and all the electric lights in the house went out.

The *Randall D* was a schooner, fifteen hundred tons, one of the biggest ships ever built in Dundee. The builder was John Osgood; the captain was his brother Asa; and she sailed in 1867 with Otis Osgood as second mate. Otis was nineteen. It was March of the following year when word came that the *Randall D* had been lost with all hands in the Bay of Biscay. She'd not been seen since she left Cádiz, making for Cardiff, and it was presumed she had broken up in a winter storm.

Beal Island heard the news before Dundee, from a coastal steamer. Percy Grindle came out to the Haskell house himself to tell Claris, and she wept as she got the children ready for the trip onto the main. Amos was six; the new baby Sallie was almost two. Danial moved around Claris silently as he made their preparations; he held a grudge against Claris's older brothers for being so different from himself and for having the knack of making Claris happy, but no one could have held a grudge against young Otis. Danial understood Claris's tears. Although by the time they were halfway up the bay he'd had enough of them.

The whole village had gone into mourning. There had been a dozen men from the village and the Neck on the *Randall D,* and scores who had worked on her or sailed with those who had sailed on her. There were services held for all hands at both the Congregational church and the Baptist. The whole town attended both.

The youngest Osgood cousins were inconsolable, feeling the loss of Otis, their playmate and champion, as terribly as the loss of their father. Claris's mother and her newly widowed sister stayed very close together. The neighbors brought in vast arrays of food, and visitors came and went throughout the days and into the evenings.

Claris and Danial slept in the bed Claris had once shared with her sister Mary. Their new baby Sallie slept between them, and Amos was on a trundle on the floor. It was the first time since her marriage Claris had spent a night under that roof. As always when they were among her family, Danial grew more and more silent. On the evening of the second day, Claris's mother asked Mary to play the parlor organ for hymns. Afterward, Leander got out his fiddle and started to play, mournful songs and chanteys. When he played "Black-Eyed Susan," their mother broke down and wept without reserve, as she had not done even at the church service.

Amos had moved to sit beside his uncle, watching Leander's hands as he played.

"That was Otis's favorite song," Leander said to him. "He started playing it when he was about your age." He began to play it again. Claris's father left the room. Claris watched him go, knowing John Osgood was suffering terribly, not only from the loss of his brother and his son and so many young friends and the sons of friends but also from the terrible fear that it was somehow his fault, that there was something in the way the boat was built, something different he could have done to it to bring them all home safe.

> All in the Downs the fleet was moor'd
> The streamers waving in the wind,
> When Black-Eyed Susan came onboard,
> "O where shall I my true love find?
> Tell me, ye jovial sailors, tell me true,
> If my sweet William, if my sweet William
> Sails among your crew?"

Their mother had learned it in England on her honeymoon and taught it to each of the girls in turn. It was always sung after supper, a duet or ensemble, the night before any man of the family left on a sea voyage.

> Change as ye list, ye winds, my heart shall be
> The faithful compass, the faithful compass
> That still points to thee.

Leander looked down at Amos. "Do you want to try?" he asked, and he held out the fiddle to him. Amos nodded solemnly. He arranged the fiddle under his chin and placed his left hand just so; he had been watching very carefully. Leander put his arms around Amos and placed his big hands over the little ones, one on the neck of the fiddle and one on the bow. Very slowly, moving Amos's fingers with his, he played the first note of "Black-Eyed Susan," then the next, then the next. Claris observed from across the room with a terrible ache in her heart. Little Otis. She saw a hundred pictures of him in her mind. She wrapped her arms around the sleeping baby Sallie on her lap, and watched Amos hungrily.

Meanwhile, Danial was also watching his son, whose face was a mask of concentration, following his uncle Leander's fingers with his, passionately studying how to squeeze music out of the box of wood and gut, as one wrings juice from an orange.

All the Osgoods remembered the night Otis had first taken up Leander's violin. Claris turned to Danial, wanting to describe that moment to him, as they looked together at their son. But as she turned and leaned toward him to speak, Danial got out of his chair and left the room swiftly, without looking at her.

—⁓—

Danial left the house the next morning as soon as it was light. He left no word for Claris as to how she should get home, and she decided to take that to mean she should pay as long a visit as she wanted. She stayed three weeks. As the days passed, the family returned to their usual pursuits. One of Mary's children had a birthday, and they had the familiar form of celebration, although the feeling was terribly muted. Life was for the living. There was a coconut cake, and there were presents; Claris's mother gave the little girl a doll that had been Mabel's; she had sewn it a new dress and a tiny muff made of rabbit fur. Mary and Claris made small patchwork quilts for the doll's carriage. Amos had the completely new experience of attending a party, and baby Sallie was given her first taste of ice cream, which Alice and Cousin Sarah had made using crushed peppermint candy canes saved from Christmas for the flavoring.

The cousins next door treated Sallie as if she were their own brand-new doll, singing to her and pushing her around in a doll's carriage. Amos made a special friend of Mary's third child, William. William introduced him to the pleasures of the pony cart, the same one Otis used to drive behind Elmer the burro. Together Alice and Mary had shared the expense of a Shetland pony, the first ever seen in the state, and Amos learned to drive it as well as to sit astride it while the cousins led him around the backyard.

Every night there was music. Sometimes Mary or Cousin Deborah played the organ while those who liked to sang, sometimes Leander or Thomas played the fiddle, and one night Neighbor Treworgy carried his bass violin up the hill to join them. Simon coached Amos so that he won the first game of Up Jenkins he ever played. Claris saw even Sallie forget her lifelong habit of clinging to her mother's skirt and begin to venture forth, toddling after the older children.

—⁓—

After the first week of mourning, the older cousins returned to school, and Amos went with them. The school had three times the number of children as the island school, and that meant many more games could be played. After school Amos usually went home with William and sometimes stayed the night. One afternoon he came home alone in a funk; he and William had had a fight over possession of some marbles, but Mary and Claris left them to sort it out themselves, and by the next afternoon they were friends again. Amos learned to play Authors, a game unknown in Solace Haskell's house, since it was played with cards. On Sundays they played a spelling game but used only words from Bible stories. Jonathan Friend conducted these. And almost every night after dinner, Leander went on with Amos's fiddle lessons.

It should not have come as a surprise to Claris when it was time to leave that Amos didn't want to go. But it did; it shocked her. Amos, her beloved son, sent to her to make her life worth living. With his face set in misery, he said, "I could stay with William."

"But your home is with us!"

"Why?"

She didn't know what to say. She looked over his head at her sister Mary; she knew that if she could part with him, Mary would willingly take him in. There were several families on the island and more on the main that had done this, kept a son or daughter when a family removed for one reason or another. She pictured Amos happily folded in with Mary's brood and was flooded with terrible feeling. Baby Sallie in her arms seemed to sense it; she began to wail.

"Hush!" Claris jiggled the baby and felt her own heart pound as the crying grew worse. Young Bowdoin Leach would be waiting for them at the landing, ready to sail them out home. She had packed the few things they'd brought and the many things they'd been given, hand-me-downs and keepsakes and new things for the baby.

"I have to go back, and you have to go with me. You'd miss us terribly if I left you behind. You're my son." She could see that this utterly rational statement of fact meant nothing to him beside the huge emotion he was feeling; he'd found the place that felt like home to him, and it wasn't with her.

Mary reached out and took the howling baby from Claris and began to croon to her. Almost at once Sallie grew calmer; then something worse happened. Claris turned on her sister and grabbed the baby back, setting off a fresh shrieking.

"Claris—I was trying to help," Mary said.

"I don't need help, I can comfort my own child!" said Claris, though she manifestly could not. Sallie was arching her back now and screaming, hysterical. Amos watched with horror the explosion of emotion he had set off. More than anything he wanted the conflict to stop, but almost as much he wanted to choose for himself. He wanted to stay.

Mary had turned to her sister Alice, who put an arm around her and whispered to her. William slipped closer to Amos and stood with him, shoulder to shoulder. Mrs. Osgood watched her daughters quietly, deeply upset. Claris tried angrily to calm Sallie. So fierce were her commands and ministrations that more than one person in the room worried that she might accidentally hurt the baby.

Oddly, it was Leander, the bachelor uncle, who solved the impasse. He came and knelt beside Amos so they were eye to eye.

"So, nephew," he said. "I have a going-away present for you."

"What is it?"

"Watch out—it doesn't work that way. If you go with your mother and take care of her, the way we count on you to do, then you can take it with you. Otherwise I have to keep it."

"Why?"

"Because that's the way the world works. Uncles make the rules."

There was a pause.

"What is it?" Amos had a glimmer of an idea, but it was so huge he didn't want to let it grow. It would be like a genie out of a bottle.

Leander made a show of thinking this question over. "I don't think I can tell you. There's a rule about that. I'll give you a hint. Then you have to decide, fish or cut bait. Bargain?"

Amos thought hard and then nodded.

Leander nodded. "All right then. It's something Otis would want you to have. You, out of all his nieces and nephews."

Amos seemed frozen, considering Leander. He hardly dared to breathe.

"That's it then. Now it's your turn. Are you going to look after your mother for us, and baby Sallie, so they won't get lost on the way home and sail off to China and never come back and visit us again?"

Amos nodded, all fifty pounds of him full of manly gravity.

"All right then," said Leander. "Get your things."

The rest of the leave-taking went as expected. Sallie finally wore herself out and fell asleep. Mary and Claris hugged each other good-bye, if stiffly, then Alice and Mabel hugged Claris in turn. Claris turned to her mother, who was weeping. She led the children next door to say good-bye to Aunt, and to the cousins, then came back to hug her mother once more. And there, standing at the foot of the stairs, was Leander, waiting to say good-bye, holding Otis's fiddle.

"Next time I see you, boy, I want you to play 'Black-Eyed Susan' with me. I'll be practicing."

Amos couldn't speak. He only held out his arms for the violin case.

—⁂—

When they landed at the Haskell dock, Danial was there to meet them. Claris was much calmer, soothed by the quiet sail and the presence of her beautiful boy.

"You took your time," was Danial's greeting. Bowdoin Leach started handing bags up onto the dock.

"Father—William can come out to visit me!"

"That's fine. He's a nice boy."

"I can play Authors!"

"Can you?" Danial was waiting for Amos to say he was glad to be home. He was waiting for Claris to start in about how he had gone off and left them. He'd been thinking about this as he lived there alone for three weeks, picturing the scene in the Osgood house. From time to time he had wondered what he would do if they never came back.

"Father, look! Leander gave me Otis's fiddle!" Bowdoin Leach was handing the last of the gear up out of the boat to Claris.

Danial stopped what he was doing and looked at his son. "Why, you're turning into a regular little Osgood, aren't you?" he said.

Claris's face burned. She heard the nastiness in his voice. "Thank you, Bowdoin, for all your help," she said, and took the bow line off the cleat, wanting no witness to the rest of the scene. At a nod from Bowdoin she cast him off and turned to Danial, but he was looking at Amos.

"You will not play that thing in our house, or I'll throw it in the bay."

Amos was shocked. He drew closer to his mother and stared at Danial.

"We are Haskells out here," he said. "Let's not forget it." He picked up Claris's carpetbag and started for the house.

"He won't throw it in the bay, it belongs to you," said Claris to Amos. "Come on, bring your things." She gathered the baby's gear and started up the wooden walk to the house.

Edith was in a fine mood the morning after the lights went out. I don't know why; it had been utterly terrifying stumbling around in the cellar, dank as a grave and darker, trying to find the fuse box. (Dot Sylvester had confirmed on the telephone that the blackout was only at our house; the lights were on in the village.) I imagined that horrible figure in every corner; I could see its sallow eyes, and if anything had reached out and touched me in the dark, my heart would have blown out like an overfilled tire.

I held the oil lamp high, casting long stretched-out shadows of Edith and me onto the walls, while Edith marched fearlessly into the darkness like Stanley searching for Livingstone, full of confidence and purpose. She found the fuse box under the stairs, and I held the lamp for her as she unscrewed one fuse, then another, finding every single one of them blackened and dead.

"What on earth could have made them all go at once?" she kept saying. "It must have been lightning."

"There wasn't any."

"There must have been. We just didn't see it."

Fortunately she had found two entire boxes of fresh fuses in a kitchen drawer, as if sudden blackout was a contingency Miss Hamor had had to contend with often.

But when I came downstairs the next morning, the sun was out, finally. The kitchen door was standing open to let the light in. Edith had made oatmeal for our breakfast and put out a pitcher of maple syrup. Stephen was already eating. I said, "Good morning, Mother." She said "Good morning, Hannah," quite civil, but when she took a good look at me she added, "My, don't you look awful in bangs." She appeared to get a real kick out of that.

When she finished her gruel she said, "Well, I'm sure you remember that Grandma Adele arrives today. Will you change the sheets in the front room, Hannah, and clean the bathroom before we go to meet the train?" I said I would just nip up to the village and get the mail first. I had no intention of spending the day with Edith. I was awfully on edge from the night before, and the crack about my bangs had made me want to smack her.

As soon as I'd washed up the breakfast things, I went into town and made the barber cut off the rest of my hair. The barber was upset; he kept saying he didn't know how to cut girls' hair and I said, Good.

The barbershop was in that tiny white cottage with the flower box in the window down past the old post office. There's someone sells gewgaws from it in the summer now. Then it had a striped pole out front. As I was going out from my haircut, Conary Crocker was coming up the street. He was going to go right past me.

When I said hello to him, Conary stopped and looked, and then he stared. You've got to remember that in those days girls didn't do things like that to their hair. I was standing there in the street looking like a convict or a mental patient.

I could see pretty quickly that he liked what I'd done, a lot. In fact, he looked at me an awfully long time. I think seeing me with my hair cut off made Conary suddenly feel that I wasn't an alien, some party girl from the big city. That I felt like him, whatever that meant.

That was the beginning of a day I will never forget, a day that seemed to last about forty hours. It was turning into a beautiful blue one, with high streaks of cirrus clouds. Conary said, "What are you up to?"

I shrugged. All I knew was, I didn't want to go home.

"We could go on over to the hospital and have something else cut off," he suggested. I said I thought I'd done enough for the time being. Then he said, "I was thinking I'd go clamming. Want to come?"

"Yes."

"Good. Let's get us a bucket."

Conary's truck was parked across the street at the Esso station. The guy in the office seemed to leer at us as we walked across the street together, but Conary ignored him. He came around to open my door for me. I thought for a minute this was a show of conspicuous gallantry, but it wasn't; it was that the door handle was off and you had to work the latch by reaching inside and doing something with a screwdriver. In all the times I rode in that truck, I never did figure out how to do it.

"Careful," he said. "You don't want to put your foot through that floorboard." That was true. I didn't. I was used to boys driving as if they thought everyone might mistake them for daredevil race car drivers and fall in love. But Conary drove gingerly, as if the truck were an ailing animal, and if it faltered he would have to carry it. I found I liked that better than taking curves at high rates of speed on the wrong side of the road, a pastime that had previously struck me as mature and romantic. There was something protective about everything Conary did, even teasing. He did a lot of teasing, but it never hurt.

As we crept onto the Westward road, the bay spread out below us to the left, a silver gray color in the morning light. It was miles from here to open sea. I could see the greenish black hump of Beal Island.

"You ever been out there?" Conary asked, seeing where I was looking.

"Beal? No."

"Want to go?"

"With you?"

"Yes."

"Yes. I do."

"All right. They got clams out there as well as here."

I hadn't realized he meant right that day, but it was fine with me. I wasn't in any hurry to hear what Edith thought of my new haircut.

We had come to Tenney Hill, and this was where I first experienced the truck's peculiar style of coping with a grade. Connie pulled into a cow path, turned the truck around, and proceeded smoothly up the hill in reverse. When he got to the top, he pulled around again and off we went forward.

Seeing my expression, Connie said, "Would you believe, Hale Bogg was going to sell this truck to Carleton Haskell for scrap?"

I laughed.

"I told him, 'Don't do that. I can make her run. Besides, you don't want to do Carl Haskell no favors, he's so mean he charges his mother to take a bath.' "

I laughed again.

"He does," Conary said. "He figures up how much the oil costs him to heat the water and makes her pay him."

I asked, "Is Carleton related to Danial Haskell?"

"The whole town's related, one way or another. Carleton would be a great-nephew or some such, I guess."

"You aren't related to them."

"Oh, yes. My great-grandmother was Elzina Haskell. Maybe great-great."

"Do you know all about the murder?"

"I know what they say about it."

"What do they say?"

"Well, Bowdoin Leach says Sallie Haskell didn't kill anybody, but she knew who did. Some thought it was Mercy Chatto, the schoolteacher. She boarded with the Haskells, and it came out she was pregnant. She wouldn't say who got her that way, but most thought it was Sallie's father. Then there's those think Sallie's boyfriend murdered Danial because he wouldn't let them marry. He disappeared the night of the murder; folks say he was spirited off the island disguised in women's clothing."

"And never came back?"

"Never came back."

"Think . . . if Sallie Haskell took the blame for him, and he let her."

"There's people say it broke Sallie's heart, that he never came back and never sent for her, and that's why she kept to herself in that queer way. Then there's Abby Gordon. At the trial they said that if

Sallie Haskell did the murder she would have had blood on her clothes, but no bloody clothes were ever found."

"She would have burned them or buried them." I was picturing myself taking a hatchet to Edith and planning how to get away with it.

"Burned them where? Her mother or Mercy would have seen her do it if she'd burned them in the house. The ground was frozen, so it would have been hard to bury them. Abby Gordon said she had it figured out, though; she said the reason there weren't any bloody clothes was, Sallie took them off first and did it in the nude."

There went my career as a murderess. I tried to imagine taking off your dress and your corset and your stockings and whatever else Sallie wore . . . I tried to picture walking naked into a room where Edith was napping, with a hatchet in my hand. I couldn't.

We rode the last half mile in silence. Then Conary pulled his truck into the yard of a house I'd passed a few times before and thought looked haunted. I was shocked when he said, "Stay here, I won't be a minute," and I realized he lived there. He climbed out over his door, and now that I knew what it took to move the latches, I appreciated why. He disappeared inside.

The house looked a hundred years old and as if it had not been painted in fifty. The front porch sagged. There was a bedspring leaning against the side of the house, and wheels and pieces of farm gear stood rusting in the side yard. Chickens wandered around looking discouraged. There was a well a few yards from the kitchen porch with a bucket hanging from the crank. There were cords of wood in a chaotic mound on the far side of the yard partly covered with a rotten canvas tarp, as if no one in the household had the spirit to bother to stack it neatly.

Then I noticed that the power lines that ran beside the road from the village to the Neck did not throw a spur down to the Crocker house. No electricity meant no pump, so no running water. I began to understand that Conary's no-fuss grooming might be something other than a fashion statement.

Conary came out carrying a pail, a long-handled tin spoon, and a large pot with scars where the enamel was worn off. He stopped at the woodpile to load some dry kindling into the pail. When he climbed into the truck, I saw that he also had a hatchet, a box of matches, and a gob of butter wrapped in wax paper in the cook pot.

"We're off," he said.

We drove in silence back toward town, enjoying the day. I was particularly aware of the sun and breeze on my shorn head. I was also absolutely aware of what Conary had said about our house; I'd been wanting to ask him why he said it ever since. I was trying to think how to introduce the subject when he saved me the trouble, as if he'd been reading my mind.

"I spent the night in that house of yours, one time. Or part of one."

I turned to him. "How did you . . ."

"After Miss Hamor died, the house stood empty. People began to say they saw lights moving inside at night. Some little boys said they'd heard someone walking around and talking inside. I thought it was funny."

He drove on a bit, knowing I was waiting. Waiting . . . I was barely breathing. He seemed to decide that if he was going to tell it right, he didn't want to be doing two things at once. He pulled off the road near the top of Tenney Hill and stopped the engine. The day was suddenly very bright and quiet. We looked down the meadow to the bay.

He sat for a minute remembering. Or deciding whether to trust me, although I think he had already decided to do that. Finally he said, "It was in the spring, two years ago. May, but still plenty cold at night, and this girl and I were looking for someplace we could . . ." He paused, looking for the right word.

I said, "Yes."

"We weren't planning to hurt anything, we just wanted to be inside somewhere, and I thought, Well, there aren't a lot of places people hide keys. I figured that even if the real estate agent took one away, Miss Hamor probably left another one somewhere around. An old lady living alone doesn't want to go out for wood late at night and find herself locked out. So, we got in. We found a room up on the second floor at the front of the house that had a stove. We figured that if people out on the road saw a light or smoke from the chimney, it would just add to the rumors. It was a dark night."

"That's my room," I said, not adding that I was afraid to sleep there anymore. What an odd feeling, to think of him there. I guess he thought the same thing. I had to prompt him to go on.

"We got a fire going, and the place started to warm up, and one thing was leading to another, when I heard this noise."

I was afraid I knew what noise.

"I thought we were caught. I heard this sound like somebody thumping on the floor with a stick or cane. At first I thought it must be in the hall, and yet it sounded closer. As if it was in the room. Then it stopped. This girl was saying, 'What's the matter?' I thought she must be deaf. Then there was silence. Then—I swear—I heard the stove door open and slam closed again. It must have been something metal banging in the hall, or on the roof, but the sound was weird. You couldn't tell where it came from. Well, by this time the girl is just staring at me, like she thinks I've gone mental, and I'm wondering why the hell she doesn't get her shirt on. No matter who's there, if it's some caretaker or what, you don't want your personal parts hanging out. . . . It seemed like an hour I sat there waiting."

It was so real to me, I could barely stand to listen to him.

"Then I realized someone was in the room with us." His voice dropped to a whisper as the memory came back to him.

He knew. Finally, someone to believe me.

"Could you see it?"

He shook his head. "I felt it. And then I heard it. It began to make this noise, like someone crying. Horrible sobbing. The worst thing was . . . the worst thing was that it wanted something. It was crying in that angry way a person does when they expect you to drop everything and make it right . . . But make *what* right? What could make any difference? It's *dead*."

I had felt that exactly. It came around weeping, but then it didn't get what it wanted, and found out that you were going to go on living . . .

"What happened?"

Long pause. "The door slammed."

"By itself?"

He shrugged. "And I nearly jumped out of my skin, and the girl started to yell."

"Had she seen it?"

He shook his head. "Never saw it, never felt it, never heard a thing, except the door, and she thought I'd done that somehow, to scare her."

I might have laughed at this, except I knew that the only thing worse than what he'd gone through was discovering you were alone, even when someone else was beside you.

"Did you ever tell anyone what happened?" I asked him.

"Are you kidding?"

"Did she?"

He smiled. "I wouldn't know. We didn't have a whole lot to say to each other after that night. She still gives me a pretty wide berth when we meet."

When Sallie Haskell was old, with plenty of time to sort through the pictures of her life glinting like pieces of beach glass in a jar of stones, she found she had only two vivid memories from the time before her brother died.

The first was her mother's birthday in perhaps '71 or '72. It was a very mild April that year, and Sallie had discovered a meadow full of snowdrops in drifts across the new grass in a glen beyond the cow pasture. She was still a very little girl but free to wander where she wanted, and this was an immense discovery; she had never before been the first in the family to find these proofs of spring. She knew how her mother longed and waited for them, impatient at the end of drawn-out winter. She knew too that everything that happened on her mother's birthday was important in some secret way. Claris examined and interpreted the events of her birthday like a priestess reading secret runes of a religion with only one member.

Sallie did not exactly know that her mother didn't see her, any more than a fish knows that water is what it swims in. That was simply there. She was aware, though, of a sense of waiting for the moment she believed up to then was inevitable, when her mother would turn from Amos to her, and her face would fill with delight and she would see that she had a daughter as well as a son. This would take nothing away from Amos. It would simply be Sallie's turn; she had reasoned that this must be the way the world worked.

She began to pick the snowdrops, laying them on the grass in the shade, and then she found that there were also violets. Her plan grew more grand, and she left the flowers where they were and ran back to the house. Her mother was in the parlor at her new loom, making a rag rug out of scraps of cloth left over from Amos's and Danial's winter shirts.

Amos, her adored brother, was down in the yard working on an elver net. It was warm in the sun. Sallie slipped in the door of the ell and into the pantry, where she stood on a chair to get a willow basket down from the peg on which it had hung all winter. Then she hurried out again and ran back to her flower glen with the basket bumping against her knee.

She picked as fast as she could. The stems of the snowdrops were tiny, like green threads, and even though it felt as if she'd picked hundreds, there were still as many as stars sparkling in the new grass, and only a limp-looking handful in her basket. She pictured herself presenting an armload of spring to her mother, and the moment Claris would turn to her, and the light would fill her smiling eyes, and she would say, "Sallie! How beautiful!" and then it would be Sallie's turn to matter. She worked and worked.

When she had picked all that she could, and waited as long as she could wait, she started back to the house with her basket.

As she came into the dooryard, Amos came whistling around the corner. "What have you got there, Little Bit?" he asked her. She looked to him hardly bigger than the basket she was carrying.

She showed him her cargo.

"Little Bit! Look at that! Where did you find them?"

She pointed.

"Look how many you've got!"

"They're for Mother."

"Of course they are! Come on, come up to the larder. Let's put them in water."

Water. She hadn't thought of that. Maybe that was why the green threads were going all rubbery. She went up the stairs behind Amos and her basket and stood on a chair by the sink while he pumped water into a pretty goblet with a fragile stem. Then he held the glass for her as she carefully lifted her limp treasures into it, stem by stem.

She was almost finished when the door to the larder swung open and there stood their mother. A shaft of afternoon sun fell across the room from the open door.

Sallie turned to her joyfully. This was the moment.

"Look!" Sallie cried.

"Look what Sallie brought you, Mother!"

"Happy birthday!" Sallie waited for the eyes, aglow with pleasure, to turn to her.

"Oh, how beautiful!" said Claris, crossing the dark little room to take the glass full of snowdrops. "Where did you find them?"

Amos was smiling broadly at his sister, happy for her triumph. Claris had carried the flowers to the window to examine them.

"There are violets too! Snowdrops and violets! What a wonderful birthday present!"

Just then Danial came in, and Claris turned to him, holding the glass out. "Look—look what Amos brought me for my birthday!"

B y the time we got down to the wharf, the wind was filling from the south. Conary's boat was a beautiful little sailing dinghy that had been so lovingly sanded and varnished for so many springs that the deck and gunwales felt like velvet and glowed as if the wood were still alive.

"My dad bought her for me from some fool who'd let her swamp and spend a couple of weeks underwater," said Conary. "She was quite a mess, but I've done some work on her since. He bought her the year my mother died."

"When was that?"

"When I was seven."

The boat's name was *Frolic*. He kept it in town because there wasn't any deep anchorage at Sand Point, where they lived. The shore turned into mudflats for half of every tide. We rowed out and loaded the gear we'd brought onto her and got ourselves aboard.

"All we got to do is hoist sail and cast off," he said. "You want to hoist, or steer?"

I took the tiller and he raised the jib; it flapped like a frustrated gull as I held us into the wind while Connie hoisted the mainsail. He moved smoothly and swiftly, winching up the sail, cleating the halyard, and then, with one long-armed motion, he unhitched us and threw the buoy overboard.

"We're a sailboat," he said, as I pulled the tiller over to get some way on.

"Oh gawd no, fill the sails to northward first . . ."

"Why?"

"For good luck. Jeez, you straphangers."

"If I come about now, I'll ram the *Molly II*."

"That'd be all right. George Black puts her on the rocks so often she's practically amphibian."

"I'd rather not. Ready about." I brought the boat around just under the fishing boat's bow, and Conary trimmed the jib. He watched me and smiled. He didn't say anything, and that felt good. I liked it that he assumed I could do what I said I could.

Frolic's mainsail was gaff-rigged, so she looked like a tiny pirate sloop scudding out to sea. A lobster boat we passed gave us a toot and a wave. As we approached the mouth of the harbor, I expected Conary to take the tiller, but instead, he handed me a chart. The mouth was narrow and had a spit of rocks jutting into it from each shore like pincers waiting to crush a little wooden hull (or a big one). There was a safe channel, but sailing it was like threading a needle. A drop in wind or a fighting tide could put you right up on Captain Herrick's lawn, and it had happened to plenty. (Before this coast was charted and marked, so many ships had come to grief trying to enter the elusive safety of the cove, lying in beyond those jaws, that early maps left the bay a blank. Just sail past Beal Island and give the whole place a miss, was the common wisdom. It was a bad-luck stretch of coast; leave it to the demons.)

"What's our tide?" I asked. I was looking at the depths noted on the chart for the channel at lowest tide.

"Middle, ebbing."

"Good." That meant the flow would carry me, not fight me. "How much do we draw?"

"Three and a half." Feet.

"Could I cut this nun?" There was a red channel marker showing the outer tip of the rock ledge.

"Could. Won't need to."

He lay back against the bulwark, apparently unconcerned that I might in the next five minutes reduce his boat to splinters.

I threaded the needle. We made three quick tacks, close-hauled, to leave the nun to port, the middle-grounds spar to starboard, and the double black cans off the eastern shore to starboard as well. Then we headed across the wind for an easy reach out to Beal Island. I felt like a million bucks as I let the mainsail out, and Connie was smiling to himself.

I think it was right about then I began to feel like singing or laughing out loud. It was euphoric. A perfect, joyous, gleaming moment. We couldn't be stopped. I couldn't run into Edith. No one could expect me to do anything except exactly what I was doing. The sky was wide and blue and bright, the sun was warm, and the colors . . . the gray water, violet-blue sky, and black-green shore lined with granite gray . . . I can see them still, more intense than any landscape I've seen since. I felt that if only I could take that vision in with open eyes and open heart, I would be able to carry it with me into the world, glowing inside me like a talisman.

Conary reached into the cuddy and produced a bottle of beer and a church key. He opened the bottle and handed it to me. "First blood."

"Thanks."

He touched my hand as I handed the bottle back. We didn't have to talk. From the beginning we could talk, and we did when we wanted to, but we never had to.

There was a thud and a hard blow to the hull. Conary sat up. "What was that? A lobster pot?"

I hadn't seen a thing. We looked at our wake; twenty feet back there was a dark shape floating.

"Come about," said Conary. We tacked and sailed back, but long before we reached it I knew what it was. A body. A baby seal. Its head lolled back and forth on the waves as if its neck were broken, and its flippers waved like kelp. I wanted to weep. Conary put a hand on my arm. I brought *Frolic* into the wind so that the sails flapped, and we wallowed in the water beside it, like a noisy wraith.

"Hannah, you didn't kill it."

"Of course I killed it. I was sailing."

"You didn't kill it. You can't hit a live seal. They dive."

"It's a baby."

"It still knew how to dive. They're born knowing."

"What's it doing way out here? It was lost."

"It was dead." He took the tiller and sculled for a minute until the boat turned and the sails filled. I felt sick. I couldn't tell if he was telling me the truth or trying to protect me, and I didn't want to ask. So in a different quality of silence we made our approach to the green-black hulk of Beal Island.

This is the other day from early childhood Sallie remembered. She was seven. It started with an argument, as did many days.

Her father was getting ready to sail to town on the main. Her mother said she wanted to go too. Her father said he wouldn't take her.

"I'm marooned here!" Claris cried.

"Get your own boat, then. I don't like to spend all afternoon staring into space while you gaggle with your kinfolk."

"You're a cold man, Danial!"

Danial looked at her, unmoved. "That may be, but you knew what I was when you married me."

"I did not!"

Danial laughed. "Then you should have. I haven't changed."

"You have!"

"That's one of your stories. I am who I've always been."

So far, this was all familiar. Claris hurled grievances, Danial let them land and fall, as if the very thought of being hurt by them amused him. But on this day he turned on her and added, "Meanwhile, you made some promises on our wedding day yourself."

"Promises! You promised to cherish me! You said it in church!"

Danial stared at her, then smiled. (This was particularly frightening, a man who smiled when he was angry, as if pleased at having his bitter worldview confirmed.) "So I did." (Smiling.) "And I'm not the one who changed."

"You won't even take me to town!"

"Not my fault if you fooled yourself," said Danial, and he went off down to his boat landing.

—⁓—

Even Sallie knew that the joke was, her mother really didn't care if she went to town or not. If she didn't go, then the minute they saw Danial away past the headland, Amos went to the schoolhouse for his fiddle. They could play music all day. Amos played the fiddle tunes Uncle Leander taught him, and Claris played the organ. They tried to teach Sallie to sing along, but she was hopeless. (A Haskell, her mother said, with a downward pull of one corner of her mouth.) But Sallie loved to listen, and she danced with her dolls. Sometimes, if he had the time, old Virgil Leach came down with his washtub bass, and young Bowdoin brought his fiddle or an empty molasses jug, which he played by blowing across the neck of it, making a sound like a tuba. Mrs. Leach would come in too, and she and Claris sang. Sallie was happy on those music days because her mother smiled and laughed. Then, when someone caught sight of the gaff-rigged sail coming up the bay, the Leaches would tip their hats and skedaddle and Amos would run his fiddle back up to the school-house.

On this morning, after Danial's little boat was out of sight, Amos came in on the run with his fiddle. It was a weirdly hot and still day in September, the kind of day when Captain Osgood would tap the glass in his barometer and watch the needle fall. Hurricane weather, he called it, or earthquake weather. But the morning was cloudless as yet, and Mrs. Leach had left her book *Songs That Never Die* with Claris so she could play through them. Mrs. Leach had an idea that if Claris accompanied her, she could offer lessons in voice to the ladies of the island.

Claris could read music and had tried to teach Amos, but Amos's ear was so quick that he could play any song through if he'd heard it once, so it was hard to get him to see the value of reading. "You're just like Otis," Claris would say, shaking her head, her eyes glowing. When they had new sheet music, as now, Claris would play through the melody, and then they'd go to town, with Amos stomping his foot and adding embellishments around his mother's steady song line.

What they didn't know, this still, hot morning, was that Danial's main halyard had parted before he was halfway down the bay. With the sail dumped in the cockpit like a heap of laundry, he'd had to turn around and beat home on his jib, feeling put out and foolish.

It was far too early for anyone to be watching for his sails. He had plenty of time to hear the music floating out over his cove as he sailed into his landing and moored his boat. He had plenty of time to listen to his wife's laughter and his son's stomping foot as he came up the path to the porch. Plenty of time to hear the sudden panicked silence as his step was heard at the door, turned into an ogre to his children in his own house, by his own wife.

The fight was terrible. Amos tried to defend his mother, which made Danial roar and turn on Amos. Sallie sat in the corner with her doll, watching in horror as the three cloud giants who filled her sky clashed together in thunder and lightning. She and the doll followed the battles with matching wide-open black marble eyes.

In the end, and it came quickly, Amos said he was leaving. "There will be no peace in this house until I'm out of it," he said. Though Sallie wondered much later what sort of peace he had thought there would be even then. "I'll go to sea, like my uncles."

"No," cried Claris, in a wail of terror.

"Good," roared Danial. "That's a perfect Osgood thing to do."

After a minute to pack a kit bag, Amos was out the door on the run to the landing.

"He's going to start by stealing my boat," said Danial to Claris.

Claris had begun to weep as if her heart were a piece of cloth and she could feel it ripping. She wasn't ready to have Amos leave. It was too soon. She'd never been able to picture him leaving, even when he would be grown. Danial looked at her with her eyes swimming, so undone by grief (and of course not for him or their marriage, never for that) that he didn't know whether to comfort her or slap her.

Finally he said roughly, "He won't get far. Shackle's broke, main halyard's parted. The worst that will happen is he'll spend the night in the woods and be back at breakfast time."

Danial went out to the backyard and spent several hours with his ax, splitting out kindling. Claris packed up Amos's fiddle (Otis's fiddle) and took it to her room upstairs. (Amos and Sallie slept upstairs also: Danial slept in a room off the kitchen that had once been a buttery.) Claris came down and put her music away and went to her rug loom, where she rocked in and back, in and back, moving the shuttle along the cotton warp threads. All the while only Sallie, watching speechless at the window, knew that the little gaff-rigged sailboat had hoisted sail, the halyard jury-rigged somehow, and had scudded out past the headland and out of sight. As the hour passed, and her father in the backyard raised his ax and whacked it down, and her mother rocked into her loom and then back, waiting for morning, when their son would drag in ready to apologize, the boat was limping far down the middle of the bay with a line squall filling in behind it.

—⁊⁊—

It was Bowdoin Leach who found the hull, demasted and floating upside down, and towed her home next morning. As far, at least, as Danial knew, his son was never seen again.

Conary sailed for a patch of lime green meadow on the ridge of the island. I looked at the evergreens and scrub hardwood that crowded the shore. It was amazing how dense it had grown in the short time since the farms there were abandoned. The island people must have felt the trees and undergrowth trying to edge them off the land every day. It must have been like living in a house where every morning you find that all the rooms are smaller, and all the walls have drawn in toward you and have to be forced back.

We put into March Cove, a small horseshoe of beach surrounded by rock. Above the rock the land slopes steeply to the ridge of the island. The hull of an ancient fishing boat had been pulled up onto the land, and it lay there among wild raspberry bushes, weathering and looking oddly at home. Just above the dark line of dried seaweed that marks the high waterline, there was a circle of beach rocks for a picnic fire, and a fat barkless log, silver with age, had been pulled into place as a bench or backrest for those around the fire. It's a true sand beach too, not pebbles. Because the tide was nearing low, the beach stretched for thirty feet or so down to the water, and the sand glistened like warm gray glass in the sun. It was utterly silent. The colors were so vivid that the cove seemed to me enchanted. It made me feel the way some illustrations did in books I loved as a child. *The Mysterious Island,* N. C. Wyeth, with the blues bluer than blue, and the woods full of apes and pirates.

As we skimmed into the cove, Conary pulled up *Frolic*'s centerboard. I could see gray boulders covered with rust-colored lichens inches below us in the clear water, but we glided over them and nudged up onto the sand with a gritty crunching sound. I dropped over the side of the boat and held the painter while Conary furled the sails. We were silent. Sand crabs played around my toes in the sun-warmed water.

When he had finished furling the sails, he cleated and coiled all his lines. I liked that. There was no one here to see us and it seemed a calm day. It would do no harm, one would think, to leave the boat in a more slapdash way, but it never occurred to Conary. When he had finished, he pulled a little anchor from the cuddy and tossed it up onto the beach. He reeled it back toward him until it bit into the sand and held; then he cleated the anchor line on *Frolic*'s bow. He'd calculated the length of rope so she wouldn't end up with her nose underwater if the tide came up under her before we were ready to go. Last, he tied a light line to the bow cleat over the anchor line and carried it up the shore, where he settled a large rock on top of it. That was the painter, for pulling the boat to us once she was floating.

*   *   *

We set about our clamming and must have dug for two hours. The sun was high, and the tide was all the way out. *Frolic* lay beached on drying sand. All over the tide flat there were holes with piles of sand beside them where we'd dug, and beside each of us where we knelt was a pile of clams like strange gray eggs. I had struck a mother lode of huge ones, and they made a proud heap, with their fat yellow bodies forcing the shells open a crack. I gathered mine in my hands and, making several trips, carried them to my bucket. The bucket was almost full of clams and seawater, and I was lazy with sun. I decided it was better to go to it than to lug it to me. Conary's hod was full too, which meant he'd dug about three times as many as I had. I'd felt pretty good about my future as a clam digger until I noticed that.

Conary looked at my catch and said, "That ought to be enough for lunch." I thought he was teasing that we could eat that many, but he wasn't, and he didn't miss by much.

He carried the hod down to the waterline to keep wet. On his way back to me he stopped by poor listing *Frolic* for the cooler and the cook pot he'd brought. Then he carried my bucket to the water; I went with him to guard my booty. He poured out their water, and a few of the clams escaped.

"Jailbreak! Run for it, boys!" Connie called. I pictured them slipping into their element and burrowing madly into the bottom with their black rubbery necks, but of course they just lay there like fools in clear shallow water, so I scooped them up again. Conary rinsed the clams and replaced the water several times. Back at the top of the beach, he got some cornmeal from the cooler and threw that into the bucket.

"They don't care for it. Makes them spit, and they spit out sand. We should leave them overnight to really clean out, but if we do we won't have any lunch. I don't guess a little grit will hurt us." He started off to look for firewood, and I followed.

"Can they live in a bucket overnight?"

"They can live for days like that. They just shrink some."

"What if one dies and you eat it by mistake?"

"It'll kill you."

I noticed Connie wasn't dead yet, so perhaps the odds were not as bad as they seemed. We soon had all the wood we needed in tinder-dry driftwood. The big pieces, thick as my leg, were amazingly light to carry. We used pine twigs for kindling, and the fire took hold easily.

We sat side by side in the sun, leaning against the driftwood log and drinking a cold beer we passed back and forth. The hair on our arms was white with salt, and white seagulls wheeled overhead. Occasionally one would drop down to investigate our clam holes. Conary told me the way gulls eat clams. They fly high into the air with them, drop them onto the rocks to smash the shells, then swoop down to pluck out the bellies. I said that sounded like tool use. I thought man was supposed to be the only tool-using animal. Conary looked at me, surprised. He wasn't used to girls caring about the same things he did. He said, "Man's got company." We sat in the sun watching the sea-gulls. Our arms touched.

When the fire was ready, hot and steady, Conary put a few inches of water in the cook pot and got it steaming. Then he put in the clams and covered them. While they cooked, the steam inside the pot rattled the lid and made it jump, as if it were chattering at us. We talked nonsense back to it, and laughed. Connie had no watch, but when he took the lid off again, they were done. He poured a cup or two of cooking liquid into a little enamel bowl, and he put some butter to melt in the overturned lid of the cook pot. (I had wondered why the handle was burned.) The clams he dumped out in a steaming heap onto a broad piece of weathered driftwood.

Once in a while I'd feel the sun or breeze on my scalp and remember that this morning I had cut my hair off. That felt just right.

This day felt like the beginning of a new life, a life that could be spent in sunshine in some new world, where it didn't feel so dangerous to be a motherless child. Oh, Conary. Beautiful wild boy.

I didn't know how to eat steamed clams. Connie could have teased me, but he didn't. He just showed me. I felt that he wasn't showing me something that was his to own and mine to visit; I felt he was showing me it was mine. My real place. He showed me the same way he let me sail out of the harbor.

The steam had relaxed the muscles that hinged the clamshells closed. They had opened in the pot. A clam lay inside the shell in a thin web of something, like a shroud. Conary picked a fat clam, eased it from the shell, and peeled the shroud off over the clam's black neck, like pulling a turtleneck sweater over your head. He dipped the yellow belly into the bowl of cooking broth to rinse it; then he dipped it in butter and held it to my mouth. I bit. He threw the neck away. I laughed with surprise at how much I liked it. He watched as I cleaned and rinsed and dipped one of my own. It was easy.

"The neck is like a handle."

"Yuh. You can eat it if you want. It's chewy."

I did another one and fed it to him. Then we settled down to eat in earnest. I told him I felt like a raccoon, eating with my clever little animal fingers; again he gave me that surprised look. He did an uncanny imitation of a raccoon eating and made me laugh with surprise and happiness. He must have spent hours sitting in patient silence watching wild animals to know how to do that. He certainly hadn't learned it by going to the zoo.

Conary came to a clam that hadn't opened. He held it up to show me, then lobbed it out onto the beach.

"You don't eat any that are closed. That's why you won't eat dead ones and die."

I picked up one that was a little open, questioning. He said heave it, and I did. It sailed through the air, and a gull followed it down and pounced.

We ate until we were stuffed, but we couldn't finish all that we'd cooked.

"I wish my stomach were bigger. I hate to waste them."

Connie pointed at the gulls. "They aren't going to be wasted." I thought this was the best way to eat I ever heard of. The seagulls wheeled above us and squawked, *scree, scree scree.*

We took the pot to the water and scrubbed it with sand, and we washed the butter and clam broth off ourselves while we were at it. Con's fingernails were ragged, like mine. In fact, our hands looked strangely alike in the clear water. We both noticed it. Connie held his right hand up, palm facing me, as if he were taking an oath. I put my left palm against his, and we stared. They were almost exactly alike. Narrow palms, long curved thumbs, very short littlest fingers, knobby middle knuckles. We turned them, palm to palm, this way and that. He even had a curved scar on his index finger like mine where I had cut myself with a jackknife when I was ten, trying to peel a golf ball to see what was inside. I showed him the scars. Our eyes met.

I put my left hand up to the light just now and looked at it. The scar is fainter; it's an old woman's hand. Would Conary's still match mine if we could lay them against each other? Two old friends and lovers who had shared a life?

Sallie Haskell had grown into a handsome girl, with her father's heavy black eyebrows and brown eyes, and large hands and feet. She looked as much a Haskell as her lost brother had looked an Osgood. But she had her mother's quick imagination and intuition, especially the knack with animals. She was always bringing home hurt raccoon kittens and birds to raise, and once she raised them, they never went back to the wild, so the barn was full of beasts that hid in the rafters when Danial was about but came down to nuzzle and perch on her shoulders as soon as Sallie came in. She needed the animals for company. After Amos died, cold anger had settled between her parents, dark in color and in the shape of silence. Her father was ashamed and grief-stricken and incapable of admitting it. What her mother felt she never said to a living soul, but Sallie knew it was hard and bitter. Claris never saw Danial as a man who was paying a terrible price for a mistake. She saw only her own loss of her angel boy, an endless unrequited sorrow that left her surviving child, who was a real child and not an angel, in the cold quite as much as it did her husband. That was the way things were, and there was no point waiting for the horse to give milk. Sallie had life to get on with.

She loved school, and was good at it. There was warmth and life at school, and the teacher, Miss Pease, made a special pet of her. The village was growing too; a man from Boston had opened a granite quarry and built a great long pier out into the reach from which the stone could be loaded onto the boats that called for it. Men came over from the near shore of the Neck every day to work, and some fancy stonecutters from away, some from as far away as Italy and Scotland, came to live in the new boardinghouse. One or two brought wives and children, and the children came to school. It was wonderful to hear the way they talked and to see the strange food they brought in their lunch pails. Sallie's lunch was always the same, mostly cold beans, except on winter mornings her mother would give her a hot boiled egg and a fresh-baked potato, and she would hold one in each mittened hand inside her pockets as she ran to school, and at lunchtime eat them.

Sallie's mother went on as she always had, tending the chickens, carving fancy buttons from bones, teaching music at the school to any who wanted it, since Miss Pease was tone-deaf. When the minister came out to hold services and baptize, he always stayed with Mrs. Haskell, and on those occasions they would have roast hen for dinner, a special treat that came otherwise only on birthdays, Amos's and Sallie's. On these days Mrs. Haskell killed her hens by wringing their necks. She taught Sallie that that was the test of your womanhood. Girls used the ax, but a woman broke the chicken's neck in one swift movement of the hands. Sallie couldn't bear the feeling of the beak struggling against her palm or the look in the birds' eyes; she used the ax.

One thing had changed. Sallie's mother didn't want to go to the main anymore. She always asked Danial if she could go in with him, to put him to the trouble of denying her, but Sallie felt she had no real wish for it. Sallie didn't know why, unless it was that she feared her family would say to her, "We told you so," about the man and the life she had chosen. Sallie never stopped hoping Claris would change her mind, show an appetite for color and life again. Take some pleasure in the child she had remaining.

One spring morning when she was sixteen, Danial was making ready to go into town, and Sallie said, "Father, Mother and I want to go too."

Danial grunted. He stood in the doorway as if he were thinking it over. Claris had all the doors and windows open, airing the stale winter air out; there was a smell of green buds and a strong scent of balsam in the air. It was going to be a lovely warm day.

"I don't have room for two more," he said to Sallie, finally. "You can come." He went out and down to the dock, carrying a wheel rim he needed to have mended, and the setover for the pung he'd broken at Christmastime. Claris left the room as if she hadn't heard him and soon was back with an armful of bedding she carried out to air on the clothes-line. She was standing on the rock ledge outside the kitchen with her mouth full of clothespins hanging a quilt when Danial and Sallie cast off. As the little boat caught the spring breeze and moved lightly off onto the bay, Sallie looked back and saw that her mother was standing, head bent in the sunlight, weeping. It hurt her terribly.

Once in Dundee, Sallie went to Abbott's first with a pail of eggs to sell, and after she'd bought two pennies' worth of rock candy, she hurried up Union Street to see her aunts and gather news for her mother. Grandmother Osgood had died the winter Sallie was ten, and Mary and Jonathan Friend lived in the Osgood house now, with their children and Uncle Leander and Grandfather Osgood, who lived in the parlor as he could no longer climb stairs.

William was there when she got there, home from Bowdoin College for Easter vacation. Grandfather was sleeping, and all the rest had gone to pay a visit to Aunt Alice's in-laws in Orland. They would be back midafternoon. Sallie knew her father would be at the blacksmith's for hours, so she decided to take a walk. The air was soft and fragrant and the sun warm after a long winter. Also, like all islanders, she loved the thought of roads different from the few she walked so often. The chance to get out South Street on her own would be a great adventure, to see what new houses there were and what folks she would see.

She was a strong girl and a fast walker. It was still mud season, but the roads were drying fast in the days of sun they had had this week, and there was plenty of traffic. She walked all the way from the village to the neighborhood on the Neck, where she met Ellen Cole, an old friend from the island school whose family had removed to the main. They were excited to see each other and had a thorough visit.

Ellen insisted Sallie stop up to the house to say hello to her mother and see the new hats the milliner had just finished for them. The milliner came up from Portland spring and fall and spent a week or more living with one family or another, making hats for the ladies of the area for the season. When she had finished at the Neck she would move up to Dundee, and from there on over to Franklin. This never happened on the island, and Sallie was thrilled to see the new styles. She tried on both Ellen's hat and her mother's, memorizing details of both to tell Claris when she got home.

It was much later than she'd meant to stay when she came to start for the village. The sun was high, and she knew the tide would be turning. If it set them getting out of the mouth of the harbor, her father would be angry and the return trip would be long. She walked faster, but she was getting tired and thirsty.

As soon as mud season was over, there began to be peddlers on the road, and they were very welcome, except for the Gypsies. There was always a tinker and tinsmith or two who could mend your old cook pots or sell you new ones. There were Micmac Indians selling grass baskets, often very beautiful, and there were the dry-goods men, with wagonloads of cloth and ribbons and fancy glass buttons from Boston. Sometimes these peddlers would even hire a boat to sail out to the island, but not very often, and to Sallie the sight of a peddler's wagon held the promise of high excitement. Almost everything they used every day was homemade; for store-bought there were the tools and household goods that Abbott's carried, the same year in and year out, but the peddlers brought the latest things from the big cities. At least they claimed they did, and Sallie believed them.

She was beginning to be apprehensive about how late she was when she heard a wagon coming along behind her. She didn't relish her father's black mood and sarcasm if she made him miss the ebbing tide. She turned, hoping she might see a relative or acquaintance, but it was a wagon drawn by a small sorrel horse with a paper flower pinned to its bridle. The wagon had staves arching above the flat bed so it could be tented over with canvas in bad weather, but today the tenting was rolled up, and Sallie could see as it pulled up beside her that the wagon was full of row upon row of shiny new shoes.

She was staring at the shoes long before she looked at the driver. There were ladies' button shoes and men's work boots and shoes and boots for children, and house slippers in all sizes and even shoes in colored leather. When she got around to looking at the man, she saw a pleasant face, neither Gypsy nor Indian, with a large mustache. He was offering her a ride.

"It's a hot day for April," he was saying. She could tell that he was noticing her shoes, her only good ones, which were not made for hiking. "Climb up, old Bob won't mind. I'll be glad of the company."

She was tired, and the sun was indeed hot. And she'd never in her life been in the vicinity of so many new and stylish shoes. She climbed up.

The peddler clucked the horse into a trot and turned to look at

Sallie. "Saw you looking at my shoes," he said. "You were looking at 'em, weren't you? Saw you looking."

She agreed that she was, hoping it hadn't been rude to do so. They jogged on for several minutes.

"Fine looking girl, looking at my shoes, and I could show you shoes," he said in a burst. He seemed excited. "Fine bosom too." He turned to look at her square in the face. Sallie was bewildered. The horse was going along at a good clip, and the countryside seemed to be whizzing by. She didn't much like the way the peddler smelled.

"Fine bosom, fine looking girl, want to see my shoes? Want to show me your bosom, I'll show you my shoes?"

"Put me down," said Sallie. "Stop right now, I'm getting down."

"I'll stop when we get where we're going," he said and slapped the reins hard on the horse's back, making it go even faster.

Sallie moved as far from the man as she could go without falling off the seat and said once more, very loudly, "Stop! I want to get down!"

"Wants to get down, I'll put you down. I'll stop when we get where we're going," he said. This man is crazy, Sallie said to herself. I've never seen a crazy person, but this is one. Her heart was pounding so that the blood hammered in her ears. This man could kill me, she thought. There are people who do such things. He could carry me off and kill me and no one would ever know. With her right hand, she reached behind her until she grasped a shoe, and she threw it out of the wagon. She reached and threw another. She threw another and another until she couldn't reach any more with her right hand. The wagon was slapping along the road, and the shoes were in the dust behind. Watching the man from the very corner of her eye, she reached with her left hand, found a shoe, and threw it. She reached for another, and this time he saw her.

His hand whipped around and caught hers with the shoe still in it. As he did this, his eye moved to the road behind, and he saw the shoes lying along it. He yelled a word at her she had never heard before, and so didn't understand, and hauled on the reins, sawing at the horse's mouth. The minute she dared, Sallie threw herself out of the moving wagon.

She landed in soft mud. A rock caught her in the ribs, and her wrist hit hard and bent backward, making her cry out once. Then she was up and running as fast as she could, waiting to hear hoofbeats galloping after her, but she heard nothing but the blood in her head. Finally, when her lungs were burning, she looked back and saw the peddler driving his horse the way they had come, going back to pick up his shoes. She kept running, fearful at every point that he would overtake her and kill her, but he must have finally retraced his way and taken another road, perhaps fearing she would reach Dundee first and tell what had happened.

She did reach the village at last, and she was so exhausted and frightened that she hadn't even noticed yet the throbbing pain in her wrist and side. Her face was streaked with dirt and tears, her skirt was covered in mud, and her shoes were broken. She stood by the town pump and breathed in great gasping gulps, then bent to wash her face with one hand, and to drink the pure cold water.

William saw her coming up Union Street and cried, "Sallie! Mother, she's here! Sallie—what happened?" He ran down to meet her, asking again what had happened to her, but all she could do was put her arms around him and cry.

Later, when she was properly washed and comforted, and her aunt Mary had made her drink a cup of hot sweet coffee, she told the story. Uncle Jonathan wanted to go out looking for the man and beat him up, but Sallie said she couldn't bear to see him again. Mary and Alice could hardly breathe for fear and relief at what had almost happened to her, at what might at any moment happen to any of them. All the while the Osgoods were listening to her and petting her and telling her what a strong brave girl she had been, her father sat outside on the porch step, looking at the sky and saying nothing. Once in a while Sallie saw a look pass from aunt to aunt, a glance toward the porch and then a shake of the head and a glance toward heaven. Danial had been waiting there for an hour before Sallie came, but he wouldn't come into the house.

When finally the aunts were convinced that she was calm again, and safe and had broken no bones, they packed up the things they wanted to send to her mother and let her go. Sallie and Danial walked away from the house, Sallie with her egg pail full of presents and Danial empty-handed; the boat would be loaded and ready to sail when they got to the dock, so she would know she had kept him waiting.

He had still not said to her that he was frightened by what had happened to her or glad to have her back. When they got to the town wharf, he stopped to look at her before they stepped down into the sloop. "Weather coming," he said.

Oh, thought Sallie, briefly angry. Weather. The sky was the Bible of the island sailor. Children come and go, but the Scripture is forever. She looked down the bay and saw that indeed a threatening green-black passage from Jeremiah was coming from the east, and she got down quickly into the boat and stowed her things.

They sailed toward home in a freshening breeze. They were taking green water over the bow by the time they passed the north point of the island. Sallie's muslin dress and light wool shawl were waterlogged before the rain began to fall, which it did as Danial made his first pass at the home dock. Sallie had seen her mother on the rocks in the wind watching for them, but by the time they had made the boat fast and climbed to the pathway, she had gone inside.

Claris stood by the window with her back to them as they came in. Her posture was as eloquent as any words. I must stand here alone, far from the fire, watching this terrible sky, while you, you who drove the person I loved most on this earth to his death in just such a squall, you have my one living child on the bay somewhere, in peril, you unforgiven and unworthy of forgiveness.

As the door closed behind Danial and Sallie, Claris turned to face them. They stood drenched, held by her gaze, which was almost yellow in anger. Sallie wanted to take off her sopping shawl and lay the wet letters and presents on the bench for Claris before they were ruined, but she didn't move.

"She had a run-in with a peddler," said Danial. "Took her up on the road from the Neck and then wouldn't let her down. She had to jump off and run away from him. She's some torn up, but your sister says nothing is broken."

Claris looked from Danial to Sallie. Her weight shifted. Finally she moved to Sallie, took her wet shawl, and looked at the swollen wrist and painful abrasions on her palms and her torn dress.

She looked back at Danial. She looked like a dog in a fight who is quivering to close his jaws on the opponent's throat but is prevented by some inner primordial prohibition that governs the conflict.

Finally she turned back to Sallie. "I thought you had more sense than to take a ride from strangers," she said, and that was all she ever said to her about it.

Finally the tide made us move up the beach. It had turned, and the clam hod was up to its handle in water. Conary fetched it and brought it up the beach to *Frolic* and left it in the shade beside her, then covered it with seaweed. I doused the fire and collected the things we had brought, all the signs of human activity, and put them back in the boat. Then we put on our shoes and Conary led the way to a path that went up the bank into the woods.

It was steep at first; we had to scramble up rocks barely covered by earth and moss, and sometimes we had to pull ourselves on surrounding bushes to keep from sliding back. Sometimes long thin branches would whip across our faces and sometimes we had to go almost on hands and knees to get through the bracken. I remembered what Conary said about the island having been cleared at the turn of the century. It didn't seem possible.

"What made this path?"

"Don't know. Deer, probably."

The undergrowth thinned some and gave way to bigger trees. This path had a clearer floor, and walking was easier. We were still climbing. Then with an abruptness that seemed almost magical, we stepped out onto a meadow, open and shimmering. There were outcroppings of rock here and there, and low ground cover, some I knew to be blueberry bushes and something silvery that looked like heather. This was the meadow we had seen from the water, and I knew Conary had been here before. He was smiling the way you do when you've arrived at something you looked forward to but feared it wouldn't be as good as you remembered.

We walked from one end of the meadow to the other. We found some ripe blueberries and picked them and ate them. They were warm from the sun. I found a little hard dry animal spoor that looked almost like a pinecone.

"Porcupine," said Conary.

"Are there all kinds of animals out here?"

"Not all kinds. No moose. No bears, anymore. There are a lot of deer. At one point there was a good deal of hunting out here in the fall, but it's dropped off lately."

"Why?"

"Well . . . people started coming back to the main with weird stories. One fella claimed he'd seen someone dressed in black floating around in a field. Another claimed he saw a light in a window where there isn't a house anymore. Then someone told a hell of a yarn about seeing a man with a rope around his neck, and how he shot at him but the bullets went right through him."

"Was anyone ever hanged out here?"

"Not that I ever heard. Besides, someone heard this sport laughing in a bar down in Belfast about the bill of goods he sold the locals when he was up here."

"Oh." I didn't know what he was telling me. If he meant it was all just stories, or if he thought there was something out here.

We walked in silence for a while. I was very aware right then that I was very far from home, alone with a boy—a man—I didn't know very well. After such sweetness, was he trying to frighten me?

We were walking among tall pine trees; the ground was soft with rust-colored pine needles. We moved almost silently, and it struck me that there should have been birds singing, but there weren't. For the first time, Connie took my hand.

"Should we be dropping bread crumbs?" I asked him. Whistle in the dark.

Conary smiled. "Are you scared?"

"Yes."

He squeezed my hand.

"Are you?"

"Yes," he said. "But less, with you."

We went on. After a time Conary said, "When I'm out here, it feels like the world on the main is gone. Maybe we'll come around a corner and find a mansion, and it will be ours. We just forgot about it, that we had a mansion with mahogany furniture and linen sheets. Or maybe we'll meet a wild red Indian, and we'll speak his language and he'll take us to his village. Maybe we were kidnapped as babies and given to those people to raise. It would explain a lot."

"Maybe we were given away as some kind of test, and if we can find our way back, we passed it." I was happy again. With him, it didn't take much.

We came to a fern grove hemmed around by trees, where tall grass grew the fantastic bright green color of the first buds in spring.

Sunlight shafted down into the middle of it so that it felt like a chapel. We soon understood the luxuriant growth; the grove was a bog. We could see that the path resumed on the other side, but the only way to get to it was through muck that sometimes only seeped up around our soles but sometimes rose to our ankles. We were halfway across before we discovered this.

"Here's a log," Conary said, after feeling in the muck with his feet. He stepped, and it was solid. It carried us about ten feet and then ended. Connie stepped off into whatever it turned out to be, and I followed, thinking of the deadly cottonmouth water snakes I had read about and reminding myself there are no poisonous snakes in Maine. Muck began to suck at my feet with each step.

"Is there quicksand in Maine?"

"Yuh," said Connie.

"Is this it?"

"Don't know. But we're still moving." He added, "Don't be scared."

"Why not?"

"Because it doesn't help."

"Oh."

Step by step, we crossed. Nothing bit us; we didn't sink in and disappear. Where the bright grass ended there was a mass of scrub birches and alders, taller than we were but no bigger around than my arm. There, the ground became firm again. Connie bent a birch out of our way to clear the path and held it till I had passed, so as not to let it swing back and whip me. I did the same for him with the next one, and in that fashion, passing each other, we made our way through to pinewoods again. Here we regained an open path, perhaps the same one we'd been on, perhaps not. The woods were crisscrossed by trails of different creatures looking for different things.

I asked, "What direction are we going?"

Connie looked at the sun. "South." Toward the outer tip of the island. Seaward.

"Have you been here before?"

"I have no idea."

"You don't?"

"I might have been. Woods change. It's been a long time."

"How long?"

"I used to come out here all the time with my sister when we were kids. We used to prowl around looking for the lost town."

"Did you ever find it?"

"I didn't."

"Aren't there maps?"

"Yes. But they're just sketches, made by the Baptist minister seventy years ago. You can't really follow them. None of the landmarks are the same as when they were drawn, and the distances are all wrong. We didn't mind, really. It was just an adventure."

"Have other people found it?"

"Sometimes. Sometimes not. At first after the island was abandoned people came out a lot. The houses were broken into. Some burned. One or two were moved. Then somebody burned off a good bit of land for blueberrying, and most of the houses that were left burned too. Woods take over fast."

A cloud passed across the sun. It got suddenly cool; it would be cold when night came. We had reached another meadow. Once again we were drenched in sunlight.

The cloud moved on. We walked in silence.

"So," I said. "There ought to be blueberry barrens here somewhere."

Connie smiled. "Ought to be."

"Look." There was a shade tree, a huge oak, in the middle of the meadow. Part of my brain registered something the minute I saw it, and then I knew what it was. We hadn't seen any hardwood like that since we started walking. Someone had planted it. Someone had cleared the land around it so it had all the root room and sunlight it needed, and it was bigger by far than any tree we'd seen since we left the beach. People plant trees like that in their dooryards. And now I could see that there was something nailed to the trunk; that was what I was pointing out to Connie.

"It's rusted something," he said. We hurried toward it. It proved to be several ancient gearwheels of different sizes composed in a pattern. They were oddly beautiful.

"What is it?"

"Art," said Conary.

"I guess." Whatever we had felt during our journey here, we felt delight now. We'd found it! Or we'd found something. We went on a few paces, and just the distance from the tree where you'd expect the house to be, concealed by waving grasses, was a cellar hole. It was lined with cut granite blocks, mostly tumbled into the hole itself. Young birches grew in a cluster in the center of it. We learned to recognize these clumps of young hardwoods as markers of a former foundation.

Lives had been lived here. Babies had played in this yard, and women in long cotton dresses had done the wash and hung the clothes on a line from this tree, and then walked back inside, just there. (We had found the doorstep.) A man with a beard and suspenders had chopped and split wood with an ax somewhere just here. Perhaps there were chickens, and the children fed them and gathered eggs in the mornings.

"Did they have glass?" I called to Conary. He seemed excited; he was pacing something off. I was excited too, imagining being a farmwife out here. She'd have loved that tree out her window!

"Did they have what?"

"Glass. For windows."

"Depends on how old the house is. But sure. You know the Jellisons' house?" I did. "Well, that one's probably older than this one here. They could order whatever they wanted from Boston, and the packet captain would bring it the next time up the coast."

That made it even more real. Not a cabin. A house. White frame, with curtains and windows and braided rugs, and iron stoves.

"Here's the barn!" Conary called. I hurried over. There was a rim of stones roughly forming a rectangle about thirty feet from the first foundation. This one had no cellar. We stood in the middle of it and tried to imagine the animals we would have if we lived here.

"Cows, do you think?"

"At least one. A horse, for riding and plowing. Or maybe oxen," said Conary.

I hoped so. I love oxen. I wished I was a barefoot farmgirl of a hundred years ago riding the horse bareback over the meadow at sunset to drink at the pond.

"Where did they get water?"

"There'd be a cistern for rainwater in the cellar. That's what we have at home. There's a hand pump in the kitchen sink brings it up into the house. But there must be a spring or dug well too."

"Where?"

"I'd guess in the back. Someplace handy for watering the animals." We went looking in the direction away from the tree. I noticed as we went that my shadow was beginning to lengthen. It must have been getting on toward midafternoon, and we'd have to go soon if we didn't want to have to dive for the clams Conary left beside *Frolic*. I didn't want to go, at all. I loved it there. I could picture Conary in suspenders, chopping wood.

We didn't find a well. We did find two small headstones. The first said, LORENZO 1872–1874. The second said, ROSELBA 1873–1874.

We didn't speak for a time. I kept looking back at where the house would have been. What was it like to grow old there, looking out at these graves every day? What could it have been like to leave them?

"Little babies." Conary sounded sad. I moved closer to him. "They must have gotten sick. Smallpox or something."

The breeze riffled the grass around the graves, and it blew Conary's dark hair on his forehead. I didn't have enough left to blow.

"Why such strange names?" I wondered aloud.

"Maybe the father was a sailor. Maybe he'd been to Portugal, or Spain." Conary took my hand. By unspoken mutual consent we moved on toward a break in the trees ahead of us, leaving this house behind. We could see another clearing beyond; perhaps two or more families had settled near each other. Or perhaps this was actually what was left of the village.

"Were there roads?"

"Not paved ones. The Duffy family ran a store near the southern tip, and there was a school, and a tavern before the temperance law. There must have been horse paths and some wagon roads there. It may have been that the families living up island just came around to the south end on foot or by boat."

"And the graveyard?"

"It's a small one. I've seen pictures of it. Some buried their people at home, and some sailed the dead over to the main to be buried with relatives in town."

"If you'd once buried a child on your own land, you couldn't ever leave it, could you?"

"You wouldn't do it expecting to. No."

Through the trees we could see a sweep of blue water.

"There's Closson Point out beyond there," said Conary. "We've come almost to the southern end."

"Then we must be near the village."

"We must. What fuddles me is, I *have* been here before. I came out here by boat once, and climbed up the ridge from the beach to about this view, and tramped around all afternoon. I never saw this before, though."

He gestured to the second meadow, which we had just entered. There were some little apple trees not far from us, and we could see from where we were that they were still bearing fruit. A little gnarled and green, and probably sour, but bearing. Beyond that was a clump of alders, like the young birches in the first foundation.

"They had a beautiful view of the water."

Conary nodded. We walked down to the apple trees and stood looking south.

"If you were up as high as a second story here, you could see all the way out to Jericho Bay."

"You could see a ship come up the bay before anyone else did. Maybe a sailor lived here. Maybe his wife had a widow's walk and spent her days scanning the horizon."

"The house would have faced the sea, with the apple trees in the backyard. And the barn was probably back there, and out at that end . . ."

"The garden . . ."

"Yes."

We walked to the foundation to pace the size, to get a feel for the house. We surprised a squirrel or something that had been sunning on a rock; we didn't see what it was, just a flurry of motion and a scratching of claws on rock as it vanished among the foundation blocks. I stepped up onto a square-cut chunk of granite so I could see the water better.

"Careful."

"I'm okay. It's solid."

Conary put a hand out to steady me. Then he stepped up to join me. We stood in happy silence looking at the blue of the bay. It was lovely. The sky to the south was cloudless now, and the air around us was still, except for a lazy summer hum of insects. On this side of the house were more fruit trees, maybe pear. We happened to look at each other at the same moment, so at peace and delighted that we glowed with it, and Conary, very delicately, leaned toward me and kissed me.

He can't have meant to do it. But once it happened, the power of it, a mere brush of lips like a moth wing, stunned me so that for a minute or two I couldn't look at him. I turned and stood looking at the sea, afraid that if I met his eyes I'd start to blither. The sea lay, serene and green-black, with light glittering on the moving wrinkles of its surface. Tall pines between me and the shore cast triangular shadows, and I looked at them with a sense that the geometry of the world had just been altered forever.

When I turned back to him, Conary, probably quite as overcome with shyness as I was, was making a sextant with his hands, calculating the size of the house that had stood in this place. I looked into the hole that had been the cellar and followed with my eyes the line of granite that traced out the foundation.

I said, "What I can't decide is, whether our couch will fit between the picture windows."

"If it doesn't," said Conary, "we'll cut the arms off."

"Can I have a porch swing?"

"I promised you a porch swing."

"So you did."

I walked, arms outstretched for balance, away from him along the foundation wall. I suddenly understood what people mean when they say that their hearts sing.

The foundation blocks were jumbled one against another and

looked unsteady, but I tested each one before shifting my weight onto it. Conary, lithe and steady as a cat, came right along after me.

"Here," I said. "I want the swing right here, so I can look out to sea, or down into the garden." And I looked down into where we'd said the garden would have been, and there, standing patiently, watching us, was that unearthly black figure I'd seen in the schoolhouse hall, with the gruesome burning eyes.

I made a noise, but it wasn't a scream. I didn't have that much control of my faculties. How long had it been there? It was not thirty feet away from us, and it was studying us, preying on us. I knew this, yet I still could not clearly see its features. It was as if it were much farther away from us than the tree it was standing under.

One thing was clear: Conary saw it too. I heard him make a noise in his throat and he touched my arm. We couldn't take our eyes from that face, with its awful eyes that seemed to pin us against some invisible wall. Conary took a step backward, and I moved with him, terrified of slipping or falling into the hole, but even more afraid of staying where I was. Without seeming to move, the thing stayed with us.

We backed away, but it stayed the same distance from us, as if it and we were linked together and all moving on another plane. This was so awful that we stopped again. It held out its arms to us, and then began to shudder . . . and then the noise began, the noise we'd both heard before in the schoolhouse on the main. The weeping.

Now when it moved it drew nearer. I tried to back away and found *I* could not move. I could not. It was walking toward us, but not exactly on the ground. It was moving on a level with us as if the ground it was walking came up to the top of the foundation wall, as indeed it may once have done. The weeping was terrible. It had an awful angry timbre, and it wouldn't stop that keening. It gave off a smell, like the earthen floor of a root cellar.

It was only about ten feet from us now, and the sobs could have been coming from our own throats. I'm not sure that they were not. It was as if its grief here was so great that it made new rules. It seemed to have gotten into *my* heart and chest, and I felt rooted in horror to the rock where I stood. Sometimes in church when you sing or pray, all the voices vibrate together and seem to come from your own being ... *Almighty and most merciful Father ... We have erred and strayed from thy ways like lost sheep. . . . We have followed too much the devices and desires of our own hearts. . . . And there is no health in us . . .*

I was crying. It was close enough to reach its hand to me (or someone it saw where I was standing). I could see its weird light eyes with no pupils. It was repulsive, reaching out for us yet not really seeing us, lost in a dream of its own desires.

Conary pushed me, freed me, and I jumped from the foundation wall and ran. I could hear footsteps running behind me, but I couldn't stop crying and I couldn't look back. I ran and ran and ran. Finally Conary caught me, running and crying too, and when I heard his sobs I had the thought that he was possessed, that the black thing was inside him, using him to chase me, and, frightened all over again, I ran away from him. At last, gasping with pain in my lungs, and balked by a great wall of raspberry brambles, I stopped and stood, shaking and panting. My legs were trembling. I was afraid to sit down for fear I'd be too weak to get up again, so I just stood there with my knees locked, trying to remember how to breathe and listening to unnatural silence. Where was Conary? What had happened? At last I turned back the way I had come. It was easy to track my course through the brush; I'd broken a path the size of a bear's.

When I reached him, Conary was lying on his back in an odd position, as if he had dropped and not moved again. His face was streaked with tears and his pale eyes were staring, at the sky, at nothing. It took me a moment to dare to touch him; I couldn't see him breathing, and his skin was an awful grayish color. I sat down beside him and got up the nerve to reach out. He was warm, but his eyes looked like dead marbles, flat as a doll's. Now my fear changed again. What was this? Was he suspended somewhere, no longer alive but not yet dead? Had time stopped? I felt I stopped breathing myself, spending all my strength trying to turn time back, to will whatever had happened to him to unhappen.

I wish I believe I rescued him, but whatever had gripped him was not something I could touch. Suddenly, though, explosively, he took a long shuddering breath, and then more, with his eyes now on mine, as if he could stay in life that way and force the horror to get out of his lungs by squeezing it out with sheer will. His face began to return to a human color. As I watched his eyes take on more and more the expressions I knew, it seemed his return was gradual, as if his spirit had been shattered and dispersed and he had to recall it from some miasma around him. Then he lay still, and then, at last, he closed his eyes. I touched his face and said his name. I could still hardly believe it hadn't killed him. I thought that parasitic black sack of fury and decay had lodged itself in his lungs and shaken him apart with his eyes staring open. He suddenly sat up and put his arms around me, and I began to cry my own tears.

Conary held me and let me feel him breathe and believe in his warmth, and he didn't try to stop me. Finally he stroked my back and whispered, "It's all right now, it's all right now," and I felt myself calm down, like a skittish horse being gentled.

Somewhere in the woods near us we heard something moving. Something large and mercifully ordinary, like a deer. It brought us both to our feet. In another moment we saw that the sun was low in the sky and would soon sink below the line of the trees. We could feel the coolness chilling our skin and knew it would deepen with darkness. Where had the day gone?

Connie took my hand and said, "Let's go home."

"Do you know where we are?"

"No. But let's try to head northwest, up the ridge of the island. We may find the meadow, or we may catch a break in the trees so we can see the shore of the main. I'll be able to tell better where we are from that."

I nodded; I was sure he could lead us to safety.

We saw nothing that we'd seen on the walk south. It was easy going, though Conary had hurt his foot and was limping. We came once to an open field filled waist-high with some bushes or stunted trees with copper leaves. It proved impassable, so we made our way around the rim of this strange rust-colored basin. It forced us off our course, and when we reached the other side, a thicket of alders forced us still farther off the ridge than we wanted to go. We went on in that fashion, zigzagging in an attempt to head for the point we wanted, like a boat tacking into the wind. I said, "It's a beat," and Conary smiled for the first time in what felt like hours.

Near the ridge of the island, the brush and woods that had been fighting us suddenly opened out to a wide heath. It lay silver and peaceful, like a naked body under summer sky. We had found one of the blueberry barrens. Most of the berries were still green, but here and there a cluster of deep blue glowed among the tiny polished green leaves, and we gathered as many as we could without stopping; we were beginning to be hungry and thirsty.

At the highest point on the barren, Conary stopped and pointed. We could see the south shore of the Neck. Conary said, "That's Allen's Nub." It was over a mile away, across the south reach, and it looked like flat black shoreline to me, but I could tell from Connie's expression that we were no longer lost.

It took perhaps another half hour to reach March Cove. I wanted to ask him a hundred questions about what had happened to us. It was already beginning to seem like a waking nightmare of some sort, except that the ache in my throat was as real as if I'd been screaming at the top of my lungs for hours. I almost started to speak then, when we knew we were at last on our way home, but the fear was too fresh, my sense of normalcy too tentative, and it must have been the same for him. We both carried ourselves carefully through the pinewoods, concentrating on our footing like people battered and fragile and frightened of falling.

By the time we reached the cove, *Frolic* was floating quietly in deep water. The anchor was holding, but the painter Connie had led up to the beach was lost somewhere underwater; we had no way to bring the boat to us. In the hours since we'd beached the boat on sand some twenty feet below what was now the water's edge, the cove had become a different place. There was no sand flat. Our clam hod was eight feet underwater. The wind had died completely, and the bay was like a mirror, its unrippled surface streaked with blue and pink and violet shadows.

I must have showed a momentary loss of heart, because Conary, watching my face, put his arms around me. We held each other for a moment. What thoughts we'd had of reaching somewhere warm and bright, with hot food and a welcome before nightfall, were gone.

Connie said, "I could swim out and tow the boat in to shore . . ."

"Don't. It's too cold."

"I don't mind that. But there's not much point. We can't sail without wind."

"Are there oars?"

"One paddle. And no light, until the moon rises. We're a couple miles from the harbor."

For a moment I had an unpleasant vision of Edith beginning to really steam about now. Conary must have had similar thoughts, because he added, "They'll probably start looking for us soon. For you, anyway. And even if they don't, the wind may come up after moonrise."

Just then the sun reached the treetops on the mainland and shot a streak of gold across the still water. It was going to be one of those heart-stopping sunsets. Conary stared at it for a moment, then leaned down and chose a small flat stone and sent it skipping across the glassy stillness, a gesture very much like whistling in the dark. I chose my own and sent it whisking toward the sunset. It sank a good ten feet farther out than Connie's.

He looked at me in surprise. "Damn," he said and skipped another one. I skipped another and beat him again.

"Wouldn't anyone come looking for *you*?"

"Don't change the subject." Conary skipped another stone. I didn't really want to change the subject, of course; I skipped another and beat him again.

"Where'd you learn to do that?"

"My daddy." I skipped one behind my back. Showing off.

"I'm going to beat you if we have to stay here all night," he said.

The fire of the sunset had hit the water and was flaring across it like spilled paint; the reach was still. Not a boat stirred. The whole world had gone to supper, and out here where once an entire village had hummed there was only the sound of a loon once in a while, and our stones whispering *plink plink plink* across the water.

In the winter of 1884, cold closed in early on Beal Island. There was heavy snow on All Saints' Day, and the night before, All Hallows' Eve, a couple of boys out making mischief claimed they saw a strange light moving in the graveyard. They said their dog had barked and barked and then tried to dig a hole at one of the graves. The story was soon all over the island, and it spooked Claris Osgood Haskell. For a month she didn't want to go out for wood after dark or to the backhouse by herself. Danial laughed at her. Sallie didn't. Patiently she went out with her mother.

Christmas came and went. The Osgoods on the main wouldn't come out to visit in winter because Danial was ugly to them, but they sent presents by way of Virgil or Bowdoin Leach. Claris and Sallie would see the cousins in the summer. Relatives and friends came out for berrying and picnics on the beach at March Cove and, when they arrived, sent one of the children to bring Sallie and Claris, and Danial too if he would come. Once in a while he did. He would never admit it, but people thought even he wished for more company, and some of the life and bustle of the town, even if all he did was stand at the edge of it and watch. But things were at such a pass between the two families that he was trapped on the stand he had taken, and Claris with him.

Sallie understood all this, though it wasn't spoken of. Her mother had chosen to lock herself to Danial, but Sallie had not, except to the extent that she had chosen to bear her mother company. Sallie hadn't yet stopped hoping that her mother would finally find that a dutiful living daughter was true consolation for the lost perfection of the favorite. She did what she could to protect her parents from each other, while growing bolder at defending herself as she saw more of the ways of the world.

Sallie was finished with school, and in fact sometimes helped Miss Pease teaching the little ones. She liked being up in the village; there was a lot going on now that the quarries were flourishing. There was a second store open, and a boardinghouse full of quarry workers, and there were often parties in the evenings. Island people didn't dance, since that was considered, if not sinful, thoroughly unwise, but there was music, and there were blueberry festivals and lobster boils and bean hole suppers, and plenty of sled riding, sleighing, and skating in winter. Sallie was a popular high-spirited girl, and several of the village boys had courted her at one time or another. At the moment she was taken with a young man named Paul LeBlond from Vermont, a fancy cutter up from the stoneworks at Barre. His people were French Canadian, and he had strong arms and high color, and could sing songs in English and French and was not afraid of dancing, though he had to do it with other boys from the boarding-house. They could do a noisy dance with lots of stamping, called clog dancing, and something called the schottische, as well as square dances from Virginia. Sallie in her reckless mood had asked him to teach her, to the mildly scandalized surprise of her island friends.

On a Saturday evening in January, a group of young people, boys from the quarries along with boys and girls from the island, came to the door to ask Sallie to go out with them. They were going to have an ice-skating party with a bonfire, and afterward Mrs. Gott had invited them for doughnuts and hot cider. Frank and Winnie Horton came in to speak to the Haskells since they had known them all their lives; the rest of the young people waited outside.

Danial said, "No." He was sitting in the kitchen knitting an eel net. Claris and Sallie had been sitting across the table with the work basket between them, darning. Sallie was already on her feet, going out for her skates, when her father spoke.

Claris looked up and stared at her husband, and Sallie stopped in the middle of the floor. The Hortons said afterward that the color rose in her face and she seemed to get bigger as she stood there over her father in his chair.

"Why not?" she said in a voice like a rasp against a metal burr.

"A gadder comes to grief," Danial said calmly, not looking up.

"That's Grandmother speaking," said Sallie sharply. "That's my grandmother speaking right out of your mouth. I don't have to listen to a dead woman."

"You could do worse," said Danial just as sharply. The young Hortons didn't know what to do. They felt as if they'd put matches to a pile of tinder without knowing what they were doing, so intense were the emotions crackling through the room.

"I'm going out," Sallie declared.

"You are *not*," said Danial, suddenly standing up. Now he was standing taller than Sallie. They looked amazingly alike, with broad shoulders and black eyebrows. Winnie said she believed at that moment it would come to blows, though she had never seen a man strike a woman, nor a woman strike a man for that matter.

Claris rose from her chair. Without a word, she went out of the kitchen to the ell, where the outer clothes were hung, and came back with her own heavy black wool cloak. She ignored Danial as she crossed the room and put the cloak around her daughter's shoulders. She put a hand on her back, as if to say, Go. Sallie looked at her, threw a look back at her father, and went out. The Hortons followed her, closing the door behind them.

Once outside with her friends and her skates under her arm, Sallie wept briefly from anger and frustration. The circle of young people comforted her. He doesn't want to lose you, some said. He lost one child, you're all he has. He's afraid you'll marry and move off island, said others. They knew. Their own parents had the same fears, or other ones, and were often unreasonable. He's not so bad, they said.

I know he's not; you don't understand, said Sallie, her voice frantic.

—m—

Meanwhile, a terrible silence filled the Haskell kitchen. Claris sat down in her chair, but she did not resume her mending. It was almost five o'clock and night had fallen. Danial too sat for a long time, not moving. It was getting on toward suppertime, but neither of them stirred to get food ready. Finally, Danial rose and found the matches in the near dark. He lit the lamp on the table. Claris got up and went out of the room; Danial sat absolutely still again waiting, though he didn't know for what. She had gone up the stairs. When she came back down, she was carrying Amos's violin, which he hadn't seen since the day the boy had died.

Danial went rigid. This was an act of defiance such as had never happened between them. She couldn't be planning to play it? Her sitting in this kitchen, cradling the thing that had caused all the trouble, was like accusing him of murdering their child.

She had sat back down in her chair across the table. The fire in the stove was close to embers, since neither had fed it wood, and the room was cold. Danial stared straight ahead, his eyes looking past Claris. Claris stared straight at him, her eyes unblinking, pinning him to the chair. After what seemed a terrible wait, she put the fiddle to her chin and, without taking her eyes from his face, she began to play "Black-Eyed Susan."

Later in the summer, I learned a great deal about what was happening at home that night while we were stranded. I had it from Dot Sylvester, the village telephone operator, after we became friends. Mrs. Sylvester was a seamstress; her house was in the center of town, the switchboard in her living room. She knew everything that was going on. If you called her and asked her to ring, say, Kermit Horton, she'd say something like, "Won't do you no good, dear, I just saw him going up the street to Abbott's. I'll wait till I see him go back home and call you back." It was a great convenience.

Sometimes Dot would get busy pinning up a hem and visiting and fail to notice the red lights on her switchboard; people would have to send a son or daughter over to knock on the door and tell her they were trying to put a call through. She was always glad when some young person at a loose end wanted to hang around and watch the board for her. She'd teach you to sit on her swivel stool with the headset on, and when someone rang to place a call, you plugged certain rods in and then twirled the crank a certain number of times. Our number was 496 ring 3. Dot wasn't supposed to listen in on people's calls, but everyone knew she did; we all listened on the party line ourselves when there was something interesting going on.

When I hadn't returned by suppertime, Edith was beyond annoyed. She was upset and angry. She rang in and asked Dot to put through a call to Boston. Naturally Dot had to check the line, to be sure the connection had gone through all right. She heard Edith saying, "She went up to the village this morning to get the mail and she never came back. She knew my mother was coming today. We waited and waited for her; we almost left Mother standing on the platform, we were so late."

As it happened, I had forgotten all about the great visit from Grandma Adele. When I did remember, I knew it was going to do nothing at all to make my life easier. If there was one thing I understood about Edith, it was that she did not at any time want to get crosswise to her mother.

I could picture my father two hundred miles away in the thick heat of a Boston summer night, listening to this rant. What was he supposed to do about it? He'd say, "I'm sorry." That was what he always said when Edith was upset, and it made her just furious. She couldn't tell if he meant "I'm sorry you're upset" or "I'm sorry the world is so terrible for you" or "I'm sorry you're upsetting me" or "I'm sorry I married you." It always sounded like all of those at once, and it tended to make her go straight up and turn left. I often wondered why he kept doing it.

This time she couldn't blow up at him, because Grandma Adele would have heard, so she didn't say anything. He asked her if she had called Ed and Frances, my grandparents.

She said, "No, I called you first. I didn't think I ought to frighten them, if there's nothing really wrong." Father said he was sure nothing really was. In point of fact, I might have been drowned or murdered by then and cut up into pieces. Every child in America expected to be kidnapped every minute since the killing of the Lindbergh baby.

What he would have known was that Edith of course hadn't called my grandparents. Edith never did, if she could possibly help it, and at the moment she was helping it by making him do it. I'm sure he was pleased at the thought of a staggering long-distance phone bill, on top of everything else.

Edith began on the litany of my horrible behavior, which Dot didn't have to tell me, since I knew it by heart. It went like this: "She's been just impossible, Milton. You cannot imagine what it's been like here the last two weeks. Thoughtless, disobedient, terrible moods, screaming in the night. . . . Now her brother is getting frightened that something filthy has happened to her, and I don't know what to tell Mother."

My father suggested she do something sensible, like ask around town if anyone knew where I'd gone. Ask who? Edith snapped at him, as if she was alone on some polar ice cap.

My father told her, "Ask Nella B. Foss. And ask up at Abbott's."

"Nella B.'s gone home by now," said Edith.

"Then ask Dot to ring her at home," my father said, almost surely knowing perfectly well that Dot was right on the line at the time.

"I didn't know Nella B. was on the telephone," said Edith.

"Just ring Dot and ask her. I'm going to try to reach Ed and Frances. One of us will call you back." He hung up.

Edith hated it when anyone hung up on her. She behaved as if someone had yanked a plate away from her before she'd begun to eat. Only of course she couldn't show that because, in front of Grandma Adele, she had to be Lady Bountiful with the perfect life.

Dot, being the saint she was, called Edith the minute she saw the connection go dead.

"Mrs. Gray, it's Dot Sylvester. How are you, dear?"

"Well, I'm—"

"I'll tell you why I'm calling. I just checked on the line to be sure your long-distance call went through, and I couldn't help hearing that you're worried about Hannah. I saw her this morning, right after she had her haircut. She was going through the village with Conary Crocker. I saw them turn down the road toward the town dock. You want me to go down to the corner and look, see if his truck is still down there?"

"I don't want you to go to any trouble," said Edith stiffly.

"I don't mind, I've had children of my own. I'll come right on back and let you know," Dot said. She closed down the switchboard and went out and trotted down to the town wharf and back. She rang Edith and told her, "Conary Crocker's truck is down by the dock, and his boat's off her mooring. I believe they must have gone out fishing and run out of air. There's not a breath of wind out there right now; they could be anywhere. I'll tell you what I'd do, I'd call Mrs. Tapley, who lives down across from Tom Crocker, have her go and knock him up and find out if Conary's still out somewhere. If he is, Tom Crocker can go looking for them."

Mrs. Sylvester talked in a rapid-fire manner as if every speech was timed and charged by the minute. She was busy and cheerful and had a heart as big as a house. I doubt if she gave Edith a chance to answer.

"I'll just go ahead and call Mrs. Tapley, dear. She won't mind, it's good for her to worry about something besides herself. Tom Crocker won't bite *her* head off anyway. If I find out anything more, I'll let you know." The switchboard was lighting up now, and it was all Dot could do to keep track of it all.

My grandfather called Edith, wanting to know if she had heard anything. Edith told him about Dot Sylvester and Mrs. Tapley, but he already knew all of that. He told her: "Jewel Eaton says Tom Crocker's clamming gear is missing and Webby Allen saw Conary going down the bay late in the morning. Webby said he had another boy with him, so there are probably three of them. Tom doesn't have any running lights on that boat of his, so he's waiting for moonrise, then he'll get out and go looking. Now try not to worry."

"But where can they have been all this time?"

"Out on one of the islands," my grandfather said to her. "Either that or they're out of wind ashore someplace, and they'll start walking and someone will pick them up. If they're on the bay, Tom will find them. It's a fine night, don't worry. Everyone in the village has pulled a stunt like this one time or another."

Edith called Dot back, sounding really scared. "Dot, I think I'd better call the police."

"Nearest police are over in Unionville. Would you like me to put you through?"

"Yes, please."

"I'll call Ham Fitch, he lives closest, and he's probably to home. Hang up, dear, I'll ring you back."

Dot told me she was worried herself, that she didn't try to talk Edith out of this. What if we were out of wind down the shore someplace and trying to walk home and fell afoul of vagrants? The woods were full of desperate characters, Hoover's Army. The Depression had taken a turn for the worse that summer, and the mood abroad was just miserable.

Mercy Chatto was half amazed when Mrs. Haskell suggested she board with them for the winter, since they didn't seem like the kind of family that would welcome company. Everyone on the island agreed that Claris Haskell was a woman not easy with strangers or those she thought not her class. Some wondered if she had the melancholia. Also, everyone knew there was a state of open warfare between Sallie Haskell and her father; even over on the Neck people had heard about it. Sallie was going about with Paul LeBlond. It was said that her father tried to lock her in at night but she climbed out the window. They had exchanged angry words in public.

Mercy had graduated from the Academy the previous spring and come to take over the Beal Island School from Miss Pease, who'd gone gouty. Mercy hadn't really wanted to leave home, but things were changing in Dundee. A man from Philadelphia had paid an enormous price for

Homer Carleton's farm, the prettiest farm on the shore between the village and the Neck. The Philadelphia man wasn't going to farm it either: he'd built a great boardinghouse on it, a barn of a place with no stoves in the rooms, for he intended to open it only in the summer. Mercy's father and her uncle Paul had laughed themselves silly over that, but the second summer the place was full, and the third year a woman from Cleveland came for the whole summer, bringing her own carriage and horses with her and a driver from Hampshire, England.

There were all kinds of accents to be heard when you went up to Abbott's to market, or even to the Grange store. Not only were the rusticators and their servants everywhere but there was a mining boom on. Three copper mines had opened within fifteen miles, and Simon Osgood built a great square brick hotel for the miners to live in. James Chatto thought his daughter Mercy would be better off out of harm's way, and the island was quieter, and less infected with change.

Mercy had started out boarding with her Aunt Gott, who was actually her cousin a few times removed, around on the southern tip of the island right next to the granite wharf. But there was sickness in the house, and Aunt Gott had to ask her to find another place. Mercy confided this to Mrs. Haskell, a tall reserved woman who was often at the schoolhouse. Claris Haskell led the children in singing in the afternoons in the schoolroom, and she gave violin lessons in the rooms above, or sometimes sat up there alone, playing for her own solace.

Mercy had been glad at first to move to the Haskells'. She thought it would be merry to have another girl in the house for a companion, and Mrs. Haskell was a lady; you could see that. But she soon found that you didn't have to know much to know that something had gone gravely wrong in these people's lives.

The house was spotless. Mrs. Haskell was a careful, even zealous housekeeper. But she hardly cooked. No one cooked. Mercy had never seen a household in which there were no regular meals, no table spread with hot and cold dishes and a time set aside for the family to gather for food and fellowship. Mr. Haskell was a dark inward man whose first thought seemed always to fancy a slight or to find himself hard done by. He got up in the mornings and fed the fire in the kitchen stove, then went out to tend the large animals. He had something wrong with one foot, and on cold days it pained him worse than common and he used a cane. She grew to dread the sound of the cane thumping on the stairs, or moving around in the kitchen below. Mrs. Haskell had given her the cozy back room above the kitchen; it kept the warmest on winter nights. It had once belonged to a son of the house, who'd been lost at sea. Mercy's grandfather Kane was a sea captain, and two of her young cousins had been drowned, one on the China Sea and one at the Straits of Magellan, so she knew the sorrow that could bring to a family.

In the mornings, once Mercy could hear that the fire had been renewed and the pump in the kitchen sink started, she would dress herself and hurry down and out to the backhouse carrying her chamber pot. Back in the warm kitchen, she heated water for washing face and hands and a kettle for tea, and cooked a pan of oatmeal. If Sallie came down in time to gather eggs before Mercy left for school, they would boil half a dozen and share them for breakfast. Sallie cooked lunch and dinner up at the boardinghouse, and took her own dinner and supper there. She was saving up to escape, Mercy thought, and Mr. Haskell may have thought so too, for she sometimes heard him rummaging about in Sallie's room trying to find out where she hid her money. One time he must have found it, for one Saturday morning Mercy was awakened by a blazing great argument between them downstairs. After that, Sallie took to paying a visit to Mercy at the schoolhouse every week, and she always found an excuse to spend a few moments upstairs by herself. Mercy assumed she had a hiding place up there. She hoped it was a good one. She didn't know but what Danial searched the schoolhouse too.

Sometimes Mercy would come home to find that Mrs. Haskell had cooked a pot of beans, or Boston brown bread, or made a pie. Sometimes Claris would have a fancy to reproduce some meal from her childhood, and Mercy would find an embarrassment of riches at the table, perhaps boiled meat and vegetables, with biscuits and butter and raisin pie.

One time she made a pitcher of switchell, a summer drink of water and ginger and molasses that farmwives used to carry to the fields for thirsty men in haying time. Mrs. Haskell set the pitcher on the table, saying, "This is Sallie's favorite."

Sallie, passing the table, simply gave her a look.

"Come sit, Sallie," said Mrs. Haskell. "I made switchell for you."

"I hate switchell, Mother. It's Amos who liked it."

Mrs. Haskell paused for a moment, and then said dismissively, "*Hate* is too strong a word for food. Say, 'I don't favor it.'"

But Sallie said nothing and went upstairs, while Mrs. Haskell poured two glasses and began to talk to Mercy about summer afternoons of her girlhood.

On such evenings Danial sat silent, fuming. After a while he'd cook a pan of whatever he found around, cabbage fried with salt pork, or some salt cod, and plop a plate of it down for Mercy and one for himself. If Mrs. Haskell wanted some, she served herself; otherwise what was left was pushed to the back of the stove and Mercy took it to school in her lard pail the next day for dinner.

Sallie brought home leftovers from the boardinghouse at night, and that often made up dinner for the next day, and even supper. But there were several nights when Mercy was so hungry she went out to the hen yard, where sometimes Danial had thrown crushed pieces of the lobster he picked up along the beach and boiled for the chickens to save corn. She discovered that he often failed to crush the claws, and she could wash those off at the well and break them open with a stone at the door rock and get enough to eat to keep her stomach from grumbling all evening.

Danial called lobsters "bugs," but Mercy's family ate them, and she liked them well enough.

Another oddity of the family was that the only one who ever went to worship service was Mr. Haskell. The services on the island were intermittent and Baptist, conducted by a lay leader except for the rare occasions when a minister came from the main. Mrs. Haskell claimed to have reverted to the Congregational faith of her childhood, while Sallie made no excuse. She simply didn't do anything her father wanted her to do. Mercy herself didn't go because she was a Roman Catholic, the family having originally been Chatteau, from Montreal.

On Sundays, either the three women were alone or all four of them were cooped up together, bored and silent. Mr. Haskell was some kind of very strict Baptist, and when someone took to a frivolous pastime on Sunday, he would stare and say that his mother was turning in her grave. Mrs. Haskell replied once that his mother wasn't in a grave, she had probably long since been dinner for the lobsters, and Mr. Haskell whipped his head around to stare at her and moved in his chair as if he might get up and hit her. He didn't, but Mercy noticed that, still, Mrs. Haskell didn't go to her loom on Sundays, which Mercy knew she was aching to do the way a drunkard aches for rum. All the other days of the week, except when she was at the schoolhouse playing music, Mrs. Haskell sat at her loom in the parlor with a basket of rags torn into strips at her side, weaving rugs. There were rugs of her making in every room of the homeplace and of the schoolhouse, and now they were piling up in the ell between the pantry and the backhouse.

What the rug loom was to Claris, the animals were to Sallie. When she wasn't working at the boardinghouse, the place she wanted to be was the barn, where she groomed the horses and talked to them, and petted the cow, and sometimes just leaned against it and felt it breathing. She had all kinds of pets out there too, Mercy wrote her mother. Raccoons and a raven, and a family of barn cats. Mercy wrote to her mother several times a week, about her classes and her scholars, and about this very odd family and their ways. The letters were later subpoenaed for the trial.

They told of how Mrs. Haskell seemed in a way to be trading places with Mercy, in that when Mercy came home Mrs. Haskell would leave for the schoolhouse, and there she would stay until dark and sometimes after. Mrs. Haskell liked to be alone there. Meanwhile there was Mercy, alone in another woman's house, and it was her first time boarding and she didn't know what was right for her to do. If no one had cooked the supper, should she? If she wanted to sit in the parlor for the evening light, might she light the stove in there? There was not much stock of preserves or pickles in the cellar, but if there was nothing else for supper, might she open a jar?

What she didn't write about was the afternoon in February when she was sitting in Mrs. Haskell's rocker in the kitchen preparing her lessons. Danial had come in and put his wet cold mittens on the stove shelf to dry and set about lighting the lamps. Then he turned to her as if he'd been practicing this speech in his mind and said, "I guess we got the place to ourselves." As if we didn't most of the time, Mercy thought. Then she saw he was starting to undo his trouser buttons.

Finally all the warm colors faded out of the twilight and there was nothing left of the day but deep blue shadows. We stopped skipping stones because we couldn't see them sink anymore. It was getting colder too, and as the darkness deepened, I began to be afraid again. What if we did have to stay here all night? I thought of Edith. I thought of supper. I thought of my brother, and the fuss at home.

"We'll be all right," said Conary. "It's just going to be black as pitch for an hour or two till the moon rises."

"Could we make a fire?"

"We could, if we hadn't left the matches on the boat."

"Oh." I looked out across the dark reach. I turned my back to it and looked at the black hulk of the island. We seemed perched between the two, on this narrow strip of rocks.

"Does anyone use that old boat hull for anything?" I saw again the rotting lobster boat in the brush above the shore.

"Yuh. Hunters use it some in the fall. They leave gear in there they don't want to truck out here every time they come. They usually clean it out pretty good by the end of the season, but there might be a match there." We made our way across the rocks and up the bank to where the boat carcass lay, cradled in brush with its prow still facing out to sea. There was a crude ladder against the hull by which you could climb aboard. Conary went first. I was frightened the boat would shift under his weight or the wood would give way as he stepped onto the ancient deck, but it seemed to be sound.

"Would anyone mind us prowling around here?"

"Don't think so."

I was stalling. I was a little afraid of the ladder, and of trespassing. "Does someone own it?"

"Yuh." There was nothing for it. I tried the ladder and it held me, so I climbed into the open cockpit of the boat.

"I own it," said Conary. He hadn't meant to surprise me. He just hadn't thought of mentioning it. "My sister and I do."

"You mean, the boat?"

"The boat and the cove. And some land. That meadow up there on the ridge."

"That beautiful meadow?"

"You liked that, eh?" He smiled. "I like it. My grandfather left it to us." He opened the door to the boat's cabin and let himself down into it. It seemed black as a tomb in there; I watched from the doorway. The cabin had one narrow bunk against the wall and some shelves and a hanging locker. It smelled dank, and it was barely big enough for one person to stand in. I guess it was unusual for a work boat to have much of a cabin at all. Conary found a rusty fork and a kerosene lamp on a shelf. He checked everywhere but there were no matches. In a cubbyhole under the bunk he found an old thin blanket.

"Doesn't even smell too he bad," he said. Taking the blanket, we made our way back down to the beach. The night was dark, but starlight reflected on the water made enough of a glow that we could see to climb down the rocks without breaking our arms, though I got pretty torn up by wild raspberry brambles. We went back to the log where we'd leaned together in the sun and eaten steamers. Conary made a tent of this blanket around us both, and when he felt how cold my bare arms were, he wrapped his arms around me too. I sat very still.

"You own that meadow."

"Yuh. We own about twenty acres, I guess. When we were little my grandfather hauled that old boat up onto the shore for us to use as a playhouse. We could explore all day. There was a tumbledown sawmill up the shore where the creek comes out that he said was ours too."

"Did your people live out here?"

"No. Some Osgood ancestor bought this chunk at some point, but they never used it."

"You're related to them too?"

"Osgoods? Most everyone in the village is. You probably are yourself."

That was true. At least I was related to the Friends. I asked him if we were cousins, then.

He said, "Could be. My mother's grandfather was an Osgood. He was captain of a ship called the *Randall D* that was lost at sea. And I remember my mother took me and Mary to visit a tiny old creature called Alice Crocker, who she called Auntie, who had a son named Osgood. That's about all I know. My father doesn't spend a lot of time keeping up with the relations."

We sat silent for a bit, and Conary laid his cheek against mine. "You're still cold."

"I'm all right."

"I felt you shiver." He stood up, leaving the blanket all for me. "Look the other way, will you?"

"Why?" He started to take off his clothes, and I quickly looked the other way.

"What are you doing?"

"Going to get matches."

"Conary—that water is freezing!"

"I'm the stupid nit left them on the boat," he said, though it wasn't true. A second later I heard a splash. Connie's clothes were in a pile on the beach, and he was swimming toward *Frolic*. It made my skin creep just to think of how cold it was; I thought there was a real chance it was the nicest thing anyone ever did for me.

He reached the boat, riding peacefully in the blackness. He pulled himself halfway onto the bow, grabbed the painter we had rigged, then dropped back into the water. I heard a tremendous kicking fuss, and then the boat started to move toward me. I could see Connie's wet black head in the water, moving like a seal's before the bow. When he got to where his feet could touch bottom, he maneuvered the hull between us and pushed the bow up onto the sand. With a sweep of his arm he grabbed a tattered flannel shirt from the tiller well and threw it to me as I pushed the blanket across the bow to him. The shirt still smelled of sun and the clean sweat smell of him; he'd torn the sleeves off at the elbows to keep them out of his way when he was handling tiller and sheets by himself. I put it on, feeling suddenly sheltered. Soon he followed me up the beach wearing the blanket and carrying the bucket that held our supply of newspaper and matches and the hatchet. As soon as he got his dry clothes back on, he split out some kindling from a piece of driftwood and in minutes had a fire going.

We sat close together warmed by firelight, waiting for the moon. A black bird, darker than the night sky, skimmed into the cove and with hardly a sound settled on *Frolic*'s stern where she floated near the water's edge.

"A shag," Connie said. "She's out late. She must be surprised to find she isn't alone here."

"What's a shag?"

"To a straphanger? Cormorant." Connie seemed perfectly glad of this stranger in our midst, but I wasn't sure I was. I'd had enough dark figures floating around half seen.

Connie asked, "Did you ever dream about being able to fly?"

"Always. For years. Did you?"

"Yuh."

"Did you ever dream about living out here?"

He smiled. "Always. I still do. I'd like to build a cabin up in that meadow, and have a landing here, and fish and farm. I'd like to try raising sheep, like they used to on the outer islands."

"You wouldn't find it lonely?"

He smiled again, maybe with surprise. He said shyly, "I hadn't thought to do it alone." There was an embarrassed but sweet silence between us. I was intensely aware of his bare arm, the flesh still cold from the icy water, inches from mine. I thought about a house up on that ridge behind us. The quiet. The sunlight. Blueberries and clams and firelight. Teaching a baby to swim in this cove.

The cormorant suddenly shook herself and rose from the surface of the cove with a flurry of black flapping. She rowed the air furiously, disappearing into the darkness. Conversation stopped again. I wanted to be somewhere light and safe. I wanted to go home. I wanted my mother.

Conary whispered, "I'll take care of you if I can." I nodded. I knew it. A log shifted suddenly in the fire, and the noise startled us both.

"Conary?"

"What?"

"The thing we saw—that weeping noise. Is that the same noise you heard in the schoolhouse?"

"Yes. Exactly."

"Me too. That's what was in the kitchen, and in my bedroom. And once I saw it watching me from the hall. What is it? Is that a ghost?"

After a time, he said, "I don't know what else it could be."

"What *is* a ghost, then?"

"I imagine," he said finally, "it's a creature that won't take no for an answer." I watched his profile. He looked at the fire. He said, "My uncle had a dog named Smokey once. He found him on the mountain when he was a pup, too small to be weaned. He would have died if Uncle Paul had left him there. He was a pitiful little thing with big eyes. They cleaned him up and bottle-fed him and let him sleep behind the stove so he'd be warm and wouldn't miss his littermates. He had huge paws, even when he was a baby. When his eyes settled down to a color, he had one brown and one blue one, and he grew up huge. My aunt believed he was half wolf.

"Smokey lived for my uncle. He followed him everywhere, slept at the foot of their bed. When he got to be three or four, he began to turn mean. Started growling at people who came near the house. Bit a hired man once who touched my uncle's toolbox. They tried to train him out of it, but he couldn't understand how to be any other way.

"When he started growling at my aunt in the house, Uncle Paul put him outside and made him live in the yard. When Uncle Paul would go into the house last thing at night, Smokey would howl and whine outside the door and fling himself against it for hours. They tried shutting him in the barn, but he upset the chickens so they stopped laying. They tried chaining him outside, and he just howled all night. Nobody got any sleep. Finally, my uncle came out one morning and shot him."

A glowing log broke in half, and two blazing embers rolled away from each other, sending sparks into the night.

"It didn't stop him," said Conary. "They still hear him whining outside the door on cold nights. Last winter when my uncle got pneumonia, the dog howled and howled every night until Paul was up and around again. Thing's been dead nine years."

The dark bay lay flat and empty. Somewhere—no way to tell how near or far—a loon called.

"So," I said, "what we keep wandering into is something that happened in the schoolhouse."

"Something that's *still* happening, I'd say," said Conary.

"It has to be the murder."

"Except that didn't happen at the schoolhouse."

"Well *something* happened there. It isn't a spelling bee gone wrong."

Conary laughed. Then more soberly, he added, "Tell you what, I'd give a lot to make sure I never get within fifty yards of that thing again in my life, whatever it is. Was."

I took my hand and wove my fingers between his. Shyly he turned and kissed my shorn forehead. We sat like that in silence for I don't know how long. Connie stroked my hair now and then. I was tired. And sad. And hungry. And falling in love.

Conary said, "Look at the water." I did. It had a silver texture, no longer as glassy still as it had been at sunset. "Breeze is coming. By the time the moon is up we'll be able to sail."

We waited, and slowly the waning moon slipped out of the trees on the far shore and filled the bay with shimmering light. We were so hungry for it after all that blackness that it seemed to us the difference of night to day. For the first time since sunset we could see the shapes of rocks and trees beyond the circle of firelight. We both stood up, and Conary started piling sand onto the fire.

"Is there enough breeze to sail?"

"Yes. Not very fast, though." Quickly we loaded our gear onto the little sailboat. In the moments it took Conary to return the blanket to the fishing hulk, I was terrified something would happen before we could leave. But then he was back, beside me. We climbed into the sailboat and with the paddle poled ourselves out into the cove. Conary pulled up the anchor; the wet line spattered freezing water as he reeled it in and coiled it. The anchor had to be dipped and dipped to rinse off the black sandy muck before he would bring it aboard. There was no way to recover the clam hod. It was many feet down in water as black as ink.

I let down the centerboard and unstopped the main. We hoisted sails. What breeze there was seemed barely to be whispering across the water, but the sails softly filled to the north, and as soon as we had way on to come about, we turned and started up the reach for home.

We were well out onto the bay, gliding directly before the breeze. Our sails were all the way out like motionless wings, and we moved softly and silently in the silver moonlight. You could barely even hear the licking of water against the hull. Conary leaned against the coaming, holding the tiller. His hair fell across his forehead, and there were dark shadows around his eyes. He was worn out. I sat down hugging my knees for warmth, but Conary held out his arm to me, and I went to him and settled in, leaning back against his chest in the warm circle of his arm. We watched the stars.

Somewhere down the bay we heard an engine cough to life. It could have been miles away. Gradually the sound grew stronger. It was coming toward us, indeed at that hour could only have been coming *for* us. Thoughts of what was now ahead of us began to crowd into my head. It occurred to me that Conary and I would be separated. I reached up and took his hand, and he squeezed it hard. We ghosted along, waiting.

I don't know exactly when I understood that the boatman was Conary's father. The boat was an old lobsterman, white with scarred pink paint on the cockpit housing, and *Ruth E* written in script on the transom. It roared up the bay and made a circle around us. The driver stared without expression at Conary, who met his gaze, and the fact that he circled at undiminished speed, throwing a huge wake, was the only sign that he was furious. Neither he nor Conary said a word. When we stopped rocking wildly in the wake, the *Ruth E* pulled up beside us and slipped into neutral.

Mr. Crocker stared at me awhile and then at Conary. He said, "Are you Hannah Gray?" I admitted to it. He said to Conary, "Her mother's looking for her." Conary nodded. Well, he'd said they'd be looking for me. What he hadn't said, but of course knew, was that he would be blamed.

Conary got up and made to drop the mainsail. I went forward to take down the jib. Mr. Crocker tossed me a towline, which I cleated to our bow. Then he pulled *Frolic* in to him and reached a hand to me. . . . I understood. I was to ride with him. I looked at Connie, and caught a flash of something dreaded, unhappy, in his eyes, but then it was gone. He said nothing and gave me no sign. So I left him.

Mr. Crocker took off the lumber shirt he was wearing and made me put it on. It didn't make me any warmer; there was no sense that it was given out of warmth. Mr. Crocker was a big man with a deeply weathered face and the same weirdly light eyes as Conary's. This I noticed during the brief moment he stood looking at me as if to say, So you're what a smart girl from Boston looks like? I wondered all the way home how cold he was, and how much he resented me. I tried to imagine by what transaction he had learned that I was missing, and that Conary and I were together.

He pushed his engine back into gear. He watched carefully, expressionless, for the moment when the towrope grew taut before he accelerated. He was too good a boatman to snap the line by starting up too fast, though I felt fairly sure that his care was out of pride in himself, not concern for Connie's comfort or safety. We picked up speed and I watched from the stern as Conary, ten feet behind us, set about furling and stopping his mainsail. Then he flaked and bagged the jib and coiled all his lines. When all was secure, he stood holding the boom to steady himself and the tiller to hold *Frolic* in line, and looked at me. I watched the air stir his dark hair. I reached a hand to my own hair, abruptly remembering what it looked like; my reaction must have showed on my face because Conary smiled. His smile seemed to say, Courage, buddy, this is only the beginning. So I smiled too, as well as I could, to say, Courage to you too.

As we pulled into the town anchorage, there was not a word, or even a look, between father and son. Mr. Crocker slowed down and made for a mooring with a little rowboat on it. Conary tied his tiller long enough to go forward and, at just the right moment, to cast off the towline. From the stern of the *Ruth E* I reeled it in and coiled it, watching as he glided on to his own mooring. We circled around to ours. I wanted to pick up the buoy for Mr. Crocker, but he never even acknowledged the offer; he just went about doing what he did every day in exactly the way he liked to do it. He picked up the buoy from the cockpit, stopped the boat by throwing the engine into reverse, cut the motor, and then walked himself forward to secure the mooring line on the bow cleat. Then he brought the rowboat around and held it for me to get in. I could feel him waiting for me to do something stupid like sit in the bow.

Side by side in silence the two men secured their oars and attached their skiffs to their outhaul. They used the same moves. Mr. Crocker, pulling hand over hand, sent the two little boats bobbing out to where they would float even at lowest tide. Then in silence we walked up the hill together. Connie and I moved toward his truck, but Mr. Crocker marched toward a decrepit sedan patched with spots of rust.

"I'll drive her," Conary said.

"*That's* a fine idea," said his father. He opened the door of his car for me, and stood waiting for me to get in. So, I did. Conary and I didn't say good-bye. We didn't say anything. I sat in the car smelling the ancient upholstery and looked at my hands. Mr. Crocker backed carefully up to Main Street and turned his car toward Edith's house.

He drove twenty-five miles an hour the whole way. He was pretty polite to me, once Conary wasn't there anymore. I said we got stranded when the wind dropped. He said it was true, there hadn't been a breath of it. He asked if we'd had anything to eat, and I said clams for lunch. He said, "Where'd you go, March Cove?" and I said yes. There was a little edge in that last question, as there is when you know the answer and mean to be insulting.

I wondered what it was going to be like for Conary when he got home. His father said to me, "Your mother must be pretty worried." I wondered what it was going to be like for *me* when I got home. I said I was sure she was. We drove the rest of the way in silence.

Spring 1886

By April the air in the Haskell house had become thick and charged, like the atmosphere that produces heat lightning. Mercy Chatto hid in the schoolhouse as much as she could. She didn't want to be alone with Danial anymore, and neither did anyone else. When he lumbered in from the cove, it was like hearing a wounded bear up on the porch, furious and lonely and unnatural. He could locate his injury but not reason past it or help himself. In fact his efforts to do so had long since broken the shaft of the weapon off in the wound, where no one could get at it.

Venom, which sometimes coursed quietly for months like an underground stream, other times erupted in unexpected places in the household. Danial roared at Sallie. Mrs. Haskell lashed out at Mercy for boiling a pan dry when it was she herself who had done it. Sallie and Mrs. Haskell fought with each other. This shocked Mercy almost more than the contemptible pokings she infrequently suffered from Danial. She'd been around farm animals far too long for virgin primness, though not for disgust, since it seemed to her that at the moment Danial wielded his swollen manhood where it wasn't wanted, he was most unmanned. She disliked pitying him but put up with him as you would a badly trained dog. Mercy was young, but she was not a delicate flower. If she had a resentment, it was less of Danial than of Claris, for not seeing what turn things had taken and putting a stop to it.

She couldn't tell her parents what they had done when they sent her out to the island to preserve her from the wicked ways of town. She didn't want to shame them. This was only what came of wanting your children to make the same choices you had. Mercy was beginning to think she would not go back to the Neck when this school year was over. She was beginning to think she would like to travel to Florence, Italy, the most beautiful city in the world according to Signor Floro, the island's master stonecutter, who came from Carrara, and whose dark-eyed twins with their long black lashes and shy foreign manners made up Mercy's entire second-grade class. These twins had brought her a stereopticon picture of the Florence Duomo as a present their first day of school, and she kept it on her desk in the schoolhouse. Out here on the edge of the island, in sight of open sea, it seemed like the easiest thing in the world to hop overboard onto a ship and be off to the wide world. It was a better thing to think about than growing up to a life like Claris and Danial Haskell's.

Spring was late in coming that year; the winter seemed to wind on and on, and the joke going around the village was that when the trees finally did leaf out it would be in yellow and orange and they'd fall right off the same day. The hackmatacks were covered in yellow fuzz, but nothing turned green. What they were having instead of spring was an endless mud season. Even in April the ground was frozen hard except for a few inches at the surface. When snow or rain fell, it had nowhere to go. The surface mud became saturated with water, and all the roads and footpaths were the consistency of chocolate pudding. Everyone's boots and hems and trouser cuffs were caked with it.

Sallie Haskell's beau, Paul LeBlond, was talking about Colorado. Sallie came into the schoolhouse one afternoon when Mercy was there alone grading a Latin essay. *Pater bonus agricola est,* it began. Sallie had been crying, hard, and her eyes and nose were red and ran with anger. She couldn't go home like that. She sat beside Mercy, weeping.

"What happened? Can you tell me?" Mercy asked.

Sallie took deep breaths and shook her head violently, less to answer no than to shake off some intolerable emotion. "Paul," Sallie said.

Mercy said, Oh. She had already heard that Paul was leaving the island. She didn't know if Sallie would go with him, and Sallie seemed incapable of saying more about it than his name. That was the way of the family. There were so many things they had secretly decided must never be put into words that living with them was like living in a glass maze. Mercy kept bumping into barriers she didn't know were there, although Claris and Sallie navigated them expertly. Mercy had thought at first that Danial was the jailer, but when she began to see more of how it worked, she wondered if it was designed by the women, a prison in which they kept their beast. And themselves, all together.

Sallie left Mercy and ran upstairs. Mercy could hear her in the front room above her head, where Claris gave her music lessons. What was Sallie doing? Nothing musical. She couldn't play a note; she couldn't even whistle. Mercy could hear a thumping, as if Sallie was trying to break something. Was she looking for her money? Was it gone? Or was it in something she had to break to get at it? Mercy was doing a poor job of concentrating on her Latin lessons.

Finally Sallie came downstairs. She was pale and grim, and crying once more. "Mercy," she said, "would you go ask my mother to come here?" Mercy said she would. She got up and put on her black cape and hood and went out into the drizzle.

Claris came straight back to the schoolhouse with Mercy. She was wearing a summer dress that belonged to Sallie. It was printed with lilacs. Sallie stared at it when her mother came in as if this were the last straw. And why? Mercy wondered, watching them. Mrs. Haskell had explained to Mercy that her own clothes were wet from the wash and wouldn't dry in this weather. Would she explain this to her daughter? She would not. Would Sallie care? She would not. Her mother was wearing her dress. Nothing she had was really her own, especially her life. All this Sallie said with the set of her head, the expression in her eyes. But Claris was a match for her.

Suddenly Sallie said fiercely to her mother, "You could go home." Mercy, amazed and embarrassed that they were going to air their laundry before her, went to her desk and sat down. They didn't want to be alone with each other, she saw. It wasn't just with Danial. She saw that Claris's eyes went cold and still.

"No," Claris said, nailing her daughter with her stare.

"Why not?" Sallie was wild. Mercy wondered, watching them, Home. What did that mean? If someone said that to Mercy, it would mean home to the Neck. Did it always mean that, no matter what age you were? Did Sallie mean Claris could go back to the house where she was born?

Claris's nostrils flared. She looked like a schoolmarm about to issue a rebuke, imposing and obdurate. The air between them almost crackled. Because I say so, and don't dare to presume to question me, was Claris's unspoken answer.

"This is your life, not mine!" Sallie cried. "I am not you! I want to go and I can!"

Mercy tried to understand what she was looking at. Was Sallie opening a cage door for Claris, angry now because the rabbit wouldn't come out? Or was Sallie rattling the bars of a cage that imprisoned herself?

"You both can stay," said Claris. There was nothing soft in this; it was a rebuttal.

"Paul? Cheek by jowl with that?" Sallie's hand jerked in the general direction of the Haskells' cove. It was a small, intense movement, like an aborted blow.

Claris turned away from Sallie. Mercy could see her face though Sallie couldn't. Claris's was dense with anger. At what? That Sallie thought she had her own choices to make?

"When your brother—" Claris began, and Sallie seemed to go off like a rocket.

"I don't remember my brother!"

Claris wheeled around and stared at Sallie as if she had violated a sacrament.

"I don't owe you any more for him! I've paid, I'm done!" Sallie spoke with force but as if she hoped, rather than knew, that what she said was true.

—⁂—

For a long moment the two women faced each other, eyes locked. Mercy stared as if she were watching spirit bodies wrestling in heaven. Though nothing moved, not even their eyes, it was like watching some huge machine blowing apart in front of her eyes. Instead of the gradual, natural exchange of places that occurs in time as children assume the care of those who once cared for them, these two had slammed together in rage, full of will, at the exact moment that they seemed to be of equal strength. All the huge spinning gears and tiny balance wheels of family feeling, so strong to protect innocence in the young and dignity in the old when running smoothly, were clutching and grinding, tearing into spiritual marrow, and the silence in which the battle was joined seemed shattering.

Mercy was the first to look away. She didn't know which of them had won or lost. She didn't know if they knew. She looked up from her desk when she heard the door slam.

Sallie was gone. Claris was staring into the space where Sallie had stood, her eyes burning as if she could see through walls and find what was no longer there. After a few minutes, she too turned and left without a glance at Mercy.

I had forgotten all about Grandma Adele. The door of the schoolhouse opened as Mr. Crocker and I walked toward the house, and there, silhouetted, I saw not only the bosomy figure of Edith I was expecting but also the smaller, squarer figure of her mother. In the next moment, they moved aside to allow a third person to emerge, this one wearing the uniform of the Hamlin County sheriff's office. Oh, Christmas, I thought. There'll be a hot time in the old town tonight.

"Hannah, what the hell have you done to yourself?" This was Edith's greeting as I stepped into the light of the entryway. That may not sound like strong language, but for Edith Gray it was swearing like a sailor. I guess she noticed I was wearing a not-very-clean lumber shirt hanging nearly down to my knees and I'd cut my hair off. And, oh yes, been absent without leave for about fourteen hours when I was supposed to be on bounds, and embarrassed her before her mother.

I didn't answer her. What was the point? What should I have expected? A hug?

Mr. Crocker said to the man in the uniform, "Hello, Ham."

"Hello, Tom. Where'd you find them?"

"They got stranded out to March Cove. They're all right. As soon as the wind came up they tried to sail home." He may have blamed Conary, but he wasn't going to invite these people to.

"This is Tom Crocker," said the sheriff, or whatever he was, to Edith. I gathered the three of them had had plenty of time to get to know each other. Mr. Crocker stuck out his horny hand to Edith and said, "Mrs. Gray." Edith had to shake it. I thought all at once that Conary's father and Edith were probably near the same age, but Mr. Crocker looked much older. He had the leathery burned skin of someone who is outdoors all day in all weathers, and although he was perfectly sober now, he had a network of tiny scarlet veins across his nose and cheekbones, like the vagrants who always have a pint bottle in some pocket. He looked, in fact, not many steps away from the men you saw in Boston those days selling apples on the street and sleeping on heat grates.

He said, "They were easy to find once the moon came up. They were drifting down the middle of the bay."

"I can't thank you enough, Mr. Crocker," said Edith. She couldn't look at me.

I said, "Thank you, Mr. Crocker," and took off his lumber shirt and handed it to him. Underneath I was wearing the flannel shirt of Conary's, and I could see Edith eyeing it. She wanted me to take it off and hand that over too, but I didn't.

"Conary all right?" asked the man called Ham.

"Seems so. Hungry, but that won't kill him. Guess I'd better get along back and see how he's doing. Sorry you all had to worry."

"All's well that ends well," chirped Grandma Adele. She smiled at me, and I was thinking it was just about high time somebody did. I smiled back, truly grateful, and she gestured to me to come in. Edith was holding her hand out to Conary's father. "We're very grateful to you for your help," she said, and I saw as I passed her that she had a green bill folded in her palm. He looked at it, then at her.

"Good night, Ham," he said, and the sheriff's man said, "Good night, Tom," and he was gone. Edith put the bill into her pocket and bustled inside. Grandma Adele and I followed. I wanted some supper and a hot bath so badly I ached, but one look at Edith's face as she led me to the kitchen told me not to get my hopes up.

The sheriff's man picked up his hat from the kitchen table, accepted thanks, and said good-bye. Edith bustled around washing coffee cups and a plate full of crumbs. I guessed they'd had a night of it. Then she went to the phone and jiggled the hook for a long time until she roused Mrs. Sylvester. Briskly she gave our telephone number in Boston.

"Would you like some coffee?" Grandma Adele asked me. I nodded. She poured the dregs from a pot on the stove and brought me the grainy half-filled cup and a bottle of milk from the icebox.

"Milton?" Edith said. "She's home. Yes, she's all right. I don't know anything more now, but I'll call you in the morning. Yes . . . yes. Good night." And she hung up loudly. She turned to me and stood staring, as if she didn't know where to begin. I looked at her and then at Grandma Adele, desperately hoping one of them would give me something to eat.

"Who exactly is Conary Crocker?" is what Edith finally decided to start with.

"A boy . . ."

"Don't be smart."

"I wasn't."

"How do you know him?"

"He's Mrs. Eaton's grandson."

Edith and Grandma Adele looked at each other.

"Mrs. Eaton, who helps at Grandpa and Granny's," I said. I knew Edith knew her.

"How do you know him?" she asked me again, so I said, "I don't know."

"Did he have anything to do with that haircut? Is that the local style now?"

I said nothing.

"What?" She moved a little closer to me.

"Of course not," I mumbled.

"It's not 'of course not,' it's not 'of course' anything," she said, really loud. "Your judgment and your behavior are not . . . you have no right to 'of course not' anyone, Hannah!" I couldn't understand what she was even saying, except that she wanted to choke me.

At that point Grandma Adele said, "I think the hair is rather nice. She looks like Saint Joan."

Edith seemed to inflate like a puff adder, but she couldn't sass her mother. Instead she snapped at me. "Did you hear me say last night that you were on bounds for a week?"

There was a silence. I knew that Edith had been harping on this all evening to anyone who would listen.

"Did you hear me?" she bore down on me.

"Yes."

"Well then, how on earth did you end up stranded on some island with a strange boy for twelve hours, instead of home here, to greet your grandmother?"

"Are you hungry, Hannah?" Adele suddenly asked me.

"Mother, please," Edith said. "Hannah, I'm waiting."

I said, "The wind died."

"But what were you *doing* there in the first place? You were on *bounds*."

"We went clamming."

"Let me ask you this, what exactly do you think your father is going to say about this escapade?"

I didn't answer. I didn't know. Edith always undertook to tell me what he thought: Your Father and I are very angry, Your father is very disappointed . . . I wasn't sure I knew what he thought about anything.

"Is this boy a clam digger?" Adele asked me, and I could see Edith wanting to clap a hand over her mother's mouth. Grandma Adele was interfering with her technique.

"No. I mean, not only that."

"Well, what does he do, dear? Is he a student?"

"No, he works. He does some fishing. Works for summer people. Paints."

"Paints pictures?"

"Houses." I knew Edith was going to have a lot to say to my father about that. As far as I'd ever been able to tell, she had one measure only for judging value in a man, and it was summed up in the term "good provider."

Edith decided to get to her point. "Hannah, there's one thing I don't understand. You were seen leaving the cove at eleven in the morning. The wind didn't die until six. Now you were . . . *clamming* all that time?"

"No."

"Well? What were you doing?"

I suddenly heard in her voice exactly what she thought I'd been doing. I was so tired of having her assume the worst about me that I wanted to slap her.

"Mother, may I have something to eat?" I said. She just kept staring at me, waiting for her answer. Grandma Adele got up and started opening cupboard doors. She found the breadbox and cut me a thick slice of anadama bread and spread it with honey. It was very hard to eat it slowly, swallowing one bite before ripping off another.

"Hannah?" Edith barked.

I swallowed. "We went for a walk."

"For how many hours?"

"We went to look for the lost town."

"What lost town?"

I told them. I was hoping one of them would ask if we found it, but they weren't thinking along those lines. Grandma Adele was thinking, though. She said to Edith, "I really think she ought to have a good wash right away. Those woods could be full of poison ivy. Yellow laundry soap."

Poison ivy. There isn't any poison ivy on Beal Island. The poison ivy was in some other woods, in someone else's childhood, but that didn't stop either of them.

There wasn't a laundry in the schoolhouse, and no yellow laundry soap. Our wash was taken to Mrs. Seavey, who had a machine with a mangle and a jungle of clothesline strung in her yard. Edith and Adele made me take off all my clothes right there in the kitchen, where the light was brightest, and watched as I washed all over with a sponge and a cake of Ivory soap. I could have gone upstairs and soaked in a hot tub in private, but that way I might have felt warm again, or been comforted. When they let me dry myself, with a dish towel, Edith carried my clothes away to the laundry hamper, and Adele brought me a wrapper. It was her own, a baby blue wool old lady wrapper with lace on the collar. It was much too short and smelled of bath powder. I felt repossessed by these two, completely. Edith asked if I wanted anything more to eat, but I was too exhausted and demoralized by then to feel hungry. Edith turned out the lights, and we all three trooped upstairs.

Outside the door to Stephen's bedroom, Edith stopped and gave me this dry little kiss on the cheek, as if to say I shouldn't forgive you but I'm so tenderhearted I can't help myself.

Her mother watched. Then Edith said, "Well. We're just glad you're safe. Of course you can't see any more of the Crocker boy. If it will make it easier for you, I'll call and explain it to his father."

I just stared. I was choked with aching in my throat, tears and anger, so I turned and went into the bedroom and shut the door. I couldn't think what she would do to me for not saying good night or thank you to Grandma Adele.

I sat in the dark wishing Stephen was awake; I thought of Conary, and wondered what was happening to him at that moment. I wanted to be near him. I wanted just to see him, so badly it was sickening. I sat in that lacy wrapper and listened as Adele came out of her bedroom again and down the hall to the bathroom; then Edith.

When the house was completely quiet I went back out and down the stairs in the pitch dark. I couldn't risk turning a light on, and I was too exhausted and angry even to care what might be waiting, anywhere, in that inky blackness. I felt my way into the kitchen and found the laundry hamper. I dug Conary's shirt out and crept back, desperate not to bump anything or make a noise that would bring the two of them down on me. Back in Stephen's room, wearing the shirt, I could finally go to bed, and to sleep.

I don't know how to explain what happened next. It was as if a high wall I'd been constructing for years had collapsed and buried me under a ton of rubble. What had happened the day before, and in the weeks since we'd come to the Schoolhouse, seemed like a phantasm. What was real was that Edith hated me. Edith stripping me naked in the kitchen. Edith, who was solid flesh and right outside my door, and was such a poor excuse for a mother to me that I hated her. I really hated her. I was so angry that I couldn't wake up, and I certainly couldn't get out of bed. I think I was afraid that if I did I would roar out black flames and say unforgivable things, even hit her. I pictured myself bringing something sharp and heavy right down on her head, and the surprised stupid look on her face. I felt motherless, homeless, and possessed.

I slept and slept and my head was filled with lurid dreams, of sex and murder, red-tinged black visions. I must have been radiating something fearsome, because Edith stayed away from me. I heard voices outside the bedroom door, often, and then I'd sleep and then there would be knocks, but I never answered. Sometimes Stephen would creep in and sit on the side of the bed and look at me, to make sure I was alive. I felt as if I'd been drugged, and all I wanted was to stay under the covers with Conary's shirt wrapped around me and stay asleep forever. Finally Edith started banging on the door to say I had to get up because my father was there. I was such a problem that with all his worries he had had to leave his job and take the train all the way up here to deal with me.

I finally managed to haul myself out of bed, but I felt as if my body was made of anchors. I thought of wearing Connie's shirt downstairs, but I was afraid they'd take it away from me, so I hid it under the covers at the bottom of the bed. Without it, I felt so vulnerable that I didn't think I could make myself leave the room.

The jury was waiting for me in the kitchen. Edith, Father, and Adele. If I had had any hope that now, finally, my father would stand up for me, that he would remind Edith that he and I at least were the same flesh and bone, it didn't survive my arrival in that room. My father didn't get mad often, but when he did, it was not pleasant. He was mad to be there, and he might have been mad at Edith for calling him there, but she was a dangerous adversary and I wasn't. I was about to become the object of all the things he had to be mad about in that long hot Depression summer.

Of course first we had to deal, again, with my hair. I'm sure he'd been told what to expect, but he seemed shocked anyway. He said I looked as if I'd escaped from Dixmont. (That was the local lunatic asylum where he grew up. Idiotic and feeble-minded persons, the inmates were called in the county records.) Father did not think I looked like Saint Joan.

He asked me what I had to say for myself. I didn't say anything.

He didn't like that. He looked worn out and rumpled, as if he'd slept in his clothes on the train, which I'm sure he had. "Do you want a good whack, young lady?" he asked me.

I said, "Oh sure, why not?" I saw his hands twitch. He really wanted to hit me. He had never hit me in his life, but this day, he wanted to.

"Keep it up, Hannah," he said. His voice was cold. Then he asked me what I thought I was doing, disappearing for something like twelve hours with some hoodlum and worrying my mother half to death. I said I thought I was going clamming. It failed to amuse him. Edith gave him a look that meant, See? See what I mean?

"I don't understand why 'clamming' takes twelve hours, Hannah."

I thought about it awhile. What did it matter what I said? Probably not at all, so why not just tell him the truth? I tried to, but no matter what I said, with them all staring at me, it sounded like lies.

A silence followed my recitation. I gathered that by now Adele had been brought up to date on my summer vacation, because she didn't say anything. Daddy's voice changed then. He began using a very mild tone, the sort of tone you'd use on a mental defective who had taken a few hostages and was threatening to shoot them all in the head. Talk sweet, boys, and she'll never figure out that as soon as she gives up her guns we're going to mow her down.

"Tell me, Hannah. Is this ghost you saw the same one that's supposed to be in this house?"

"Yes."

"I see. Well, can you tell me, how does it manage to be here and out there at the same time?"

"I don't know that it is. Was it in this house on Tuesday at four thirty in the afternoon?"

Nobody answered.

"I guess it wasn't, then. So it wasn't here at the same time. It was there." Surprise, I thought. Even a mental defective can be a smarty-pants. I wanted so badly for him to understand me, defend me, but we were going from bad to worse.

He said, "Hannah. Why would a ghost from Beal Island come all the way into Dundee to make trouble?"

He in no way wanted an answer, so I didn't bother to give him the obvious one: Because the town on Beal Island is gone. There's nobody there to haunt. Out loud, I said, "This house used to be the schoolhouse on the island. I don't think the ghost cares that it's been moved." That stopped them for a minute.

My father was surprised and asked Edith if it was true about the house. She didn't know. He asked me how it got here, and I told him. He was pretty interested. He seemed to remember, briefly, where he and I had met before.

He said, "So. You think there's some connection between this house and whoever this ghost is supposed to be?" He made it sound as if it were a cartoon ghost, something cuddly and white with pop eyes.

"We think so, yes. Ghosts have their places. Maybe we found the house where it lived, maybe we found the old schoolhouse foundation; we don't know."

"We?" Oh, what a patient smile he gave me. I almost fell for it.

"Me and Conary."

That was all they needed to hear. They were all over me like wet blankets trying to smother a fire. What was the matter with me. What would happen to me if I so much as spoke to young Mr. Cracker again. (My father deliberately and repeatedly called him Young Mr. Cracker.) I was rude. I had bad morals. The whole list of my crimes, plus the kitchen sink.

I stopped listening.

When my father was gone, back to Boston, Adele gave me a bowl of graham crackers in milk for supper. I ate it, and was suddenly so hungry I could have eaten the box, but she put it away. I tried to read a story to Stephen while we waited for his mother to come back from taking Father to the train, but I kept crying. Stephen leaned against me and looked frightened, so I told him I was sorry and went back upstairs to bed.

Edith, or someone, had searched the bed and taken Connie's shirt. I never saw it again. She must have burned it.

*   *   *

Late that night, or in the early morning, I had finally cried so much and slept so much that I couldn't do either one anymore. Lying awake in the dark room listening to my brother breathe, I was visited, most unwillingly, by thoughts of the Haskells. They began playing on the screen behind my eyelids, like a movie I didn't want to see but couldn't turn off. On a Sunday morning, when the meeting house bell was tolling for worship, something unthinkable happened. Someone walked into the parlor with an ax. I saw that much—I saw the ax raised, then I saw it fall, then I saw it again, a figure walking soundlessly into the parlor with an ax.

According to Phin Jellison, it had been going on noon when Virgil Leach called in to borrow something and found that someone had lost a battle against anger and split Danial Haskell's head open like an acorn squash, wrecking at least five lives with one stroke. Six, if you count Sallie's lost brother, and you might as well since he was certainly part of the toll. They all would have been dead by now in any case, but one of them refuses to have it. One of them walks and grieves for its life so relentlessly that it wouldn't mind sucking the life out of you or me, as if that would give it another chance.

I thought about them all—Danial, Claris, Sallie, Mercy, Amos—and I began to be angry at *them* as well as at Edith for blaming me for her own unhappiness, at my father for not protecting me from her, at Grandma Adele for that sugarcoated malice that made Edith the way she was. People made their own choices and mistakes and then shoved the consequences onto other people, and I was mad at all of them. I was furious at the ghost. I thought about what little I'd learned about the Haskells from this one and that one, from Bowdoin and Nella and Phin Jellison's gory pamphlet. I thought people were fools to make such a mystery of it. Sallie was young and passionately in love and she wanted a chance to live her own life. Her father said no to her once too often for no good reason and she bashed his head in. Why would they have tried her twice if it wasn't that? But Paul LeBlond had left her anyway, and she was weeping weeping weeping, the tragic heroine, except when she ran across living people, who didn't think that life itself should stop because of what she was feeling . . .

I thought about the thing we saw, Connie and I, down in the yard behind where the house had stood. What was it wearing? Something black, a cloak, or shawls. I didn't know. I knew I couldn't describe it, it hadn't been that kind of . . . I could hear that grotesque weeping and feel the ache in my throat. I was afraid that recalling the ghost would, literally, recall it. Call it back to me.

I tried to stop thinking. I tried to recite poems. "The Wreck of the *Hesperus*." "The First Snow-Fall." A strange choice in summer, but it kept starting up in my head: "The snow had begun in the gloaming, and busily all the night . . ."

Suddenly I knew that Whitey was awake. He was listening to something in the hall outside the door, something I couldn't hear. I heard a soft growl.

It was out there, preying, waiting for an opening. I went clammy with fear. I pulled all the blankets off my bed and went and sat in the chair by the window with my back to the wall. I sat up in the dark and looked out at the sliver of bay I could see from there, and waited for the moon to set.

Mercy didn't go back to the Haskell house to sleep. She wasn't used to the kind of raw conflict she had witnessed, and she didn't want to be under the same roof with it. She was afraid it would somehow explode and besplatter her. She wanted to go home.

She spent the night upstairs in the schoolhouse. She would later testify that in the morning, which was fine, she took a long walk around the corner of the island to visit her Aunt Gott, but when she got there, she couldn't go in. She couldn't shake off a feeling of worry and sickness, she said. Finally, mindful of the open weather and the laundry that never dried in the wet, she said she walked back and went down to the wash-house in the Haskells' yard, which was, by agreement, hers to use on Sunday mornings. She said she was in the yard when she saw Sallie run out of the house and off toward the schoolhouse. Mercy said she left her wash in the tub and followed. Why? she was asked, over and over. Because it was her schoolhouse. She was the schoolmistress.

When she got to the schoolhouse she saw smoke coming from the chimney in the upstairs front room. She went up and found Claris and Sallie sitting together. Sallie looked up. Claris didn't. Claris had the iron stove poker in her hand, and she was knocking it rhythmically on the floor as she rocked in the chair, as if it soothed her.

Mercy stared at her, then looked at Sallie again. She suddenly wondered what was in the stove; it didn't smell like firewood alone. There was a scorching smell, the same smell as when you leave a hot iron on the cloth too long. Also something animal, and metallic, like blood. Mercy opened the door to the stove and then shut it again. There was a dress in the fire.

"My father's dead," Sallie said. Mercy sat down on a stool.

"Somebody killed him." Sallie looked at Mercy calmly as she said it.

Danial, they meant. Danial was dead now.

"Now she can marry Paul," said Claris.

Mercy turned and looked at her. Sallie merely said, "Paul's gone, Mother." To Mercy she added, "They're looking for him."

Looking for Paul? But why? Paul had gone yesterday, or the day before. As she understood it.

Sallie added, "Now we're helping Mother."

Mercy sat still on the stool and watched them.

"Where were you?" Sallie asked Mercy suddenly. Her voice had an odd quality, loud and flat, as if she'd gone deaf overnight.

"I spent the night here, on the cot. This morning I went for a walk."

"Alone?"

"Yes."

"Did you meet anybody?"

"No."

Mother and daughter looked at Mercy.

"It will be best not to talk about it," said Sallie.

These people think I can read their minds, thought Mercy. That's the way they carry on. Maybe if you treat each other like that, you get to where you actually can. Maybe she could. They were thinking, If none of us will talk about it, nobody can do anything to any of us. We live in our own bubble, we make our own rules. It's nobody else's business anyway.

The two Haskell women were looking at Mercy, and she suddenly saw that they knew all about her feeling of sickness in the morning, and what it meant. What if, when the police finally came about Danial, mother and daughter turned to her and pointed?

I know Edith wanted me sent away, home to Boston, or anywhere else, but apparently it was impossible. Father was working harder than ever; there would be nothing to keep me from running wild at home. Boarding schools were not in session, and it was in all ways too late for summer camp. Typical. When I was low and upset and wanted to go, she wouldn't let me. Now, loving Conary, I was desperate to stay. Edith said if I must stay with her, I had to have a job. Someplace out of the house, where I could be watched. I said I would rake blueberries when they started hiring. Edith said no; she suspected that outdoors with no one much watching me, side by side with a lot of Micmac Indians, I would find a way to see Connie, and she was right. Not only that, raking was miserable work but it paid real money. Money bought freedom. Nobody thought I should have any of that. In the end, I designed my own prison; Dot Sylvester took me on to help her with the switchboard mornings when she scheduled her fittings, and I persuaded Mrs. Pease and Mrs. Allen to let me volunteer at the library in the afternoons. They were glad to have me; there were periodicals unarchived going back years. There were books to mend and shelve. I knew enough of the Dewey decimal system to be useful.

Everyone in the village seemed to know that Connie and I had gotten into some kind of trouble. The first week Edith would walk with me to Dot's in the morning and come back to the village at five o'clock to walk me home. Sometimes when girls my age came into the library, girls who had grown up with Connie, they would find excuses to hang around the front desk until they could get a look at me. I didn't like it. But I discovered something that surprised me and gave me some courage. Mrs. Pease did not like Edith. Not at all. She had heard somehow that Edith had tried to tip Mr. Crocker for bringing me home, and it got her back up.

Sometimes in the evenings at home, the phone would ring. Edith always answered, and several times she found the line dead. One night I said, "It's the ghost, Mother." Edith shot me a poisonous look, but not before I saw a flicker of discomfort in her expression. A phone that rings when no one is on the line is an eerie thing. Stephen stopped eating and looked at me.

"I found an article in a magazine I was filing yesterday," I said to Stephen, sounding helpful, informative. 'Do the Dead Make Phone Calls?' was the title."

"Do they?"

"Yes," I said. "Quite nasty ones. They send telegrams too . . ."

"Stop it, Hannah," Edith snapped at me. "You're scaring him on purpose. I've never seen such horrid behavior."

"You've led a sheltered life," I said. I couldn't seem to help myself. I was full of foul humor, and it was stronger than I was. I *didn't* want to scare Stephen, but I knew I was doing it.

"Leave the table," said Edith, and I did. I went upstairs. I knew perfectly well that it was Conary calling me, and it made me wild that he couldn't reach me. Where was he? At the pay phone outside the drugstore? I shut my door and thought about Conary being here, right in the front room. With another girl, but I didn't care about that. I wished he were with me. I knew that I was the girl he'd been looking for, and that he of all the souls in the universe was for me. I thought about the expression on his face when I obediently left him to get into his father's boat. I wanted to tell him I would never do that again.

One day when I was at the library shelving novels, I saw a girl of about fifteen come in. She and Mrs. Pease spoke pleasantly to each other, and then she made her way over to me. At first she pretended to look for a book, but she soon saw Mrs. Pease was busying herself with something else.

"Hannah," the girl said softly to me.

I looked at her, surprised. I hadn't seen her before, but once I saw her light eyes, I knew who she was.

"I'm Mary," she said. Conary's sister.

"Is Conary here?"

She shook her head. "Dad hardly lets him out of the house. He's on a tear."

"Is there any way I can see him?"

"He was afraid they'd sent you away. He tried to call you the other night from the Jellisons'."

"I know. Could I come down to your house?"

"I wouldn't recommend it," she said. "Don't worry, he'll get out. He always does."

A woman in overalls came into the library, and Mary turned away from me very suddenly and took a book from the shelf and opened it. After a moment, she turned her back to the room, and she whispered, "I thought that was Aunt Etta. I don't know why; she can hardly read."

I looked at the woman in the overalls. It was the painter from the Colony; I'd seen her out with her easels, painting things she thought were picturesque, like Bowdoin Leach working.

"Connie said we should choose a book. When he has a plan, the book will be pushed in on the shelf, and that means there's a note in it for you."

We both looked at the book in her hands; it was *A Christmas Carol* by Charles Dickens.

"That one," I said. "Nobody's going to check that out in August."

Mary nodded and put the book carefully back on the shelf with its spine aligned with the other volumes. Then she left me and went to browse in another section, and I went back to putting the Jalna books in order. When I looked up, she had left the library.

I probably checked that book ten times a day after that. Finally, about a week later, on my fifth visit of the day, I found it stuck back on the shelf inches deeper than the rest of the Dickens. I hadn't seen Mary or Connie come in, but someone had.

The note said, "Come up to the Indian Burial Ground as soon after five as you can get there."

There was no signature. And I didn't know where the Indian Burial Ground was. I spent about an hour fretting about it and prowling in old memorabilia about the town. Finally I figured it out; I could ask Bowdoin. He would know, and, better, he wouldn't care why I wanted to know.

At five o'clock I hightailed it up to the blacksmith shed, and I thought my heart would stop when I saw it was closed and dark. I had no backup plan. I stood in the yard staring at the door, as stupid as a turkey in the rain. Just as I was about to despair and go, the kitchen door opened and Bowdoin came painfully out of the house.

"Miss Gray," he said. He had seen me and was coming out to see what had brought me.

I knew it was going to seem odd, but I was wild to be away. I just baldly asked him my question.

"Why that's an interesting thing," he answered. He stood looking toward the village, thinking. "When the first fathers chose a place for a cemetery, they didn't put it beside the meeting house, like you'd expect. I suppose that they had need of a burial place before they had a meeting house. They certainly did before they had a settled minister. In those days, in fact right up to when I was a boy, the Indians had their summer camp down there on the shore this side of the Neck. Where the summer people put their golf course. Them and the settlers lived cheek by jowl together and were a great help to each other, and it must have been natural to share the Indians' burying ground. Anyway, they did. All the earliest folks of the town are up there."

"Where is it?"

He took a good look at me.

"What do you call that haircut, now?" he said, instead of answering.

"I thought it would be easier in the heat," I said, wanting to scream. He saw at once I wasn't in the mood for teasing and let it go.

"You know where the Pottery is?" I did.

"You go right up past there, maybe quarter of a mile. It's on the left, where the old road came into town before there was a bridge over the falls."

"Thank you." I took off. If Bowdoin wondered why I wanted to know, he never asked me, and I was grateful.

*   *   *

I went as quickly as I could; I didn't dare run, for fear it would attract attention. If I got there and Connie was gone, I thought I would lie down and die. At least I would be in the right place for it.

I found it easily enough. It was in a sheltered copse, off the road. Once sunny, with a view of the bay over farmland, it was now set around with tall evergreens, dark, and hardly visible from the road, unless you went right in.

Connie was there. He had pulled his truck in on a spur of abandoned farm road, where it couldn't be seen. He was sitting on a headstone, very composed, just waiting. I thought he was the most beautiful man I had ever seen.

When we kissed, it felt as if the trees around us had grown there just to give us a safe hiding place; we came together as if our thoughts had kept pace and we had never once misread each other since the moment we had parted.

When we could bear to let go of each other, we moved to a spot in the late afternoon sun and sat on an almost illegible stone slab. By tracing nearly vanished grooves in the stone with our fingers, we read the name Mehitable, and the date 1801. I told Connie everything that had happened to me on the night we were parted, and afterward. He said that his father was violently angry; he had never seen him stay so mad for so long. Edith had made him feel like a servant.

"She wrote him a letter saying that it wasn't suitable for us to see each other, and she was sure he would understand."

"Suitable!"

"Yes, well, that's the word that's done it. He'll calm down for a long time and then something will make him think of that letter, and he just goes off his head. He's hitting the bottle pretty hard, and it isn't improving him."

"Mary said he was keeping you in—I got the impression he had you locked up."

Conary shrugged. "He pretends to lock me in and I pretend to let him. That house has more holes than a basket. I've been able to get out since I was ten. But I try not to make it too obvious; I don't want him to get huffed and take it out on Mary."

"Does he know you're out now?"

"Yes. I've been released. He was forced to it, since the blue-berries are coming in and he needs the money I earn. We're raking up on the Kingdom Road this week."

I had tried to get Connie to talk about his family the day we spent together, without much luck. Now it was like the kissing; once he started telling me what he never told anyone else, he didn't want to stop. It was as if he wanted me to know everything about him so I could keep his story safe and make it come out right.

"He wasn't like this when our mother was alive. I think everyone was so surprised she had married him, it gave him some pride he needed."

And what had she seen in him? I thought about Edith and wondered why my father had married her. Why did people marry people who were mean?

I didn't ever want to stop touching him, listening to him. "How long can you stay?"

"Not long. It took me a while to find a place we could meet. Is this all right?"

"Yes, I like it." I did. It felt peaceful and safe. Conary kissed me again, and time must have slipped a cog, because almost at once the clearing was filled with long shadows.

"We have to go," he said, and we kissed some more.

"Can you come tomorrow? Can you get away?"

"Yes. They pay by the bushel, not the hour. If I want to leave early it's my lookout. Can you?"

"I'll try to get off a little early. Connie—can I have something of yours?" I had told him about Edith and the flannel shirt.

He grinned, that gorgeous smile, and unbuttoned his work shirt. I was about to say I wanted something smaller, that I could hide, when he stripped off the white undershirt he wore underneath and gave it to me. It made me smile like a fool to see him standing there, pleased to have been asked for something it was in his power to give. The shirt had an intense smell of sun and sweat and him. They said raking was hard work, and I believed it, and was glad of it.

Connie kissed me again, and when I put my hands on his bare back, I was shocked at how different it felt from touching a body clothed. I wanted to say something, but there were no words.

"We've got to go, or we'll never get out again."

"I know."

We went on kissing.

Finally we parted and Connie put on his work shirt. He said, "I forgot . . . I found something. Look at this." I followed him across the clearing. There were some almost unreadable headstones, many from the eighteenth century, and then one much newer. It read, AMOS HASKELL. 1862–1874. GOD IS MY MARINER.

I said, "But . . . I thought he was never found."

"I thought so too. I had looked for him in the Haskell plot in the new cemetery." The new cemetery was opened just before the Civil War.

"Maybe it's some other Amos Haskell. Would the dates be right for Sallie's brother?"

"They would."

*   *   *

I thought about the grave marker all the way home. It was odd enough for anyone to have been buried there at that late date. Could the Osgoods, could Claris herself, have been so cruel as to withhold from Danial the news that the body had come in? To bury Amos privately, among Osgoods, so that . . . what? So that he would never lie alone on a deserted island, instead of being where his relatives could remember him and tend his grave? But Danial couldn't have agreed. If he had, the grave would have been in the new cemetery. And no matter what he had done, he was still Amos's father . . .

I was thinking there must be some kind of record of burials at the church, and even considered stopping, until I saw on the steeple clock the lateness of the hour. Edith would be furious, and suspicious as a snake. If she guessed that I'd been with Connie, I didn't know what she would do.

Life is full of surprises. When I got home I found Stephen by himself in the living room eating cinnamon toast and feeding Whitey the crusts. From the mess in the kitchen, I knew he had made it himself. He was reading the *Bangor Daily* funnies and getting butter on the carpet.

"Where is Mother?" I asked him.

"Upstairs," he said, and then began to tell me about his excitement of the afternoon. Kermit Horton had invited him to see his pig, which had the thumps.

"She made a noise like this," cried Stephen, and he began imitating a pig with hiccups. "And you know what he told me? He said the pig has a stomachache, and when Mrs. Foss has a stomachache, she eats a spoonful of gravel! She got the idea from her chickens!" We laughed and laughed, Stephen because it gave him the giggles, and I because I was in love and felt as if I'd swallowed a planet full of joy. I had Conary's undershirt hidden in the bag I carried with me for my books, and my wallet and my diary. The smell of it utterly thrilled me.

Edith appeared eventually and cleaned up the mess in the kitchen without saying anything about it. She made us canned hash with poached eggs on top for supper. She looked pinch-faced and puffy-eyed. She had already heard about the pig, but she let Stephen make the pig noise twice more, and even tried to laugh. Then she said, "I have news, children. It's quite exciting. Your father has been offered an important job, and he's moving to Chicago."

That certainly stopped things cold. Stephen stared at her, chewing with his mouth open.

I said, "We're moving to Chicago?"

Edith looked at me with hard eyes. Trust you to find the painful point and bring your weight down on it, the look said.

"*He's* moving to Chicago. The company won't pay to move the whole family, at least not at first."

"He's moving away without us?" Stephen got the picture very clearly.

"It's a promotion," Edith said. "We should all be proud. When he gets established, we can join him."

"I don't want to live in Chicago," Stephen said. "I won't know anybody."

"If you have to, you'll make new friends," said Edith. That was all that was said on the subject for the rest of the meal. Edith was eager to get away and go upstairs, and Stephen wanted her to go, so he could ask me what it was all about.

I didn't know what it was all about. I wasn't at all sure that the cover story was the true one, but there was no way to find out. I did know that Edith was plenty upset, and I wondered what would happen.

Spring 1886

All the while the people of Beal Island were in an uproar over the murder, the three women who might have been presumed to know most about it sat together in the upstairs room of the schoolhouse. The men of the town could be heard rushing around outside shouting orders at each other. It seemed to the still, silent women as if they were playing some game out there. Someone had been sent to the main, and by afternoon more men arrived from Unionville. There was a photographer and Dr. Bliss, acting as coroner, and a couple of reporters from *The Citizen*. Naturally the crime scene had been thoroughly disturbed by people of the village being officious and helpful. The rumor was already abroad that Paul LeBlond had fled at dawn wearing women's clothing. No one seemed to be able to find much of anything telling except the disgusting details which would later be released by Dr. Bliss about the contents of the victim's stomach.

The women of the household, Mrs. Claris Haskell; her daughter, Sallie; and the schoolteacher boarder, Mercy Chatto, were waiting quietly when the men from the sheriff's office got around to them. By then the men were pretty excited about the foreigner Paul LeBlond and deep down the rumor well about Sallie's rows with her father. The early betting was that if Paul had done it, with or for Sallie, she too might try to flee. An ancillary theory was that Paul had gone ahead, and Sallie had killed her father to keep him from following them.

The women, sitting silent together, had not guessed that that was what would be said about them. They were all thinking about something else. They were thinking that if none of them talked about what happened, all the noisy ones outside would have to go away.

It had been said that the Haskells were arrogant, but had they stopped believing that anyone outside themselves could judge anything they did? Apparently. The sheriff's man was ready to disabuse them.

A reporter from *The Citizen* described the scene. When the deputy said he was placing Sallie Haskell under arrest, she started and turned to her mother. That seemed natural. At such a moment, you would turn for protection to the one who had always sheltered you before, even knowing that you had done the unforgivable. Thousands read, the following Thursday, of the terrible and suspenseful event. Later the reporter was made to describe it again and again during the trials.

Sallie looked to her mother, and the reporter watched the dawning horror in her eyes as she saw that her mother would or could do nothing for her. Minutes later, the mother stood at the upstairs window of the schoolhouse and saw her daughter being helped into a rowboat with her hands cuffed together in her lap. The daughter stared intently from the boat up at her mother with an expression that befitted a murderess. The mother watching from the upstairs window returned the gaze, with a look, the reporter thought, of one who was watching her whole world drawing away from her, and quietly going mad.

Edith's concentration on my crimes and punishments had been broken, and, with it, the blights of the summer seemed to vanish. There were no more strange noises in the house, no fuses blown, no doors latched at night found standing open in the morning. I spent my days in freedom; I left the library early and came home late for supper, and Edith didn't seem to notice.

Mysteries that had been beyond my reach now started offering their secrets, like jammed knots in a high wind that suddenly free themselves, allowing the mariner to ease sail and avoid disaster. Mrs. Allen asked me to take her in her husband's car to Unionville; her husband was in the hospital there with gallstones and she had never learned to drive. I drove her there three times, and while she visited I was free at last to wait in the Unionville library, poring over brittle yellow news accounts of the murder of Danial Haskell and Sallie's trials. The accounts were florid and repetitive, but reading them was like finally shining a flashlight into all the corners of a blackened room. Curiosity is an underrated passion, in my view. Even if I never knew the truth about the Haskells any more than anyone else, it was a relief to finally learn what could be known.

Paul LeBlond emerged as charming, shallow, and weak. That was clear, and so was the fact that he'd left the island the afternoon before the murder; one of the Duffys had helped with his trunk and seen him off on the packet boat. His leaving may have provoked a crisis in the Haskell house, but it didn't seem to the men who'd known him best to have been any crisis to him. He was a rolling stone, a traveler; he had a useful trade and thought he'd try his luck in San Francisco. So much for Phin Jellison. I might have felt sorry for Sallie, if I didn't have reason to believe she was doing a bang-up job of feeling sorry for herself.

The prosecution established that Sallie's passion for Paul was painfully real, at least. Her childhood friends, the Hortons, Bowdoin Leach, were also made to describe the anger she'd often expressed at her parents. They took care to point out that Sallie was if anything more bitter toward her mother than her father. But then, her friends didn't want her to hang.

The friends agreed under oath that Sallie had a wild temper, but only a waitress at the boardinghouse where she cooked would give examples. She claimed she'd seen Sallie nearly kill a man with a blackpan when he wouldn't stop flirting. She had a good time with the reporters, the waitress, but was never called as a witness. She was possibly not the most reliable soul in town.

Sallie never testified at either trial; reporters had to confine themselves to describing her clothes and demeanor. There were drawings of her being led in and out of the courthouse surrounded by sheriff's men, more to protect her it seemed than to prevent her escape. A very fat man traveled all the way from Ohio to propose marriage to her, and give interviews. She got pounds of mail, more proposals, expressions of support, many screeds full of hatred. Her guards at the jail were the sources for this; Sallie never talked to reporters.

Nor did Mercy or Claris. Mercy was a favorite with the reporters even so. She was young and almost pretty, with smooth brown hair and clear skin and the teasing mystery of her pregnancy. Reporters pointed out that there were very many unwed mothers in island communities, owing to the infrequent visits of justices or clergy, and it was common for island people to take their own view of their domestic arrangements. One reporter cited a diary of Rev. Jonathan Friend of Dundee, who recorded the many cases he found in island households of children whose fathers were also their uncles, or their grandfathers. Reporters thought Mercy betrayed an odd sort of sympathy for Danial Haskell when she was forced to speak of him. She was self-possessed and not petite. She could well have taken an ax to her host if his attentions had been unbearable, but if she had, they seemed to hope she got away with it.

Claris Osgood Haskell was hardest for reporters to read, and to like, I gathered. Unlike Sallie and Mercy, she didn't seem to grant that they had a job to do. She behaved as if they had no right to exist and, therefore, didn't. Her testimony was terse and given grudgingly, as if the murder and its consequence had happened principally to her, not first to Danial and now to Sallie. Off the record people began to wonder why Sallie had not killed the mother instead of the father.

Through two long trials, the three women never varied their story. None of them had done it. None of them had seen it. None of them had anything more to say.

When I was done with the papers, I asked if there was a copy of Reverend Friend's diary on the shelves. There was, a handsomely bound book published by the Unionville Historical Society. It was almost time to collect Fern at the hospital, but fortunately I knew what month and year I was looking for, and I found this:

Date: Sept. 22, 1874.

After ten days in the water the body of my nephew Amos Haskell came ashore on the Neck yesterday morning. Fortunately Claris stayed on with us after the funeral and is still here on the main. She asked to have him buried in a place dear to him, where she says he and our William were used to play. This we have done this afternoon, with only Claris, Mary and Leander attending. R.I.P. I hope it has been a comfort to her. I wonder how she will break this news to the boy's father.

I wondered too. I copied it out to show Conary, whom I met every afternoon at the burial ground. Often we stayed there, kissing and talking and growing closer and closer, but sometimes we grew bold and drove here and there in the countryside. I never cared where I was when I was with him. Edith noticed none of this. She was shaken, and I almost felt sorry for her, up here alone, far from her mother and her snippy friends.

This was the sunniest time of my summer, and maybe of my whole life. I thought of Mercy, with her baby that was nobody else's business, and felt that Boston and its scolding strictures were very far away. In Boston there were rules to shield girls who were being fooled or making fools of themselves. Here there was life, shimmering and tremendous, and, more important, here for me and Conary was true union, which has its own rules. There was a wild field strewn with boulders where Conary and I first made married love to each other.

There was a freshwater pond back in the woods where we jumped naked from a bold granite ledge into warm peat-stained water and swam, laughing at how yellow our bodies looked under the water. "This is my private bath," said Conary. He brought a bar of soap and we took turns washing each other's hair.

We stopped fearing or even thinking about our parents' disapproval; together we felt immune, invincible, beloved of God. How could there be anything wrong with the expansive joy we felt together, our faith in the future, the communion we felt with the town, the countryside, the planets in their orbits? How could this be anything but a blessed thing in the universe?

Not that being recklessly happy had rendered Conary docile, mind you. In town I was hearing rumors about him; I heard he was hanging around with the migrant berry rakers in the evenings, drinking and carrying on. One night he came to my house after midnight and threw blueberries at my window. They made purple splat marks all over the pane, and I wanted to scold him, but I couldn't stop laughing. I put my head out, listening for Edith, and saw him standing below me. I'd been about to tell him to shush himself, but he looked so handsome standing there, all I could do was put a finger to my lips and try not to laugh out loud.

"Come down," he said in a stage whisper. I was sure we were about to be caught, but he was obviously in a wild mood.

"I can't—keep your voice down."

"I can't—I'm in love. Come down."

I hesitated, wondering if there were some way out of the house that didn't take me past Edith's door.

Connie whispered, "Jump—I'll catch you." I pulled my head in and turned to see if Stephen was awake. He was, but I put my finger to my lips, and he nodded. I crept to the bedroom door to see if the house was quiet; maybe I could risk going down the stairs. Instead, I saw a thin line of light beneath Edith's door; she was still awake. I hurried back to the window.

"Go away, Connie—she's awake. We'll be caught."

"I want to marry you," he said in this whisper the whole neighborhood could have heard. What had he been doing all evening? It looked as if his hair was wet, and I was fairly sure he'd been drinking. There was a lot more moon than the first night, and I could see pretty well, but the light seemed really to be coming from Connie's face looking up at me.

"Will you?" he asked. I was gazing at him, dumb as an oyster; I'd forgotten I hadn't answered. "Will you?"

"Connie, go away, I'll see you tomorrow. We'll be caught."

Of course it didn't matter what I said. He already knew the answer.

"Tomorrow," he said.

I nodded, grinning like a fool.

"Try to be early." Finally he turned to go. Just before he disappeared into the darkness, I saw that he must have hurt his foot; he was limping. Minutes later, far up the road, I could hear his truck start up.

The next day in the library two girls were talking in the stacks where the magazines were; I heard Connie's name. I couldn't hear what it was about, though it was clear that someone's feelings had been hurt.

"I'm sick of it," said the one who was upset. She was quite pretty, but with teeth that made her look like a horse. "I'm sick of the way he treats people."

"It'll pass," said the other one. "He has reasons." I was dying to know what had happened. They stopped talking as they took their books to the front desk, and while Mrs. Allen stamped them, I got a look at their faces. I didn't know their names, but I knew them; they both were working at the drugstore that summer.

"I'm tired of him being such a bastard," said the one with the teeth, still fuming, as they reached the door.

Her friend sighed. "So is he," she said. They went out.

I met Connie at the burial ground at four thirty that day. He was as elated as he'd been the night before, although he had dark circles under his eyes.

"Do you remember saying you would marry me?" he asked when we stopped kissing.

"I did not say that. Where had you been? You hurt your foot."

"It was nothing. I had supper with the Indians, and later we went swimming at Friend's Pond."

"And that made you realize right then that you had to marry me?"

"Yes. It was the moon. The water was so warm, and there was a silver ribbon across it that led right to the moon. I wanted you to see it."

I understood. I wanted him to see everything beautiful I saw. I wanted him right beside me, to share everything good.

He began to sing. "There's a wee baby moon, sailing up in the sky, with his little silvery toes in the air. . . . And he's all by himself in the great big sky, but the wee baby moon doesn't care."

"What is that?" I was delighted. His voice was sweet, like everything about him.

"That's what my mother used to sing. Whenever there was a new moon."

"Sing it again." Every time I learned something new about him

I felt as if I had captured another nugget of the only story I wanted to be told. He sang, unself-consciously. We kissed. It was amazing, just astonishing, to be so completely happy.

Fortunately we were well back in the grove, hidden by standing stones and a large maple tree; we had a chance to jump apart and straighten ourselves when we heard a voice demand, "Who's in here?"

Standing at the open side of the clearing was an odd apparition. It was dressed entirely in men's clothing: baggy corduroy pants, a man's shirt under a baggy V-necked cardigan, even a beaten-up fedora with no hatband. But the gray hair was long and wrapped into a soft knot behind the head, and the voice was a woman's.

"Miss Leaf! It's me, it's Conary Crocker."

She peered at us across the grove. "Who's that?" she asked again. She was annoyed about something, and her eyesight could not have been good.

"Conary Crocker, Miss Leaf," he said, taking my hand and leading me toward her. He stopped when we stood in bright sunlight before her, and added, "Tom Crocker's boy."

She peered at him. Her eyes were dim, but her expression was keen.

"Oh!" she said. "You're Tom Crocker's boy!" She still seemed annoyed. She looked at me. "Who's this?"

"This is Hannah Gray."

"Never heard of her."

"You knew her mother . . ."

"Who?"

"Sara Grindle."

Miss Leaf examined me carefully now, with the same intense expression.

"Oh, you're Frances Friend's granddaughter. Your mother used to come to my art class. Married that man from Boston, didn't she?"

"Yes," I said.

"I knew it," she said, as if I'd been trying to trick her into believing otherwise. "Are you the ones been stealing my flowers?"

I looked at Conary for guidance.

"Miss Leaf has the beautiful garden just below here. It's the pride of the village, isn't it, Miss Leaf?" He said this as if repeating an oft-repeated phrase. Pennsylvania, the Keystone State. Miss Leaf's garden, the pride of the village.

"Would be, people'd stop stealing my flowers. I'm not the town florist, you know. People want flowers can plant their own."

"We haven't taken any of your flowers," said Conary.

"Well, somebody has."

"Have they?"

"Yes, all summer. Finally I tracked him up here, and what do I find? You two!"

"We didn't take them, Miss Leaf."

"Well, I'd like to know who did! Look at that there!"

She pointed to the north corner of the burial grove, and I could see an orange flash of color lying on the ground back there. It surprised me, now that she pointed them out, that I hadn't seen them when I came in.

She was leading the way toward her flowers now, and we followed her. She couldn't see faces from any distance, but apparently she could see daylilies. That's what they were, quite a bunch of them, closed and wilting. They were lying on the grave of Amos Haskell.

Mercy Chatto could hardly conceal her pregnancy. She was big as a washtub as the first trial got under way, and delivered the baby at her mother's house on the Neck shortly afterward. It was a boy. She named him Seth, and her mother raised him as a Chatto. She seemed dazed through the trials, unable to remember anything out of the ordinary about the time leading up to Danial Haskell's death. She gave the impression she was waiting for something to happen that never did.

It was easily established at the trials that, like Claris, she had clear opportunity and quite possibly motive to commit the murder, and it was this as much as anything else that prevented the juries from reaching a verdict against Sallie. The prosecutor convinced jurors that the victim had been murdered. He almost convinced them that the murderer was in the courtroom, but he never could persuade them without doubt that he had the right person on trial.

When it was finally over, Mercy left for Europe, with her parents' blessing. They couldn't help but agree that there would be no normal life for her in New England unless she changed her name, and maybe not then. She made her way to Italy and finally settled in Rome, where again she taught school, this time to rich American girls who were being "finished" abroad. She came to speak fluent if heavily accented Italian, and when she died she was buried in the Stranger Cemetery in the shadow of the pyramid of Gaius Cestius.

Seth Chatto was her only child. She left her effects to him, though she had seen him only once since 1890, when he had been three years old. The effects consisted of a small amount of jewelry, some watercolors she had made of street scenes in her neighborhood of Campo de' Fiori, and two small tables with inlaid tops of *pietra dura*, one of which has found its way to the parlor of the Dundee Inn, where it holds the guest book.

Miss Chatto had attended an Anglican church in Rome, because they held services in English. Acquaintances from the altar guild there had undertaken to pack her belongings for return to the States. In a drawer in one of the tables Mrs. Pym found a stack of papers in Miss Chatto's hand.

"My goodness, what's this then? It looks like a confession."

Rather hopefully she handed the papers to Miss Turner, who opened to the middle. Scanning, Miss Turner said, "I believe it's a story." This surprised neither of them. Many ladies attempted stories, hoping to sell them to glossy magazines. To be published under noms de plume, of course.

"Is it any good?" asked Mrs. Pym.

"Oh, I'm no judge," said Miss Turner, although she thought she was. She was very partial to the works of Mary Roberts Rinehart. "What do you think we should do about it?"

"Perhaps we should leave it in the drawer."

"But not if it's going to . . . you know. Embarrass her."

"There must be someone in the congregation who would give us an opinion."

We couldn't go back to the burial ground. At least, I couldn't. I knew it was probably just kids annoying Miss Leaf, or a tourist who'd heard about the famous garden, but I was upset about those daylilies. Conary was troubled too, but for a different reason. He didn't want to keep running into Miss Leaf. She wasn't a gossip, but like most people in a village, she liked to know what was going on around her, and she might have said something to somebody.

The next day was Friday of the last weekend before Labor Day—we had barely one more week together. I hoped all day for a message from Conary and watched the library door for him or Mary. It was almost five o'clock when Mrs. Pease turned around to where Mrs. Allen and I were mending Oz books.

"You know that Micmac boy come in here a little bit ago?"

Mrs. Allen did.

"I filled out a temporary card for him, and you want to know what he went out with? *The Maine Woods,* Henry David Thoreau!"

"No!" said Mrs. Allen.

"I thought, wouldn't Mr. Thoreau be pleased?" said Mrs. Pease.

In my head, the light went on. Micmac! I made a beeline for the Dickens shelf, and sure enough, the book was pushed in. He'd been a handsome boy, not more than twelve. I hadn't thought they let them rake that young, but I'm sure they pretended to believe he was older.

The note said,

Be at the top of Jellison's road 11 am tomorrow. As soon as I can, I'll pick you up. Bring lunch.

All I had to do was think what to say to Edith. Just then a boy named Ralph Ober came in, returning a stack of history books. "Your grandfather all set to defend his title?" Mrs. Pease asked him.

"Yes, he is," said Ralph. "Are you going?"

"We wouldn't miss it," she said.

"Are you going, Miss Gray?" He was a nice boy. I'd met him over at the blacksmith shed, where he and some others were playing horseshoes, and he always called me Miss Gray after that, because Bowdoin Leach did.

"What is it?"

"Old-timers' race. All the old sailors turn out in boats, begged or borrowed, even some who were hands in the big ships in the days of sail. It's good fun." Now that I think of it, I suppose Ralph was flirting with me.

The next morning I said to Edith that I was going with some

friends to watch the Retired Skippers' Race and would be gone all day. She said that was fine, but be home by dark. I promised.

I packed a lunch for two and put a sweater into my book bag—I kept that bag with me always now; I couldn't take any chance of Edith snooping in my room, reading my diary—and set off. I stopped to see if Kermit's pig had recovered from her thumps. The pig was named Gloria Swanson, and she appeared to be enjoying life. No more than I was, though; I was on top of the world.

I sat on the swing in the playground beside the road to the point, across from the primary. The day was gorgeous, and while I waited for Conary I wrote in my diary. I wrote that the sun and the smell of gardens and the glow of beach roses growing wild made the day seem good enough to eat.

Soon I heard a motor coming, smooth and humming, so different from the sound of Conary's truck that he practically had to run over my foot before I looked up.

The car he was driving looked like a yacht, there was so much polished brass and gleaming wood and plush leather. Conary, beaming, got out and came around to open the passenger door for me.

"What is this?" I must have been gaping. I couldn't understand the car, and meanwhile Conary looked so handsome smiling in the sun that I could have fallen over and died.

"It's a Packard."

"No, I mean . . . where did you get it? And how?"

"It belongs to Mr. Britton," he said.

"Who's that?"

"He's a big bug over in the summer colony. He leaves it here, and I put it away for the winter for him."

"Did he say we could use it?"

"He trusts me. They're gone for the year; he had to go back down to Philadelphia. I'll polish her up and put her to bed tomorrow."

"It's *beautiful*." It was. I didn't know a machine could be so beautiful. Just standing near it I felt I'd been transformed into some other order of creature. If I'd had a white linen dress and a parasol, I'd have been Mrs. Eleanor Roosevelt on a picnic from Campobello. I stepped into the car, and Connie closed my door with a flourish, then walked gravely around to the driver's side. That took a minute; the car was about twelve feet long. My seat was like a leather armchair, and the dashboard was made of mahogany, gleaming like precious metal.

We were off. Conary drove carefully out the Eastward road, and at first all I noticed was the purr of the engine, the smooth satiny feel of the leather, and a wish that everyone who had ever been mean to me in my life would see me pass in this car, driven by the handsomest boy in the world, and fall down gibbering on the ground in a jealous faint. I came to when Connie turned onto the road to Unionville.

"Where are we going?"

"To the Bangor Fair," he said.

I don't know what I said. Probably screamed. Connie knew I had wanted to go to a state fair, but Bangor was miles and miles away, much too far to attempt in his rattletrap. He had done this for me, stolen a car; we would be sent to jail. I pushed a chrome button on the dash before me, and a door opened. Inside was a little compartment full of driving gloves. There was a large brown pair with ridges sewn into the backs, like the ridges your fingerbones make in the back of your hand. There was a soft creamy white pair that . . . somehow got onto my hands, the long soft cuffs reaching halfway to my elbows. They smelled of lavender. I looked at my hands in the gloves, and it seemed that my body parts were capable of independently coming to belong to someone else. I wished I had a wide-brimmed hat with a frothy veil, which I could tie beneath my chin.

We passed a farmer driving a tractor toward the village who

tipped his hat to us. Obviously we were millionaires from Philadelphia. I said, "We have to go back."

"Want to see how fast she can go?" Connie answered. I was scared, but of course I did want to. Connie gunned the motor, and the car took off down the deserted road. I had to hold on to the seat to keep from falling over.

"Slow down!" I yelled over the noise, not because I wanted to but because it was too thrilling. It felt like a pleasure that didn't belong to us and would lead to ruin.

Connie was smiling as if he owned the world, but he did slow down. "How are you doing?" he asked me over the noise of the wind in our ears.

"I'm afraid. We shouldn't be doing this." I was also afraid that I might talk him out of it. I wanted this day, the perfect buttery sun like peach ice cream, the speed, the satin leather of the car seat, the fair. Forbidden fruit, a day like no other. Most of all, the picture we made, a young couple in love with no cares in the world. I wanted it, and I wanted it to last forever.

"Wouldn't he mind, if he knew? Mr. Britton?"

"I drive for him when he wants me. I drive his boat when they go out fishing, or for picnics. I drive the cars when someone needs to go to the train. He talks to me about my life. He said I should let him know if I want to go to college." Conary looked at me and made a comical face. It made him feel proud that this big man respected him. He had wanted me to know about it.

We were passing a meadow filled with sheep. They were all trying to huddle under the shade tree, a huge maple.

"Do you? Want to go to college?"

"Do you?"

"I do if my father can afford it. I don't know if he can, though."

"I thought about it," said Connie. "But I don't know where it would lead. I know who I am here. If you go to college, then don't you have to go off to Boston or New York and have one of those jobs where you sit indoors?"

I guessed you did. And Connie, out under the summer sky, his hair ruffling, looked as if he were made for wind and sunlight. He was a master of the physical universe, at home with beaches and sea, with animals and engines, with Micmacs and with me. It was hard to imagine him in a suit, at a desk, you'd have to kill off so many parts of him to make it possible. And so easy to see him coming down some lovely island meadow, spending his days outdoors tending his boat and his animals and his children.

"I don't know that I see the point of looking all over when you've already seen what you want." As he said it he looked right at me. "A gadder comes to grief," he added. "That's what they say."

Of course, gadding was what we were doing to a fare-thee-well, but I had never felt more flooded with joy in my life. Whatever grief there might be waiting for us seemed to belong to some other universe. That perfect, heartbreaking day. We thought we would store it in our brains and bones for the long separation that was coming. That was how I justified it, anyway. We weren't doing any harm, and it would give us so much strength for what was to come. As if I knew what that was.

It's lovely driving in the open air, because you aren't looking through the windows at a picture; you're in the air, part of the picture, able to feel the slight change of temperature on your skin in the shade of tall pines, able to smell the sun on the earth, the spicy scent of gardens, the aromas of farmyard. You could see into people's lives as well, the swings beneath the trees, the open parlor windows with filmy curtains blowing, the clothes out back on the line. Most farmhouses were built close to the road so as to be easier to dig in and out of after snow. Nowadays those old houses are often falling to ruin, unfashionably near the road, but in those days when traffic was light, the road was entertainment and company. People came to the window to see what was passing.

Many working farmwives and playing children stopped to stare as we sailed by. A car like the one we were driving was not as rare as a circus wagon, but it was far from a common sight. We waved, like royalty. At noon Connie pulled into a farmer's yard and went to the kitchen door to ask if we could picnic in their field. The farmer came to the door in his overalls; he stared out at the car, gleaming under his shade tree, incongruous as a runaway train. He looked Connie up and down and then stared at the car some more. When Connie came back to me he had a pint bottle of cold buttermilk and a plate of fingerprint cookies filled with homemade jam.

"I told them we were on our honeymoon," he said sheepishly. "I tried to pay her, but she wouldn't let me."

"You are a terrible person."

"So my daddy tells me," he said, opening the door for me. Then he opened the trunk of the car and took out a plush maroon blanket. I saw a thing like a wicker suitcase in there too; Connie said it was full of plates and cups and knives and forks and spoons, all packed in special compartments and strapped in with little leather belts. We looked at each other, tempted, but decided against it. What if we lost or broke something?

We spread the blanket in the sun in a copse back from the road. I produced the limp brown bag that held the lunch I had packed. It suddenly looked rather modest. Sandwiches and bananas.

Conary took a bite of his sandwich and stopped to look at it.

"What's in this?"

"Maple sugar."

He started to laugh.

"Well, I couldn't find the jelly and I didn't like to ask," I said.

Conary tried to look solemn. "Good thinking," he said and then burst into laughter again.

It was true, I didn't know much about cooking then, but I thought these sandwiches were rather a success, and I said so. Conary passed me the buttermilk, and from time to time through the rest of the meal erupted in laughter again. I still don't know what was so funny. Later in life I came to put both the maple sugar and the bananas into one sandwich. My children swore by them, and it made one less thing to carry on a picnic. I'd put anything you could name into a sandwich if I could hear Connie laugh like that again. I guess he wasn't used to girls who weren't brought up in the kitchen.

The cookies were delicious. We washed the plate and bottle in the stream and left them on the kitchen porch, and got back into our chariot, fairly sure that everyone in the house was at one window or another, memorizing the details of our equipage. It was a new experience for both of us to be the envy of anybody, and it was fun. I was amazed at how much fun.

Once the story was told to the farm couple, it became our truth for the rest of the day. We were on our honeymoon. We had done the trick somehow, gotten cleanly away, with only sunlight and tipped hats and purring engines and happiness before us. It was only a wonderful joke, we knew that, but that made it better. We spent that afternoon as if we believed the sun would never set.

We could see Bangor in the distance. It was the first city I'd seen besides Boston. Bangor was very different from Boston; it had grown up rough, a true boomtown, the market loggers boomed their timber down the Penobscot. On the outskirts we passed huge white

houses with wide porches and widows' walks, and carpenter ginger-
bread all around the eaves, built by lumber barons and shipping millionaires in the great days of sail. I wanted to go explore the wicked
downtown, to see where Baby Face Nelson was gunned down by
G-men, but Conary wouldn't take me. The fair was on the near side
of the river, and he said that was as close to the big city as he was
going, in that car anyway.

The fair, of course, was magic enough for one afternoon, or for
many of them.

We parked our car in a field in a long row of others. Men from
the sheriff's department directed traffic. I was momentarily worried
they would take one look at us and the car and arrest us, but they just
tipped their hats and called Conary "sir." There were a few Cadillacs,
and even another Packard or two, but nothing so fancy as ours. Along
the rows of Model T's and A's, of farm wagons and trucks, that car
began to draw a crowd as soon as we left it.

"Will it be all right?" I was fearful that someone would harm it,
or steal my lavender-scented gloves.

"Don't worry. The sheriff will watch it. Mr. Britton just walks
off and leaves it. He always slips them something when he comes
back, though." Conary had clearly learned everything he could from
the way Mr. Britton dealt with the world.

"Will you do that?"

"Depends how much money we have left."

Money! Fairs cost money, of course. I knew that, but had forgotten it, since I'd never actually been to one.

"Do we have any?"

"You forget—I am the fastest blueberry rake in the county." But
his blueberry money—I thought he had to turn that over to his father.
I decided not to ask.

Conary took my hand as we walked toward the gates to the

fairground. Inside we could see rows and rows of sheds and stalls for I didn't yet know what, and beyond that the shrieks and music of the rides and the grandstand and, crowning it all, the Ferris wheel.

We were in a different country. Nothing from the past could follow us here. We were different people, beginning the future we would live together. No darkness from Edith Gray or Tom Crocker or anything else could have anything to do with where we were going. That was the point of being in love. It washed you clean, made you new, gave you a blank slate to write your life on.

Conary paid our way in, and as we started for the midway, barkers began to call to us. There was a shed near the entrance with big painted pictures on boards of what you would see inside.

"Con—look!" I was pointing at a picture of a baby with two heads. One head was wailing, and the other, smiling and cooing. "Can we see it?"

"No, it's terrible. It's not alive."

"What do you mean?"

"It's in a jar. Pickled. It never was alive."

He was marching me past the shed, but I found it hard to look away from that picture. Now *there* was wickedness. The barker was chanting, "See the amazing two-headed baby," and a family with three little girls in party dresses was paying for tickets.

We passed the hootchy-kootchy tent, where men were lined up waiting to go in. There were paintings of beautiful girls dressed entirely in feathers, or in highly colored silk veils. The barker there was crowing about Seleema the Oriental Wonder.

"Are they in jars too?"

"No, but by Oriental they mean Skowhegan." He put his arm around me and the barker didn't even bother trying to tempt him.

We came to a row of games. Games of skill, games of chance, Try your luck, little lady, Show the little lady how strong you are, Duck the clown, Step right up.

Conary stopped at a game where you threw baseballs at wooden milk bottles. "My wife wants to try," he said, handing the man a coin and receiving three baseballs, which he handed to me.

I wound up and heaved. A miss. I threw again and again, two hits. The pitchman whistled as the milk bottles trundled along on a little motorized track as if in a miniature dairy. Conary paid for three more balls, and this time I scored all three.

"Any prize from the top shelf, take any prize you choose," toned the pitchman, not quite as pleased as before. I chose a teddy bear in denim overalls.

"Our firstborn," said Con as we walked away.

"Yes, and it's a bear."

"I don't care, I always wanted a son with a lot of hair."

"What shall we call him?"

"Earl. How are you at darts?"

"I don't know."

"I'm wonderful at them. Let's try for a daughter."

We stopped at a booth where you threw darts at water balloons. Connie bought us three darts apiece, but my aim was poor and he said I threw darts like a girl. He bought himself another round and won us a daughter in the shape of a pig.

"Do I get to name her, since you named Earl?"

"Of course."

"Eleanor, then."

"She has very nice eyelashes," said Conary. "I like that in a pig."

He bought me some fried potatoes in a newspaper cone, sprinkled with salt and vinegar. We carried our babies over to look at the

sheepdog trials, and then to the prize pigs and goats and rabbits.
"Don't worry," Conary whispered to Eleanor, "we'll never put you in
the county fair."

I said, "Conary—let's run away."

"We already have." He put his arm around me and walked me
toward the grandstand.

"I mean—let's not go back."

He stopped walking and turned me to face him.

"Let's not go back. Let's leave the car at the train station and
go west. We can send a telegram to Mr. Britton telling him where
it is."

We walked again. I was frightened now of what I had said because I didn't know if it was part of the game or not. Anyone in the
village could have told you, you shouldn't dare Connie to do a thing
if you didn't want it done.

"Where would we go?"

I had no idea. I'd never been anywhere. I said, "Idaho."

Connie laughed. "Idaho! What's in Idaho?"

"Potatoes."

"Oh great, potatoes! Do I look like a potato farmer?"

"Why not? You're from Maine."

Conary pulled me into the shadow of the grandstand and kissed
me. He kissed me for so long it was like a conversation. I could feel
yes, and no, and why not, moving from him to me, and I could feel
it through my body down to my knees. When finally he ended the kiss
and looked into my eyes, I waited and waited to know which choice
had won. And what did I hope for?

"Why not?" said Connie. And then we both laughed and
laughed. I could think of ten dozen reasons why not, and I knew he
could too . . . and yet . . .

We didn't speak for a while after that. Connie led me around to the side of the track where the trotters would race at sunset. They had an ox pull going on; oxen pulling wooden sledges loaded with boulders. The driver would crack his whip and shout and the oxen lean into the load and drag it down the track with the owner yelling and yelling, trying to get them to keep it up, trying to keep them pulling straight. When they stopped, three officials with tape measures ran onto the course and measured the length of the pull. The strength and patience of the animals was amazing.

Connie watched me watching. He liked it that I cared about farm animals as much as about house pets. I was trying to imagine clearing a meadow with such oxen, myself a farmwife going into the dark barn made fragrant and warm by the animals' breath in winter. We'd have a barefoot daughter who could throw a baseball or drive a team, and a son to go fishing with Conary.

Idaho. Mountains. Trout fishing. Why not?

"Time for the merry-go-round," said Connie. He led me toward the rides, where the calliope and the barkers made more noise than anywhere else. We stood in line with little children, feeling like Gulliver with the Lilliputians.

"Which do you want?" Connie asked me as children rode past on bears and camels and swans. I couldn't decide. Neither could Earl or Eleanor. When at last it stopped and it was our turn to get on, I decided to take the place of a country lady in a flowered dress who'd ridden a horse in a decorous sidesaddle seat. I had watched her staring straight ahead as her painted steed carried her round and round. Conary lifted me onto the horse and mounted the ostrich next to me.

This was my first merry-go-round. What I loved was that our beasts stayed side by side. I rose, Connie fell, the landscape whirled by, but always we were hand in hand, side by side. With my other hand I held Eleanor, while Connie showed Earl the sights. A little boy on a camel managed to grasp the brass ring, and everyone clapped.

We tried another ride, one where you sat in swings hanging from a pole that began to spin. You whirled up and up and out far over the fairground while music played. I had to hold on rather hard, in fear of the height, and a little girl behind me started to cry. Conary loved it, as I could see from his shining eyes when we came down to earth.

"Want to do it again?"

I shook my head. I could feel the fried potatoes rioting in the pit of my stomach. I could also feel the shadows of the day beginning to lengthen.

"How much money do we have?" I asked suddenly.

Conary led me away from the crowd and took his cash out to show me. I didn't count it, but I was surprised at how much there was. I guess he was paid in dollar bills. Anyway, he must have brought all he had, in case . . . in case we didn't go back? Was there enough there for train fares? Surely.

Connie put it carefully away, then took me in his arms and kissed me. There was something so bittersweet in his kiss that I almost started to cry; I didn't know if it was the first kiss of a life we were beginning, or if it was good-bye.

When he let me go, he took my hand and said, "Now, the Ferris wheel."

I went right with him. We stood in the line, and I craned my neck looking up to the top of it. It seemed higher than a skyscraper. Connie was excited; I could feel it in him.

"Frightened?" he asked, looking down at me. I shook my head. A lie. He put an arm around me and held me close to him. "I'll take care of you," he said. I nodded. I knew it was true. He would always take care of me the best he could.

The Ferris wheel began to let people off and take new people on. The line moved forward swiftly; it was so big it could carry more people than I imagined. Soon it was our turn.

We were buckled into a swinging seat, and the ground whooshed away from us. We stopped again, dangling just above the heads of the crowds as people got into the car behind us. Slowly we ascended in this way until we were nearly at the top.

"Isn't that something?" Conary said. "Look—you can see past the city, way up the river—I bet you can see farther than you could walk in a day!" I looked, and nodded. I was clutching the edge of the car with one hand and Conary's hand with the other. I couldn't look up and out; I was looking at all the bolts and rivets or whatever they were that held the thousands of parts together. I was thinking how easily one might fail—shaken loose during the long trip to the fairground, how could you check them all? What if the man who checked got drunk, or had a fight with his wife? What if one cog slipped and we were dumped down down down into the machinery . . .

"And look, here comes the moon!"

And it was true; slipping up into the sky in the evening light came the same baby moon he had sung to me about in the burial ground. It was older now, and we were far away. On our way . . . Conary kissed me. For a moment I forgot to be scared. We had escaped from everything, even gravity.

When it was finally over and we had been put back onto our feet again, Connie led me toward the shadow of the grandstand, around behind the shed where they were judging prize squashes and afghans. He found a place where we were out of sight and held me.

"I love you," he said.

"I know." I did.

"But I have to take that car back."

For a long moment, I couldn't tell what I felt. Then, I felt the obvious: that it was the right thing to do. Then, dread. Of Edith. Of how soon we would be apart. Of how long it would be before we could meet again and make our plans, how hard they would make it for us . . .

We kissed. I cried a little. Connie was sorry but calm; it was the only thing he could do.

"You understand?"

I nodded. A big part of me was screaming inside, that if we missed this chance we'd never get away, but I didn't say it. I didn't know for sure it was true, and I did know that this was the only choice Conary could make.

There was a roar from the grandstand above us; the trotting races had started.

"We better go," Connie said. "They'll have the law out on us again if I don't get you home before dark."

It shouldn't be that one moment can change your life, alter or end all your chances. Life shouldn't be so cruel, but it is. You slip and break your neck, you step in front of a runaway bus. Everything that was possible a minute ago is gone, for years or forever.

We drove home in the gathering dusk, chattering some, still laughing from time to time. Connie had to put Earl and Eleanor in the backseat and speak to them sharply to keep them from quarreling. We turned on the radio (a radio in a car!) and at first got nothing but static, but then a voice came in quite clearly, KDKA fifty-thousand-watts clear channel from Pittsburgh, Pennsylvania. A band began to play, and then a girl to sing, "More than you know, more than you know, boy of my heart, I love you so . . ." We listened to the end of it. That was the only song we got. A man began droning about the stock market, so we turned the radio off.

"What do you think will happen next?" Connie asked me when we had gone about halfway.

"Edith wants to send me to boarding school. She doesn't want to deal with me by herself."

"Do you know where?"

"No."

"How will you let me know?"

I pictured the post office. If I wrote to him, Mrs. Foss would just hand the letter to Mr. Crocker when he came in. "Conary's got a letter from Massachusetts, Tom," she'd say to all and sundry.

"Bet he can't even spell Massachusetts," Kermit or someone would add, and everyone would have a laugh.

"What if I wrote my address to Mrs. Pease? Or Mrs. Sylvester?"

"I don't know . . ." I didn't either. It was one thing to like me and Conary, quite another to keep secrets from our parents.

"Bowdoin?"

We both thought about that. Bowdoin was a possibility. Bowdoin knew a great deal more about everything than he ever told anyone. He might hold a piece of paper from me to Conary and hand it over when asked for it. He might not too, but at least I didn't think he'd tell.

"Wherever they send you, I'll find you. Wait for me," he said.

"I'll wait for you," I said. "But I'll be the loneliest person in the world."

He smiled at me. We rode a long way in silence, with a piercing sadness sinking deeper and deeper in us. I felt so shot through with love that it was like quicksilver in my veins.

We could see the familiar rise of the back of Tenney Hill. The air was full of violet shadows; we had only minutes more together before home, and the warm bright clatter of closed-in evening rooms would make separate prisoners of us.

On the road ahead lay the long downward slope past the burial ground, and then the Pottery, and Miss Leaf's gardens, the library and the village. I wanted this moment never to end, to just lengthen into eternity.

Up ahead I saw a glimmer of white at the side of the road, a figure. It was just that hour of evening when your eyes begin to fail you and headlamps don't yet do much good, but in another moment I saw there was a woman there, all alone near the road, in a flowered dress, with arms nearly bare, and maybe feet too—something utterly wrong in her demeanor; something must have happened to her. She turned to the sound of our car with an air of such desperation, waving, that Conary pulled up beside her. Before he could ask what help she needed she had opened the door and gotten in behind me.

"Careful you don't sit on Earl and Eleanor," said Conary. He put the car back into gear and started down the hill. I believe it must have been at the same moment that we looked into the rearview mirror and saw the horrible featureless face right behind us, staring at us with eyes like dry ice with pinprick pupils that had no need of light to see with, and understood what we'd chosen.

Almighty and most merciful Father,
We have erred and strayed from thy ways like lost sheep.
We have followed too much the devices and desires of our own hearts. . . .
And there is no health in us. . . .
Spare thou those who confess their faults.
Restore thou those who are penitent.

For a long time, I couldn't understand what was happening. Mrs. H lived in a world of her own. She didn't know others could be hungry if she wasn't. She didn't know there were any feelings besides hers. I don't know what she thought the rest of us were. She could eat the same food at every meal eight days in a row and never notice or care, as if it were stage food in a play, and the rest of us were actors in a story she was watching. I was hungry all the time I lived in that house.

Once she put a pan of milk on the stove and then went to her weaving. When she found the pan burnt black at suppertime, she yelled at me. I cried and went upstairs; I hadn't touched the milk. I hadn't even been there. Days later when she asked me why I shied from her, I told her it was because she had been so angry with me about the pan. She looked amazed. She expected me to love her. I think she thought I *did* love her.

Mr. H was a walking bad mood. He wasn't pleasant, but you could understand him. Nobody loved him. Nobody liked him. He was heavy and sour and smelled of fish, and yet he didn't deserve what life was serving him. Not such utter disdain and loneliness.

Miss H

Miss C was in the schoolhouse preparing her lessons. Miss C was young and had never lived from home before. She lived with the H family, because her aunt had fallen sick and couldn't keep her. The H family were nothing like people she knew at home and they made her unhappy and she was always hungry there, but

Miss C was in the schoolhouse preparing her lessons. It was her first time living away from home and she boarded with the H family. It was spring and had been raining it seemed for weeks. Also Miss C had not been feeling well. Something had happened that she could not explain and did not wish to tell her mother so she was not sure where she would go when school was over.

Miss C was young and pretty and dreamed of

Miss C was in the schoolhouse one afternoon when Miss H came in. Miss H was older than Miss C, and very brave, and reckless, people said. Miss C admired her, but was worried by her headstrong nature. Miss H was in love with a handsome artist named Raoul. He was popular and gay, and flirted with other girls besides Miss H, but everyone believed they were engaged. Miss C believed it. She boarded with the H family, which consisted of the mother, the father, and the daughter. There had been a son but he died.

Mr. H was an angry and sad man. He was crosswise with everybody but especially his daughter. He was always telling her she couldn't do this and couldn't do that, when it just made her rail at him, and didn't stop her. She did what she wanted. Miss C couldn't see why he did that; he couldn't seem to help himself. Show him a way to be kind and another way to make everybody mad, and he seemed to have to do the mean thing. Tick, tock, tick, tock, as if someone were winding him up and setting him off to go lumbering across the landscape. He was very lonely too.

Miss H came into the schoolhouse and she was crying. Miss C knew she had come there because she didn't want them to know at home she was upset, nor neither at the store where she worked in town. Miss C flew to her side and cried, "What's the matter? What has happened?" for she was a tenderhearted girl.

Miss H replied, "Raoul is leaving tonight. He is never coming back, and I want to go with him."

Miss C thought that Miss H loved Raoul very much, and she knew that Miss H longed to go away and have a different life from what her parents had.

"Are you going to elope?" Miss C cried, hoping that Miss H planned to be married.

"He says I must go with him right now, or never see him again, he won't be back. He is tired of being called names by my father." It was true that Mr. H often said ugly things about Raoul. Then Miss H began to weep again, very angry. Suddenly she seemed to take a decision. "Miss C, would you please go get my mother and bring her here?"

"Of course, dear," said Miss C, very upset to see this high-spirited girl so undone. In a trice she had put on her black cloak and hurried into the rain.

She found Mrs. H at home rocking at her rag loom. Mrs. H was upset by the wet weather, in which no clothes would dry. She came willingly back to the schoolhouse, where there was a great scene.

"Raoul is leaving town. Father has been ugly to him and he says he doesn't believe I'll ever leave home," cried Miss H bitterly.

"There's no need to leave home," declared Mrs. H. "You can both live right here in town after you're married."

Miss H flared and her eyes blazed. "It would be a proper mare's nest, the way Father behaves to Raoul. He cannot stay in this town."

"You cannot leave," cried the mother. "I don't want to be left all alone here!"

"You don't have to be!" cried the daughter. "You can go to your family, they would be glad to have you back!"

The mother looked cold and hard as she replied, "I can't do that."

"Why not?" asked the girl.

"They would mock me and say, Everyone told you so."

"They would not!" cried the daughter. In any case, Mrs. H didn't listen to her daughter. She believed what she had decided to believe, and could not be talked to. She didn't want her daughter to leave town, and that was that. The daughter was torn, for she wanted her mother to love and esteem her. Miss C thought this was like the brindle cat at home who never would stop sidling up to the ones who liked cats least. The more it got kicked, the more it tried again.

After they had both gone off in the rain, Miss C was most upset. She was used to kind and happy people and even when her brother in a fit of pique knocked her down and sat on her and broke one of her ribs she forgave him because

Miss C spent the night in the schoolhouse and was very uncomfortable for the only bed there was the cot she used for pupils who felt ill during the day or came out in spots, and there was only a thin blanket and no pillow. She had bad dreams and wondered if Miss H was at that moment running away with her Raoul, and if so, would they be happy? She was not at all sure that she would be since she had seen Raoul making eyes at Miss Horton one day on the stoop of the general store.

In any case the day dawned quite bright, and with it the girl's mood lifted. She thought she would go home to the H's house and wash and get some breakfast. When she got there Mr. H was just finishing a peculiar breakfast of hot broth and boiled eggs. Mrs. H was sitting looking out the window. There were two dirty plates on the table, and from that Miss C guessed that Miss H and her mother had both recently breakfasted.

While Miss C went out to the hen yard to see if there were more eggs, Mr. H apparently went into the parlor and lay down to take a nap. He often did this on Sundays as he was an early riser and by breakfast time had already spent several hours tending the animals and put in a stretch with his Bible. The nap in the parlor was his Day of Rest, he would say when Mrs. H made remarks about it. Mrs. H didn't like him to nap in the parlor because he snored loudly and prevented her going to her loom, and because she said men in her family went to sleep in proper bedrooms instead of making pigs of themselves in public (this was the way they talked to each other). Miss

C came into the kitchen with her eggs in her pockets, one daubed with straw and chicken dirt, and set a pot of water to boil on the woodstove. The kitchen was empty, but she could hear Mr. H beginning to snore in the parlor.

As she waited for the water to boil, and wished there were bread and butter to eat instead of eternal eggs, she became aware of someone on the stairs. Sallie, she thought. She didn't go to look. The door to the mudroom, the front door properly though it was almost never used, opened and closed. No one ever went that way, except to go to the woodpile.

The water came to the boil and I put my three eggs in. I looked at the kitchen clock to time them because I like them hard-boiled, I can't bear that slimy gush of yellow yolk on the plate. It was going on ten, and in town the bell was ringing for morning worship. The front door opened again and I turned to see Mrs. H coming in. She was carrying the ax from the woodpile.

I'd never seen the ax brought in the house. It was sharpened in the barn on the grinding wheel. Wood was split outside. Mrs. H didn't use it even to kill chickens, which she did with her hands. (We had chicken for dinner once, on Easter Sunday.) I don't think she saw me. As usual with Mrs. H, you couldn't tell what she saw. She saw what she wanted to.

Mrs. H stood in the dark hall for minutes. The only sound in the house was the snoring in the parlor and the tick of the kitchen clock. I could see her from where I stood at the far side of the stove, not her face, but her back, stiff and straight. She was wearing the summer dress from yesterday, I think it was Sallie's. I didn't know what was going to happen.

Mrs. H walked forward, out of my sight. She was heading toward the light, toward the parlor where you could see the bay. Her shoes made a soft tapping noise. She made no effort to be quiet, she was very matter-of-fact. My egg water was bubbling on the stove and that seemed loud.

In the parlor there was a sudden sound like the sound of a knife going into a pumpkin, loud but not sharp. Also Mr. H made a noise, not a word but an uuuhfff noise, like a horse exhaling. The snoring stopped.

I stood in the corner of the kitchen listening to blow after blow falling in the parlor. They fell in the same rocking rhythm she used at her loom, as if instead of weaving rugs she was chopping the sofa apart. Finally footsteps came running down from upstairs and Sallie screamed. Just once.

All the way in the kitchen I could smell the blood. I knew I was going to be sick and didn't want them to hear me. I was trying not to gag, picturing them in the next room staring at each other. Finally I heard Sallie say, "Mother, it's all over your dress," and then the two of them left by the door down to the side yard, where the washhouse was.

I left the eggs on the boil and never did learn what happened to them

—⁓—

The sleek young Englishman who had once sold a story to *Scribner's Magazine* turned over the last of the manuscript pages to see if there was any more. Then he stretched his long legs and bounced the pages together against his desk to square them up before handing the whole back to Miss Turner.

"There's a rather good sentence about a brindle cat," he said.

Miss Turner waited to see if he wouldn't have something more to say about it than that. Apparently he didn't.

"Oh, dear," she said. "Poor Miss Chatteau."

When I woke up, I was crying. I didn't know where I was, but I'd had a dream. Someone was throwing pebbles at my window. I went to it and looked out, and Connie was there outside, looking up at me. He was smiling and calling to me, and I tried to shush him, but he laughed and said, "I want to marry you." His hair was wet and dark. I said I couldn't come out, and he said, "Then wait for me. I'll find you." And then he started to go away, but I noticed as he went, he'd hurt his foot, and was limping.

I didn't know where I was. In the dream it was night (and Conary was there), but when I opened my eyes it was bright, and my head ached, and Conary wasn't there. I tried to turn my head, but it made me want to scream, so I moved my eyes.

White ceiling. White window shades. Sunlight. White metal dresser. Bedclothes tucked tight around me so that I couldn't move my arms. Something else hurt, besides my face and head. Almost everything. My arm, and my whole side. And an ankle.

Somebody reached over and wiped the tears that were sliding down my neck. What was I crying about? Oh, yes, the dream. Whose hand? The owner of the hand stood, and I saw it was my father.

"Hello," he said softly. He looked very glad to see me, and this was such a change from the last time that I tried to smile.

A nurse poked her head in and, seeing my father standing by my bed, came in to look at me. She looked into my eyes and smiled at me and then said, "Hello, sunshine. I'll just tell the doctor you've decided to come back to us." She hurried out. I probably went back to sleep, because the next instant there seemed to be a convention of large seagulls, all in white coats, gathered around my bed, bobbing and poking.

One dug my wrist out from under the covers and held it. Another told me to follow his finger with my eyes. I tried. Another stuck a thermometer into my mouth.

"Do you know what day it is?" one asked me. That seemed like a trick question. My father said to me, "It's Tuesday, sweetheart."

Tuesday! Tuesday . . . of what week?

"Do you know who the president of the United States is?" asked the first doctor. I did of course but didn't know why they wanted to know.

"Who is it?"

I said Roosevelt. It came out *Ro-svel.* My lips were all swollen and cracked. The first seagull turned to my father and said, "Well. Congratulations."

"This is it? Is this what you were waiting for?"

"Yes. There's still plenty to be on the lookout for . . ." He went on and on. He seemed to know why my head hurt. I went back to sleep.

When I woke up again it was still light, or light again, and I was hungry. I tried to sit up, but that was a very poor idea and I stopped. I found out, though, that Edith and Father were both in the room, and they crowded around.

Edith stroked my forehead and said, "I think her fever's down. She doesn't look so dopey." My father nodded. I wished my arms weren't all wrapped up so I could punch her. Who wants to hear not so dopey?

My father touched my head, and I realized he was touching bandages, not my scalp. It was like finding out you were wearing a hat when you didn't know it. Bandages. And my head hurt . . . so, head injury. And . . . they must have shaved my head again. I wondered what I looked like this time. Father must have been getting used to the shorn look by now. At least Conary liked it.

Conary.

I suddenly understood—again—that a big section of time was missing. I remembered Saturday morning. I remembered Mr. Britton's car.

Mr. Britton's car! Please, God, don't let us have done something bad to Mr. Britton's car.

I said to my father, "Conary?"

It took me a long time to get him to understand me. Finally Edith came up behind him and said, "She's saying 'Conary.' Asking for the boy."

"Oh, yes," said my father. "Don't worry."

Don't worry—what did that mean? Where was he?

"Is he . . ."

"Yes, he's fine. There was an accident."

I had worked that out for myself, in fact. So how could he be fine? If we'd done as much damage to that car as we'd done to me, we'd have been lucky if he didn't wind up in Thomaston.

"Don't try to talk, dearie. There's plenty of time." I think then a nurse came in, and we began the drama of whether I could have any solid food. (I gather I'd been living on something they were drooling into my arm.) The seagulls all came back, and sometime later that day I was given ginger ale to sip through a bent glass straw.

The next day, I think, there was Jell-O. And more of the day, the lost day, came back. Earl and Eleanor. The Ferris wheel. Our future, free and pure in Idaho, which I pictured as just like Maine.

I asked the nurse, "Where am I?"

"Dundee Cove, dear. In the hospital."

So that was all right, I was in the right town.

"Do you know Conary?"

"Conary Crocker?" she said. She almost pulled it off. "Of course, dear. Known him from a tot."

"Can I see him?"

"Not right now, dear."

"Is he in the hospital too?"

"No, he isn't." She had to go rather suddenly.

There was either one person they forgot to prime, or else one who had some objection to lying. That was Mr. Gilbert Davidson, the Congregational minister, a rabbity sort of person I'd seen hopping and gnawing around the library stacks but never spoken to. One morning I woke up and found him sitting beside my bed. When he saw I was awake he introduced himself. "I thought I ought to see if there was anything I could do for you."

I thanked him. I wasn't really feeling up to starting new relationships.

"Is there?"

What I wanted was some answers to my questions, which so far everyone treated as whimsical. No harm in trying him.

"There was an accident?"

"Yes. A car accident."

Oh. This was new, someone who didn't dance around it.

"The car?"

"There's not much left of it. It hit the phone pole right outside Miss Leaf's house. She was the first one to reach you, but I think I was the second."

"Is Conary . . ."

He waited mildly for me to frame my question.

". . . in trouble?"

"No. He is not in trouble."

"Even though we wrecked the car?"

"He's out of trouble, Hannah. He's dead."

I looked at him, and his eyes met mine, steadily, truthfully. I closed mine, and began to cry.

He sat with me and held my hand. It was awful, the crying. It made my head hurt so much, and I made a sound like the sound the ghost made. Is this what it wanted? *My* body to cry with? It had *had* its own life; what right did it have to mine?

I tried as hard as I could to stop, because it hurt so much in my head and my heart, and after a while I managed it, sort of. Mr. Davidson kindly brought me tissues and, most surprisingly, neither fled nor offered false comfort.

When I could speak I said, "I had a dream. It woke me up." I told him about it.

He said "What day was that?"

"Tuesday."

He nodded, as if that was about what he'd expected.

"He was with me, and then I woke up and he was gone. I want him to come back," I said and, horribly, began crying again.

Mr. Davidson said, "No, dear, you don't. Your grief is for yourself, now, for your loss. But not for Conary. He's left you his blessing and gone to peace."

This sounded enraging to me, like those people who say that heaven is a big cloud house and everyone you love and miss is up there together with a man with a big white beard. How did he know?

My anger passed, though, as I remembered that it was true that the feeling in the dream of Conary was intensely peaceful. Unlike the hell of feelings I had awakened to. But it wasn't true that I didn't want him back. I wanted that dream, or I wanted him himself outside my window. I wanted it so much I didn't know how I could survive. I said so.

He said, "I hope it won't shock you if I say that your dream is not exactly what I would call a dream. You know our creed names Father, Son, and Holy Ghost. If there is a Holy Ghost, am I likely to deny there are others?"

I don't believe I said anything, and I hope I am remembering fairly what he said after. Of course I came to know him well in later days and to believe he was far more truly a man of spirit than his appearance had led me to think when I was still young enough to judge people by appearances.

He said, "You remember that when our Lord left the body, he was seen two days later, though not exactly as he had been in life, by people who were grieving for him? That he continued to appear for some days, it depends on which Gospel you read, and then finally was gone? If his was a pattern life for us all to follow, why is this not also what we should all expect of death?"

I didn't know the answer, then or now.

"I believe," he told me, "that the moment of death is something like waking up in the morning. At first, you don't want to leave the state you've been in. There is then a period . . . a few days, maybe longer . . . when the soul, or spirit, the same one that was in the body, but changed, is still present in this life. It visits people and places, it appears in the dreams of loved ones, it says its good-byes. And all the while it is . . . growing less, thinning out, or diluting, like drops of dye in a basin of water, until finally what had been a person lets go and becomes—I think—dissolved into the universe. Willingly, joyfully."

"All of us? Dissolve?"

"That is the problem, of course. Not all. That is why I said you don't wish Conary back. Not that wishing makes any difference."

I asked him to go on.

He said, "I believe there are those who . . . for whatever reason . . . are so unfinished with the life they have lived, so unwilling . . . there are those who somehow refuse, and get stuck in whatever the state is, not alive, but not released. And they are not for the most part the souls one would wish to see more of. The holy ghosts are the ones like Conary, who let go."

Still I asked, "Why does it . . ."

"I don't know. I tend to think it's like a kaleidoscope, in which the same bits of glass and rock form and re-form to make patterns of endless variety. As we move through our lives, all made of bits and pieces of lives that have gone before, sometimes we must form patterns that existed before. Suddenly there's a match, or something that looks like one, and it's something that such an unfinished spirit can make use of . . ."

"To do what?" I could hardly speak above a whisper.

He shrugged. "Defy God. Try again to change the pattern."

"Can it?"

"Oh, yes, but not in a way that will do it any good. Not if, as I believe, the pattern itself is God."

No. I could see that there was not any good likely to come of that, for anyone.

I know this whole conversation sounds like a hallucination. Maybe it was one. I was very deep in grief, and also full of medicine. But I think he said something like that. Much later, when I'd come back here to live, he told me what had happened to him in the Haskell house. How he knew at the time it was what I needed I have no idea. After he left, for days and days, I mostly wept.

Mrs. Pease came to see me, and Mrs. Allen, and Dot Sylvester and Nella B., and my grandparents. They none of them stayed long; I was so glad to see them, because I knew it meant they cared for me, and so glad when they left, because I didn't have to try not to cry. They gave me back my book bag that had been in the car. It didn't have that much blood on it, and I so much hoped the blood was Connie's. After a while I began to write in my diary again. My left wrist and collarbone were broken, but my right only hurt like hell.

During the time I was there I had two other unexpected guests. The first was Miss Leaf. She marched in wearing her baggy corduroys and slouch hat and plopped herself down in the chair beside me and started talking.

"They told me you were mending, but I had to see for myself. Once on a road down in New Jersey I stopped to help a lady in an accident. Cars didn't go so fast in those days, but she was pretty bunged up. I had a ways to travel still, so I didn't stay to learn how she came through it, and I've always been sorry. So here I am, came to see for myself, how are you?"

It reminded me so piercingly of the day she surprised me and Conary in the burial ground that I burst into tears.

"Oh, gorey, now don't cry," she more or less yelled, and then slapped herself on the knee and said, "Why say a stupid thing like that, Maude? What else is there for her to do?"

So I cried, and she sat there, and after a while when I subsided she handed me a tissue.

"I'm a waterworks," I said.

"I know, I know. I brought you something." I dried my eyes and looked at her and saw she was carrying a paper bag. She opened it and took out Earl, and then Eleanor. The bear and pig, our children. She carried them to me and put them on the bed. I had to hold my fists to my mouth to keep from going off again.

"They were in the backseat. The horn was going, you were moaning, and the boy was dead, you could see that much. But here were these two little fellows. I thought if you lived you'd be wanting them."

I gathered them up in my arms and said thank you with my lips. I couldn't manage a voice. She said, "You're welcome," and got up to go.

I held up my hand, and, kindly, she gave me a minute, until I could speak.

I said, "When you . . ."

"Found you, yes." I nodded.

"Was there . . ."

"Blood?" she boomed. "You went right through the windshield . . ." But I was shaking my head. Not blood. I tried again.

"Someone . . . ? We stopped for . . ." Oh, hell, I was thinking. I knew the answer. But the last words Conary said in this life were "Careful you don't sit on Earl and Eleanor."

"Someone else in the car? Honey, his head hit the tree, yours went through the windshield. That was enough. Anyone else in that car would have been thrown in the road."

Of course. I knew that, and Conary knew it. There was no one else there.

The other visitor was Conary's sister, Mary. She came in very shyly, and when we saw each other we both wept. That was a relief—the one person in the town (who was likely to talk to me) who had loved Connie as much as I did.

She told me about the funeral. Baptist, church full, for her unendurably painful. Her father had behaved like a wounded bear and was now mostly drunk. The Britton family had been kind, even sent a wreath. (The car had been insured.) Mary brought me a copy of the bulletin, and the newspaper clips about the accident, and Connie's obituary. Obituary. Connie's obituary. I still can hardly bear the words.

Before she left, she took a book out of her purse and laid it on the bed beside me. It was *A Christmas Carol* by Charles Dickens. She hadn't gone out and bought one; it was *the* copy. She had stolen it from the library. I didn't know whether to be shocked or to weep with gratitude.

Mary stood and said, "Connie told me to bring it to you. Please don't ask me to explain." I looked at her for a long time, and her gaze didn't waver. I didn't need her to explain.

I whispered, "Thank you," and she went out.

Gilbert Davidson had not been born when Sallie Haskell was tried for the murder of her father. He was a twinkle in his father's eye in Redfield, South Dakota. When he was called to minister to the Congregational church in Dundee, Maine, he was twenty-five. Dundee was off the beaten path, not a prestigious appointment, but he found the village beautiful and tranquil the summer he arrived, and he reasoned that the winters couldn't be any worse than they were in South Dakota.

His duties were not heavy at first. In July and August, retired men of the cloth who summered in the area made it clear that they would be pleased to preach a Sunday or two, and the new minister, still insecure (with good reason) about his abilities in the pulpit, was only too glad to let them. This left Gilbert free to concentrate on some fresh ideas about stewardship he was eager to put into practice.

He studied the records of the ways the church members were accustomed to raise money for the minister's salary and aiding the poor: a white elephant sale in the summer, the blueberry pancake breakfast, the Christmas crafts bazaar. In his opinion a great deal more could be done by way of tapping inhabitants of the summer colony, who more and more filled the beautiful airy meeting house on summer Sundays (while more and more members of the year-round congregation chose to worship their Maker under the blue dome of his heaven at this time of year). The outgoing minister had not died in harness, but he had come close, and in Gilbert's opinion he had let slide the obligation of visiting elderly members of the parish to discuss, along with spiritual matters, the final disposition of their worldly goods.

He spent days in the basement of the meeting house with the church secretary, Flossie Eveleth, getting the lay of the land.

"Sylvanus McGraw," he would say, and Flossie would answer, "Scratch him off. He went over to the Baptists after his wife died."

"Catherine Bowey."

"Yes, she'd like a visit. She can talk the handle off the pump, though."

"I don't mind. Sallie Haskell."

Flossie paused. What to say about Sallie?

"She's given a little every year. Yes, she does that in memory of her uncle Leander. He stood right by her always."

"Perhaps she could do more," suggested Gilbert.

Flossie looked at him, thoughtful. "She doesn't come to service at all," she offered.

"Why not? Isn't she well?"

"I don't know. I haven't seen her in a good while."

"It can't hurt to try," said Gilbert, completely missing the signals Flossie was sending. He asked directions to Sallie's house and made notes on his list.

—〰—

The afternoon he arrived on her porch was a lovely one, with light golden over the bay, which was dotted with sailboats. The front curtains in Miss Haskell's house were all drawn, but there were many of her generation who kept the sun out of the house to save the furniture. Behind him on the sidewalk a group of girls wearing straw hats and carrying a picnic basket stopped to stare at the man up on Sallie Haskell's porch. He nodded, stiff in his clerical collar, and they nodded back and walked on, whispering to each other. He supposed that they were pleased to see an attractive young man arrived in the village.

He knocked. He listened for footsteps within and heard nothing. He knocked again. (He would learn, later, that these days the people who brought Sallie her groceries and mail walked around to the back porch and left them without knocking.)

The third time he knocked, he heard something inside, and finally the curtain in what he guessed to be the parlor moved slightly. He smiled and waved at the unseen person, then waited some more.

The front door opened a crack.

"Good afternoon," he said. "I'm Gilbert Davidson. Is Miss Haskell at home?"

The door opened very slightly more. He could see now that he was talking to a woman dressed in an old-fashioned style, as if she had put on a full black Victorian mourning costume for some pageant or play. She was a tall woman with a strong jaw and large hands and feet. Nevertheless, she gave the impression of grave frailty. Her yellow-white bun was partly tumbled down in the back, as if she had lacked the energy to contain it. He began to be a little unsure of the wisdom of this visit; not everyone liked company.

"I am Miss Haskell," said the woman, speaking so softly he could hardly hear.

"I believe you are a member of my flock," said Gilbert, trying to be light. "I've come to take over from Reverend Beech."

"A member of your flock," she said, as if this were a novel thought. "Well. I suppose I am. In some sense." She spoke carefully, as if the atmosphere inside the house was thick with something other than oxygen and she had to conserve her breath for words that mattered.

"Could I come in?"

Sallie Haskell appeared to be thinking this over carefully. At last she opened the door wide enough for him to enter, and he popped in, now as much curious as anything else.

The house was furnished very simply and was painfully tidy, as if long ago someone had picked it up by the neck and squeezed the life out of it, and then put it down again, arranged in a natural-looking pose. He stood inside the front door with his hat in his hands, waiting. Miss Haskell seemed to have completely forgotten the conventions of a social call.

"Perhaps we could go somewhere to sit down," he said after a bit.

"Oh," she said. She examined him again, but just as her eyes were beginning to make him uncomfortable, she turned and led the way slowly through the dark dining room and into the sunny kitchen at the back of the house. She moved painfully. "This is where I sit," she said, when she had achieved the kitchen. There was a rocking chair facing the window and beside it a basket piled high with needles and wool.

She sat down facing the window, and he drew a chair from the kitchen table and sat beside her. Seated, he could see that her view led down to the shore and out across the bay.

"Lovely view," he said.

"Yes."

Then, "I see you're a knitter," though he knew it was a pathetic conversational gambit.

"Yes," she said again. He looked down rather desperately at the pile of woolen work in her basket. He couldn't imagine what it was.

"What are you making?"

"Bandages."

Now he was feeling like a fool. He wondered what ailed her, and how soon he could excuse himself. Suddenly, though, she made an effort.

"You remember, we were all asked to knit bandages during the war. I know the war is over; and yet I keep knitting them. Habits are hard to break. I tell myself that sooner or later there will be another one."

Was she making fun of him? Of herself?

"Another war?"

"Yes. What was it you came for?"

"I hoped to get to know you," he said lamely.

"Why?"

If all his parish calls were going to be like this one, Gilbert Davidson decided he would hang himself.

"Miss Haskell. I'm new in town, and one must start somewhere. I understood you had lived here all your life."

After a pause, she assented to this.

"I hope to make it my home too," he said. She looked at him, as if wondering what that could possibly have to do with her.

"Miss Haskell, are you in health?"

This was a question nearly as stupid as the remark about the knitting, and he braced himself for a recitation of symptoms. Instead, she said, wheezing, "I was not brought up to discuss such things with strangers."

An old lady who didn't want to talk about her health? What sort of place had he come to?

He couldn't simply grab his hat and flee. For one thing, she was certainly not in health. She seemed to be slowly drowning, or strangling. Was she getting proper medical attention? "Have you family in the area, Miss Haskell?"

"I have my mother," she said simply. Mr. Davidson was rocked by this. It had not occurred to him that Miss Haskell could have a parent living. He had been thinking of a niece or nephew. He tried not to show his surprise.

"Here in the village?"

"Out there." She motioned with her head. She seemed to indicate that her mother lived in the bay.

Seeing that he did not understand, she said, "On the island."

He was startled. "I thought no one lived there anymore."

"She does," said Miss Haskell. "I would know if she was dead."

By the time he left the house, which was very soon after that, Gilbert Davidson felt in need of spiritual counsel himself. He could not have said exactly what had disturbed him so profoundly about this visit; it was something far deeper than social awkwardness. He thought of going, hat in hand, to his brother in the cloth, the Baptist pastor, although there had been a certain competition, if not enmity, between the two denominations in the town for many decades, but the Reverend Mr. Stover had gone to rusticate at Lake Moosemeguntic. Gilbert wrote a letter describing the visit to his mentor at divinity school in Lincoln, and by the time he received his reply, Sallie Haskell was dead.

—⁂—

It was Bowdoin Leach who ferried Mr. Davidson out to the island. Only he was quite sure where the landing was for the Haskell house. The dock had long ago blown off in a hurricane, and the birch and alder had grown up blocking the view of the house from the water. There was a path, barely visible, remaining. If the old lady needed supplies, she wrote a note on a piece of cloth and tied it to a tree branch on the shore. Some fisherman passing on his way to or from the main would stop for it and leave what she needed on the beach the next time he passed. Every few months Mr. Abbott would take her bill over to the bank, and the banker would pay it. It had been years since Claris had come down to the beach to chat, or say please or thank you. Nobody knew how it was with her, but all respected her privacy and her right to live as she chose.

Gilbert Davidson sat amidships in the little sailing dory with the warm wind in his hair, thinking it was ironic that instead of bearing the news of the old lady's death to the daughter, he was carrying sorrow the other way. But when he got to the house, he found he was not doing that either. It was impossible to say which had died first, the mother or the daughter, or who had died more alone.

Claris Haskell was lying awkwardly on the floor in her nightdress. It looked as if she had fallen and been unable to rise, and was trying to drag herself or crawl somewhere. She was shockingly thin, thin enough to have starved to death, although there were beans and molasses and flour in the house, and vegetables in the overgrown garden. He went down to the beach to tell Bowdoin what he had found.

"What should we do?" the young minister asked the older man. "Should we . . . wrap her in something, take her with us?"

Bowdoin paused, looking at the sky. "I guess I'd rather not," he said finally. Mr. Davidson was relieved, as he would also rather not. He asked Mr. Leach if he would come up to the house while he covered the body and said a prayer, but Mr. Leach said he would rather not do that either. The new minister went back and prayed for the safe repose of the soul of Claris Osgood Haskell by himself.

—⁂—

Claris had left a will, including orders that she be buried alongside the graves of her stillborn daughters, with no minister and no mourners. "In my experience," said Mr. Davidson to the lawyer, "when the elderly say they want no service it's a vanity; it's not the service they object to, but the fear that a service would not be well attended." He was picturing something rather stark and lovely, with himself in black and a small contingent from his choir to sing "Now the Day Is Over."

"You didn't know Claris Haskell," said the lawyer, who had. She was buried as instructed, with only the undertaker and his man there to dig the hole and lower the coffin, and the grave was left unmarked.

"There's nobody left alive who'd have any business looking for it," she had written. By the time he heard that, Mr. Davidson knew more of the history of this unhappy family, and thought he understood.

Because there was no way to tell who had died first, it could not be determined whether the house and belongings should be donated to the village poor farm, as in Claris's will if her daughter predeceased her, or parceled out among village charities and various far-flung Osgood, Friend, and Crocker cousins, as in Sallie's. It was more curiosity than self-interest that caused Gilbert Davidson to visit the island once more that fall, though the reason he gave to the boatman he hired was that if Sallie's will should be honored, the house she had grown up in would belong to his church.

He found the house much changed from his earlier visit. It had been thoroughly picked over by curiosity seekers and vandals. People had tried on the clothes in the closets, and taken many of them away. More were left scattered about where they fell. They had taken books from the shelves and rummaged through letters in a desk upstairs. In an upstairs bedroom he found a very old doll with a china head and brown hair that seemed almost human; it was wearing an old-fashioned lawn dress, made with tiny hand stitches and a double row of pearl buttons down the back. The dress was so fragile it looked as if it would crumble if you touched it. Someone had turned down the bed and put the doll into it, leaning up against the pillow like a tiny girl. He reached out a hand to touch the doll's hair, and the head slid sideways. The doll had been decapitated.

At the moment he made this discovery, he heard a door slam somewhere downstairs, and the sound of laughing. Since he was utterly alone in the house, it sent through him a shock of terror that he could later describe to himself only as unholy.

He left the house so precipitously that he was halfway to the safety of the beach and his boatman when he realized he was still holding the Haskell family Bible, printed in England in 1610, which he had found in a downstairs bedroom. Unwilling to return to the house, Gilbert wrapped it in his coat and took it back to the main with him. Not long afterward the island house and outbuildings burned to the ground by accident or arson. (There was no doubt that the burn was a great convenience to the blueberry growers who were harvesting out there those summers.)

By the time the wills were settled, it seemed awkward to Mr. Davidson to mention that he had the Bible. He had learned by then how much it was worth on the rare book market, and it was too much for him to either keep or sell without explanation. He did some research on the early Haskells whose births, marriages, and deaths were listed in the front, and found that an Efraim Haskell had gone to Harvard in 1688. He wrapped the Bible in brown paper and mailed it off to the university, with a note declaring an anonymous donation from an old Harvard family.

When I was well enough to make the trip, Edith drove me and Stephen home. Boston was hot and loud and felt as if it had a disease that brought fever. Our apartment had been shut up since my father left, with dust sheets over the furniture. Something had rotted in the icebox, and the smell soaked into the corners of the house and could not seem to be aired out. Edith had tense conversations on the telephone with Father, but he did not come back. I was still Edith's prisoner. Or her charge. I needed help dressing and bathing and going to the bathroom, and she gave it as kindly as she could. Stephen was my comfort. He sat in my room by the hour, and we listened to the radio or played Parcheesi. One weekend Father came home to be with me, and Edith went to her mother's. When she came back she was in tears over Grandma Adele and a silver pitcher that was given to Aunt Hester, when everyone knew it was Edith who had always wanted it.

My injuries healed, but my sickness at heart was no better. I couldn't eat properly and stopped having my monthly. At first I believed I was pregnant, and it gave me the most unholy glow of hope, but the doctor told Edith I was in danger of beriberi, and after that she made me eat three meals a day and cooked everything in lard.

Once I wrote to Conary's father. It took me a week, writing and rewriting. I wanted to tell him I would love Conary all my life and was sorry for his loss. It didn't matter how hard I worked on it, it came back marked REFUSED. Much later we used to run into each other in Abbott's now and again. Toward the end of his life when he couldn't fish anymore he worked for a time at the Esso, pumping gas. He even filled my tank once when he couldn't avoid it, but he never spoke a civil word to me. He believed that if I had kept to myself, with my big city ways, and obeyed my elders, his son would be alive. That was hard. It was hard when we met, and it's hard now.

At Christmas my father came home and Edith packed her bags and Stephen's and left for good. Father kept saying everything would be all right again, the bad time was over. I couldn't figure out what on earth he meant; I didn't think the bad time would ever be over, and I missed my brother. It turned out he meant that he and Edith were getting a divorce. He thought all my wildness that summer, my "summer fling with the town rebel," was all about him and Edith. Stephen was having nightmares too and a rash, but now all that would stop, according to Father. He had a new "friend," a widow who worked in his office. He'd known her quite a while, and he was sure I would like her.

I thought Stephen had plenty of real things to be having nightmares about, but I didn't say so. I made sure I wrote to him, and most weekends he was allowed to come spend a night with us, though it seemed strange, him arriving with his little suitcase. Edith lived with her mother briefly, then got a job as a hostess at the Chilton Club, where they also gave her a room, so for a while Stephen moved back with us. Then Father married his "friend," a fattish woman with no children of her own and no interest in them. Edith, who was furious, lost her job, so off Stephen went again to live at Grandma Adele's with her.

It's all pretty much a daze to me. In fact, the bad time did end, as most things do. I never did go back to school, but it didn't matter. I didn't want to anymore. It was looking more and more as if a war was coming, and everyone was worried about whether we'd be drawn into it. I took a course in typing and got a job in an office which I liked quite well. I gained some weight back and began to care about things I hadn't for a long while.

My grandmother died in the spring of 1940, in mud season. I went up to Dundee with my father for the funeral. Mr. Davidson did the eulogy, and I thought it was fine, though my grandfather complained that the landscape had done something to Mr. Davidson, that he wasn't a Christian anymore. "Listen to him preach; he never mentions our Lord or the Trinity. We pray about rocks and trees and the eternal sea." Grandfather called him the Druid.

I'd seen Ralph Ober at my grandmother's funeral, and when he came through Boston on his way to the war, he looked me up; a lot of the boys from the county had enlisted. Soldiering was a paying job. Ralph and I wrote to each other while he was in the service, and when he got out we got married, and in the summer started coming back to Dundee.

*   *   *

The Schoolhouse is gone. One of the volunteers in the fire brigade told me that the night it burned he saw a figure in the window upstairs just before the roof fell in. Scared him so much he quit firefighting. They never found anything human in the ashes though.

Conary's sister, Mary, is still alive. I used to see her sometimes. She's gotten immensely fat and is thought never to leave her house. I know she does, probably at night, because when I go to visit Conary's grave, there are often flowers there. She plants primroses on it in the spring, and when they need it, I water and weed them. It's like a secret message going back and forth between us, like the notes she used to leave in the book for me.

I keep that book up here in the shelf to the right of the fireplace. It's one of the reasons I like to be in this house, even in winter. I can see it from my desk here by the window. I can watch it, as if someday I was going to find it pushed back an inch or two on the shelf.

It's been a strange experience, rereading that diary after all these years. It's as if the girl I was is still inside me, and the broken-down old body she carries around belongs to somebody else. Maybe to one of those old women I knew in my youth who seemed to have been old always.

Not that I haven't changed. I have; I've had a quiet life, with much of the kindness and patience I wanted as a child finally coming to me from my husband. So many things have come to me that never came to Conary, both good and bad. It's my hope that Ralph never knew how much that ache of missing Conary remained with me. I know it would have made him unhappy, and he was a good man and never deserved that.

Ralph and I went through a lot with our middle daughter, who seemed possessed by some banshee about the time she turned fourteen. She's turned out pretty well, but the bad times are not completely forgotten on either side. There were times I wished I could have talked to Edith about it, but she never allowed it, and now it's too late.

I find myself thinking about Bowdoin Leach, saying his life had been a circle. I think of mine that way, as if being old and alone has brought me around again to that moment in my life when feelings were shimmering and huge, and you felt you were the first person on earth ever to really be in love. It hasn't been easy to visit again the girl I was. Yet it seemed important, not to pretend that the present changes the past. I believe the past changes the present much more than we know, but we don't like to think about what we can't ever understand.

I suppose in going back to that time in my life I hoped I might come to understand where that evil came from. And where did it go? There's a sage plant in my herb bed now that winters over. It isn't an evergreen, but it doesn't lose its leaves. They go limp and silver gray and then freeze and hang there, looking like dead bats hanging upside down from the rafters. Then spring comes, and the green comes back into the same leaves and the thing is alive again. I suppose a really bitter winter would kill it, but nothing has yet.

How does harm pass in patterns the way it does from one generation to the next? Is there any more sense to it than to that sage plant? I hoped to find out, but I can't say that I have. Now that I've done the last thing I could, by telling this story, I suppose I should study on the most mysterious thing we have to do, that each of us does alone, and for the first time, and hope that it's not the end of understanding.

I know things about true love and ghosts, but I don't know the thing I've wanted to know most. I know there are feelings that survive death, but can they all? What if only the bitterest and most selfish are strong enough? That would explain a lot, wouldn't it?

I expect I'll know sometime. I don't think it will be long now.

Coda

The Hamor nephew who owned the Schoolhouse tried to rent it one more summer. The tenants left after a week and made him refund their money. They complained of bats, but that didn't make any sense. No one else had seen the bats, and besides, everyone wanted bats; they ate the mosquitoes. After that the house stood empty, but for some reason the field in front of it became the best place in the village for fireflies, and the children used to go there on summer evenings to catch them in mason jars.

Then there was the day late in summer when some hikers from Mt. Desert got turned around and fetched up at Dundee when they'd been aiming for Hancock Point. They finally staggered into the post office saying they'd been told that someone there could arrange a ride for them back to Northeast Harbor. Kermit said he probably could, but who had they been talking to? There was no one living up the road they came in by. The hikers said they'd had a nice chat with a lady in a flowered dress in the house out on the point, the one that looked like a schoolhouse.

—⁓—

The Hamor nephew grew tired of paying upkeep on a place that wasn't earning him any money. He put it on the market, but it never sold, though the real estate agent said she was sure it would go if he'd rewire it and put in two more bathrooms. He said he was damned if he was going to throw good money after bad. He offered it to the volunteer fire department, and they accepted it gratefully. They always needed houses they could burn down to practice on.

The night before the Schoolhouse was to burn, Bowdoin Leach walked down the road to have a last look at it. He had known it on the island and he had known it on the main. There were not many things left he could say that about, and he thought he'd just go down there by himself to say good-bye.

Bowdoin had always said that Sallie hadn't done the murder, she just knew who did. But saying it hadn't made it true, and it bothered him not to know. The one thing he knew was the person who could do that murder was a person who would take something of value from someone else, even though it was useless to her. Killing Danial Haskell hadn't given a new life to anybody else. Not a new life anyone could have wished for. The person who could refuse to see that coming could refuse anything. It was a thought more frightening than the blade of an ax, a soul like that, but Bowdoin was too old to be more frightened than curious.

He stood in the road a good while, looking at the old place. Its face was dark, as if its eyes were closed and it was ready to go. But after a while he walked around to the back, and there he could see the light in the window. It was very faint, but what was clear and growing clearer as the sun set was the sound of fiddle music. He listened a long time. It was an old-fashioned tune he hadn't heard since his youth, but he knew it well. It was the sailor's song Mrs. Haskell used to play with her son, called "Black-Eyed Susan."

Acknowledgments

I am deeply grateful to friends who have read and responded to various versions of this story and offered invaluable reactions that helped it toward its final shape. Tina Nides and Ben Cheever went so far as to read two different drafts, and their advice helped more than I can say. Maurice Gordon read a late draft on deadline over a holiday weekend and I still don't know how to thank her. Jerri Witt, Lucie Semler, Jenny Mayher, Lucy Buckley, Shelley Jackson, and Geri Herbert all gave immensely helpful readings when they had better things to do. I am grateful for the prompt and useful reactions from all the staff in Wendy Weil's office, most especially Emily Forland. For research assistance I thank Lee Austin, and I owe Gloria Tarr, Fern McTighe, B. G. Thorpe, and all the ladies of the best library in the world eternal gratitude. Robin Clements and David Gutcheon know how much I owe them and don't seem to mind. I'm especially grateful to my wise and funny editor, Meaghan Dowling, and my agent and lifelong friend, Wendy Weil.